ABOUT THE AUTHOR

Paul Theroux's highly acclaimed books include *Blinding Light*, *Dark Star Safari*, *The Great Railway Bazaar*, *The Old Patagonian Express*, and *Fresh Air Fiend*. *The Mosquito Coast* and *Dr Slaughter* have both been made into successful films. Paul Theroux is also a frequent contributor to magazines. He divides his time between Cape Cod and the Hawaiian islands.

The Elephanta Suite

PAUL THEROUX

PENGUIN BOOKS

PENGUIN BOOKS

Published by the Penguin Group
Penguin Books Ltd, 80 Strand, London WC2R ORL, England
Penguin Group (USA) Inc., 375 Hudson Street, New York, New York 10014, USA
Penguin Group (Canada), 90 Eglinton Avenue East, Suite 700, Toronto, Ontario, Canada M4P 2Y3
(a division of Pearson Penguin Canada Inc.)
Penguin Ireland, 25 St Stephen's Green, Dublin 2, Ireland (a division of Penguin Books Ltd)
Penguin Group (Australia), 250 Camberwell Road, Camberwell, Victoria 3124, Australia
(a division of Pearson Australia Group Pty Ltd)
Penguin Books India Pvt Ltd, 11 Community Centre, Panchsheel Park, New Delhi – 110 017, India
Penguin Group (NZ), 67 Apollo Drive, Rosedale, North Shore 0632, New Zealand
(a division of Pearson New Zealand Ltd)
Penguin Books (South Africa) (Pty) Ltd, 24 Sturdee Avenue, Rosebank,
Johannesburg 2196, South Africa

Penguin Books Ltd, Registered Offices: 80 Strand, London WC2R ORL, England

www.penguin.com

First published by Hamish Hamilton 2007
Published in Penguin Books 2008

1

Typeset by Palimpsest Book Production Limited, Grangemouth, Stirlingshire
Printed in England by Clays Ltd, St Ives plc

ISBN: 978-0-141-03697-7

www.greenpenguin.co.uk

Contents

Monkey Hill

I

They were round-shouldered and droopy-headed like mourners, the shadowy child-sized creatures squatting by the side of the sloping road. All facing the same way, too, as though silently venerating the muted dirty sunset beyond the holy city. Motionless at the edge of the ravine, they were miles from the city and the wide flat river that snaked into the glow, the sun going gray, smoldering in a towering heap of dust like a cloud-bank. The lamps below had already come on and in the darkness the far-off city lay like a velvety textile humped in places and picked out in squirts of gold. What were they looking at? The light dimmed, went colder, and the creatures stirred.

'They're almost human,' Audie Blunden said and looked closer and saw their matted fur.

With a bark like a bad cough the biggest monkey raised his curled tail, lowered his arms and thrust forward on his knuckles. The others, skittering on smaller limbs, followed him, their tails nodding; and the distinct symmetry of the roadside disappeared under the tumbling bodies as the great troop of strag-gling monkeys moved along the road and up the embankment towards the stringy trees at the edge of the forest.

'They scare me,' Beth Blunden said, and though the nearest monkey was more than fifteen feet away she could feel the prickle of its grubby fur creeping across the bare skin of her arm.

She remembered sharply the roaring baboon in Kenya which had appeared near her cot under the thorn trees like a demon, its doggy teeth crowding its wide-open mouth. The thing had attacked the guide's dog, a gentle Lab, bitten its haunch, laying it open to the bone, before being clubbed away by the maddened African. That was another of their trips.

'I hate apes,' Beth said.

'They're monkeys.'

'Same thing.'

'No. Apes are more like us,' Audie said, and in the darkness he covertly picked his nose. Was it the dry air?

'I think it's the other way around.'

But Audie hadn't heard. He was peering into the thickening dusk. 'Incredible,' he said, in a whisper. 'I think they were watching the sunset, just lingering for the last warmth of the sun.'

'Like us,' she said.

And Beth stared at him, not because of what he'd said but the way he'd said it. He sounded so pompous, chewing on this simple observation. They traveled a lot and she had noticed how travel often made this normally straightforward man pretentious.

They were at the edge of a low summit, one of the foothills of the Himalayas, above the holy city. Farther up the ridge from where they were staying – a health spa called Agni – on a clear day they could see snow-topped peaks. They had come to Agni for their health, planning to stay a week. The week passed quickly; they

4

stayed another, and now they renewed their arrangement from week to week, telling themselves that they'd leave when they were ready. They were world travelers yet they'd never seen anything like this.

Still, the file of monkeys hurried up the road with an odd skip-drag gait, the big bold monkey leader up front, now and then barking in his severe cough-like way.

'Good evening.'

A man emerged from the twilit road, stepping neatly to allow the monkeys to pass by. The Blundens were not startled. Their three weeks here had prepared them. They had not seen much of India, but they knew that whenever they had hesitated anywhere, looking puzzled or even thoughtful, an Indian had stepped forward to explain, usually an old man, a bobble-headed pedant, a man urgent with irrelevancies. This one wore a white shirt, a thick vest and scarf, baggy pants and sandals. Big horn-rimmed glasses distorted his eyes.

'I see you are in process of observing our monkeys.'

Like the other explainers, this one precisely summed up what they'd been doing.

'Do not be perplexed,' he went on.

It was true – they had been perplexed.

'They are assembling each evening. They are taking last of warmth into bodies.' He had the voluptuous and slightly starved way of saying 'bodies', giving the word flesh.

'I figured so,' Audie said. 'That's what I said to my wife – didn't I, Beth?'

'They are also looking at smoke and fires at temple in town.'

That was another thing they'd found. Indians like this never listened. They would deliver a monologue, usually informative but oddly without emphasis, as though it was a recitation, and did not appear to be interested in anything the Blundens had to say.

'What temple?' 'What town?' the Blundens asked at once.

The Indian was pointing into the darkness. 'When sun is down, monkeys hasten away – see – to the trees where they will spend night hours, safe from harm's way. Leopards are there. Not one or two, but abundant. Monkeys are their meat.'

'Meat' was another delicious word, like 'body', which the man uttered as though tempted by it, giving it the sinewy density and desire of something forbidden. But he hadn't answered them.

'There's leopards here on Monkey Hill?' Audie asked.

The old man seemed to wince in disapproval, and Audie guessed it was his saying 'Monkey Hill' – but that was what most people called it, and it was easier to remember than its Indian name.

'It is believed that Hanuman Giri is exact place where monkey god Hanuman plucked the mountain of herbals and healing plants for restoring life of Rama's brother Lakshman.'

Yes, that was it, Hanuman Giri. At first they had thought he was answering their question about leopards, but what was this about herbals?

'As you can find in *Ramayana*,' the Indian said, and pointed with his skinny hand. 'There, do you see mountain beyond some few trees?' He did not wait for a reply. 'Not at all. It is empty space, where mountain once stood. Now it is town and temple. Eshrine so to say.'

'No one mentioned any temple.'

'At one time, was Muslim mosque, built five centuries before, Mughal era, on site of Hanuman temple. Ten years ago, trouble, people inwading mosque and burning. Monkeys here are observing comings and goings, hither and thither.'

'I have a headache,' Beth said, and thought: *inwading*? *Eshrine*?

'Many years ago,' the Indian man said, as though Mrs Blunden had not spoken – was he deaf? Was any of this interesting? – 'I was lost in forest some three or four valleys beyond here, Balgiri side. Time was late, afternoon in winter season, darkness coming on. I saw a troop of monkeys and they seemed to descry that I was lost. I was lightly clad, unprepared for rigors of cold night. One monkey seemed to beckon to me. He led, I followed. He was chattering, as though to offer reassurance. Up a precipitous cliff at top I saw correct path beneath me. I was thus saved. Hanuman saved me and so I venerate image.'

'The monkey god,' Beth said.

'Hanuman is deity in image of monkey, as Ganesh is image of elephant, and Nag is cobra,' the Indian said. 'And what is your country, if you please?'

'We're Americans,' Beth said, happy at last to have been asked.

'There are many wonders here,' the Indian said, unimpressed by what he'd just heard. 'You could stay here whole lifetime and still not see everything.'

'We're up at Agni,' Audie said. 'The lodge. Just took a walk down here to see the sunset.'

'Like the monkeys.'

The Indian wasn't listening. He was scowling at the valley he had described, where the mountain had been uprooted.

'How old do you think I am?' he asked. 'You will never guess.'

'Seventy-something.'

'I am in my eighty-third year. I do yoga meditation every morning for one hour. I have never tasted meat, nor alcoholic beverage. Now I will go home and take little dhal and puri and curd, that is all.'

'Where do you live?'

'Just here. Hanuman Nagar.'

'Your village?'

The old man exploded with information. 'Township of Hanuman Nagar is substantial, with a market and textiles-weaving and sundry spheres of commercial enterprise, including ironmongeries, pot-making, clay-baking, for house tiles, kilns and enameling.'

'No one mentioned a town,' Audie said.

'As well as fruit and nut trees. I myself am whole-saling nut meats. Also, as mentioned, Hanuman eshrine. Ancient temple. I bid you good evening.'

With that he stepped into the darkness. The Blundens walked up the road in the opposite direction, remarking as they went on the poise of the old man, his self-possession, his pedantry. How easy it was to jeer at him, yet he had told them several things they hadn't known – the town, its industries, the Hanuman story, the temple business. He was faintly ridiculous, yet you couldn't mock him – he was real. What they had been thinking of as simply Monkey Hill had a history, and drama, an Indian name, and now on that lower slope a neighboring settlement.

'Did you understand what he said about the mosque and the temple?'

Audie shrugged and said, 'Beth, you get these Indians talking and they flog a dead horse into dog food.'

They had a surprise on their way up the road walking back to the lodge. They passed through a large gateway. They had seen the gateway coming down but they had not seen the signs: *Right of Entry Prohibited Except by Registered Guests* and *No Trespassing* and *Authorized Vehicles Only*.

'This means you!' Audie said, shaking his finger into the darkness. 'Get your happy ass out of here!'

'You're awful, Butch,' Beth said, and giggled because it was dark and they were in India, on this broken road, alone, dust in their nostrils, the obscure sense of smoky air, a smell of burning cow dung, a rocky hillside and here he was making a joke, being silly. His unruly behavior was usually a comfort, she had loved him for it and regarded it as a form of protection for more than thirty years of marriage. She felt safe in his humor.

Beyond the gateway they saw the lights of the lodge, and Agni itself, the former maharaja's residence, a baronial mansion, and in the bamboo grove the spa buildings, the pool, the palm trees, the yoga pavilion, glowing in spotlights, the whole place crowning the summit of the hill they had been told was Monkey Hill, though it had a local name too, the one that old

Indian had used that they found impossible to remember.

Staff members passing them on the path pressed their hands in prayer and said *namaste* or *namaskar*, and some of the Tibetans in an attractive gesture touched their right hand to their heart. Mr Blunden did the same in return and found himself moved by it.

At the entrance to the restaurant Mrs Blunden saw an Indian couple smile at them.

'*Namaste*,' she said, and clapped her hands upright under her chin.

'Hi there,' the Indian man said. He was quick to put his hand out and pumped Audie's reluctant hand. 'I'm Rupesh – call me Bill. This is Deena. Looks crowded tonight.'

The Indian girl at the door said, 'Very crowded. There's a wait, I'm afraid. Unless you wish to share a table.'

Audie smiled at the girl. The nameplate pinned to her yellow and white sari was lettered *Anna*. She was lovely – he'd seen her at the spa in the white pajamas the massage therapists wore.

'No problem here,' the Indian said.

'If you don't mind,' Beth said.

'I could seat you quicker if you sat together,' the Indian girl Anna said.

Audie tried to catch his wife's eye to signal 'We'll wait' – eating with strangers affected his digestion – but she had already agreed. He hated to share, he hated the concept, the very word; he had spent his life in pursuit of his own undivided portion of the world.

Within minutes of their being seated, the Indian

(Bill?) had told him that he lived in Chevy Chase, Maryland; that he owned a company that leased vending machines ('bottled and canned beverages and mineral waters'), his budget projections had never been better, he had an acre of warehouse space and a large house; his elderly father lived with them, and he had two children, one attending Georgetown, a boy, economics major, and a daughter, a Johns Hopkins graduate now a stock analyst for Goldman Sachs, doing very well, loved her work. This was their second day at Agni, they had family in Dehra Dun, one more day and they'd be back in Delhi, preparing to take the direct flight to Newark, a new service, so much better than having to make stops in Frankfurt or London.

'Very spiritual here,' he said after an awkward pause, having gotten no response from Mr Blunden.

Mr Blunden smiled. How was it possible for people to talk so much that they were oblivious of their listener? Yet Mr Blunden was relieved – he didn't want to give out information about himself. He did not want to lie to anyone, and knew that if anyone asked a direct question he would give an evasive or misleading reply. Talkative people made it so easy for him to be anonymous.

'What do you do for a living?' he was sometimes asked.

'Whole bunch of things,' he would reply. 'I've got a bunch of companies, I'm involved in some start-ups and rebrandings. We're in housewares. Hard furnishings. White goods. We used to do a lot of mail order, catalog inventory, and now it's mostly on-line.'

The Indian woman said to him, 'Where do you live?'

'Tough question,' Audie said. 'This time of year we're usually in our house in Florida. We've got an apartment in New York. We mostly spend our summers in Maine. We've got a condo in Vermont, ski-country. Take your pick.'

But the woman wasn't listening to him. She was talking about her daughter, who lived in New York City and was now twenty-seven and a little overdue to be married. They – mother and father – were in India to meet the parents of a boy they hoped would be a suitable husband. The boy happened to be living in Rochester, New York, where he taught engineering.

'Arranged marriage,' she said. 'Best way.'

She seemed to be twinkling with defiance, challenging Mr Blunden to question her adherence to the custom of arranged marriage. He enjoyed hearing her overselling it.

'Rupesh and I were arranged by our parents. Americans find it so funny.' She shrieked a little, and wobbled her head. 'I didn't know his name. Only his horoscope. He was almost stranger to me. Almost thirty years together now!'

While insisting on her approval of the custom of arranged marriage she was also presenting herself as an antique, if not an oddity, and wished to be celebrated that way. She lived in the USA, she had shocked her American friends with this sort of talk and was defying Audie to be shocked. But Audie decided to defy her in return.

'Beth was a stranger to me when we met, too,' he said. 'Picked her up in a bar.'

He overheard the Indian man – Bill? Rupesh? – say,

'Vas vesting away' and 'His own urine' – and he turned away from the man's disappointed wife.

'My father,' the man said, glad for another listener. 'He was in intensive care at Georgetown Medical Center. They said they couldn't do anymore for his condition, which was inoperable cancer of pancreas. "He will be more comfortable at home." They were abandoning him, no question. He was wasting. As last resort we saw a yogi. He prescribed the urine cure. My father was instructed to drink a beaker of his own urine first thing in morning. He did so. After a week he grew stronger. Appetite came back. Hunger was there. Thirst was there. Second week, my God, he began to put on weight. Skin better, head clear. Third week, he was walking a bit. Balance was there. Two months of this, drinking urine, and body was clear. Doctor said, "Miracle."'

That was another thing – one minute it was budget projections and stock analysis, and the next minute it was horoscopes and arranged marriages and the wonder of drinking your own whiz.

'I tell you, India is booming,' the man said, when Mr Blunden did not react. 'There is no stopping it. Bangalore is next Silicon Valley. Innovation!'

'So I heard,' Audie said, 'but all I see in India' – and he smiled at the couple – 'all I see in India, is people reinventing the flat tire.'

Soon after that the couple smiled, and said they'd enjoyed meeting them, and excused themselves; and only then did Mr Blunden take notice of them, because he was unable to tell from their manner whether they were offended and abruptly ducking out or else actually meant what they said. It was a kind of inscrutability he had not associated with Indians. He was impressed.

'He seemed nice,' Beth said.

'Nice doesn't seem like the right word for Indians,' Audie said. 'It's a little too bland. Lavish, outlandish, pious, talkative, overbearing, in your face, slippery, insincere, holy – I'm thinking they are Indian words. That talk about drinking number one – did you ever hear anything like it?'

'I wasn't listening. I thought he was handsome. That's the trouble with you – you actually expect them to make sense.'

'What do you do?'

'I look at them talking. I don't listen. Didn't you notice, he had lovely eyes?'

They had gotten up and were leaving the table, when they heard a sharp 'Hello.' An Indian man was bowing, another one who'd materialized next to them. He was carrying a clipboard.

'Doctor,' Beth said – she had forgotten his name but he too wore an Agni nameplate lettered *Nagaraj*. 'Doctor Nagaraj.'

He had said that he would see them at dinner, and they had forgotten they'd promised they'd see him. But he was unfussed, saying 'Not to worry' as they apologized and again Mr Blunden smiled at his inability to read the man's mood – whether or not he minded their having forgotten him.

'We've already eaten,' Mr Blunden said, seeing the waitress approach, and he saw it was the girl who had seated them, Anna. She held three menus and stood next to the table, looking serene, patient, attentive. She had a pale, round, Asiatic face, like a doll; her hair in a bun, drawn back tight, gave her prominent ears. She was small, quick to smile when she was smiled at.

'Is that short for something – maybe Annapurna?'

'No, sir. Mother of Mary. I am Christian, sir.'

'Imagine that.'

'Anna Hunphunwoshi, sir. From Nagaland, sir. Kohima, sir. Very far, sir.'

'I've seen you in the spa.'

'I also do treatments in daytime, sir.'

'Are you eating, doctor?' Audie said.

'Thank you, no. I don't take food after six p.m.' He spoke to Anna. 'I will take some salted lassi.'

'We should follow your example,' Beth said.

'As you wish.'

'Three of those, Anna, please.'

'Thank you, sir.' She stepped silently away, clutching the menus.

'Where did you say you went to medical school?' Audie asked the doctor.

'Ayurvedic Institute in Mangalore.'

'That makes you a doctor?'

'Ayurvedic doctor, yes.'

'Can you practice outside India?'

'Where ayurvedic medicine is licensed, indeed, I can practice ayurvedic, without hindrance,' Dr Nagaraj said. 'May I see your right hand, sir?' And when Mr Blunden placed his big hand in the doctor's warm slender hand, the doctor said, 'Just relax,' and scrutinized it, and made some notes on his clipboard.

'That Indian script looks like washing hanging on a clothes line,' Audie said.

The doctor, intent on Audie's palm, said nothing. And even when the waitress returned with the three tumblers of lassi, he went on studying the big splayed hand. He made more notes and, what was disconcerting to Mr Blunden, he wrote down a set of numbers, added more numbers to them, subtracted, multiplied, got a total then divided it and underlined the result. Still holding Audie's palm, the doctor raised his eyes and did not smile.

'You had a hard life until age thirty-five,' Dr Nagaraj said. 'You prepared the ground, so to say. Then you reaped rewards. You can be helpful to a politician presently but avoid it. Next ten years very good for name and fame. Madam?'

He offered his hand to Beth and she placed hers, palm upwards, on top of his.

'Those numbers,' Beth said.

'Good dates, bad dates, risky times.'

'How long will I live?' Audie asked.

'Until eighty-five, if all is observed,' the doctor said without hesitating. He went back to examining Beth's palm and scribbling notes.

'I don't want to know how long I'm going to live,' Beth said. 'Just give me some good news.'

'Happy childhood, but you have no children yourself,' the doctor said. 'Next ten years, excellent health. Never trust any person blindly, especially those who praise you. Follow intuition. Invest in real estate. Avoid crowds, smoke, dust.' The doctor strained, as though translating from a difficult language he was reading on Mrs Blunden's palm. 'Avoid perfume. No litigation.'

As the doctor tensed, showing his teeth, Beth said,

16

'That's enough,' and lifted her hand and clasped it. Audie glanced at her and guessed that she was also wondering if Dr Nagaraj was a quack. But that thought was not in her mind.

Dr Nagaraj perhaps sensed this querying, though he seemed calm again. He sipped his lassi, he nodded, he tapped his clipboard.

'I took my friend Sanjeev to Rajaji National Forest to see the wild elephants. They are my passion. Did you not see my collection of Ganeshes in my office?'

'I remember,' Beth said. 'The elephant figurines on the shelves.'

'Quite so.' The doctor drank again. 'We encountered a great herd of elephants in Rajaji. They are not the same as the working domesticated elephants but a separate species. They saw us. We were near the banks of the river. Do you know the expression, "Never get between an elephant and water"?'

'No,' said Beth.

'I guess I do now,' said Audie.

'The elephants became enraged. I saw the bull elephant trumpeting and I ran and hid in the trees. Sanjeev was behind me, rooted to the spot, too frightened to move.'

As he spoke the waitress came back, paused at their table, then asked whether there was anything more she could get them.

'We're fine,' Audie said.

When she had gone, Dr Nagaraj said, 'I watched with horror as the huge elephant bore down on Sanjeev, followed by the herd of smaller elephants, raising so much dust. Seeing them, Sanjeev bowed his head and knelt, knowing he was about to die. He couldn't run, he couldn't swim. But he did yoga – *bidalasana*, cat position, instinctive somehow.'

Flexing his fingers, making a business of it, Dr Nagaraj straightened the mat in front of him, tidied the coaster under his glass, then dipped his head and sucked at the lassi.

'And what happened?' Audie asked.

Dr Nagaraj went vague, his face slackening, then, 'Oh, yes,' as he pretended to remember. 'The great bull elephant lowered his head as though to charge. But instead of impaling Sanjeev on his tusks as I had expected, the elephant knelt, trapping Sanjeev between the two great tusks. Not to kill him, oh no. I could see it was to protect him from the other elephants trampling him.'

He seemed on the point of saying more when Beth said that she was exhausted, that she would be a basket case if she didn't get some sleep.

'I call that another miracle,' Beth Blunden said, as they strolled under the starry sky to their suite.

2

They woke to a brilliant sunrise and felt there were no days like this anywhere but on this hilltop in India. The rest of India and the stormy world were elsewhere.

Was it two weeks they'd been there? With a clarity of mind and a lightness in their bodies that was new to them they had lost their sense of passing time. Being at Agni had strengthened them, and they were surprised, for it was like a cure for an obscure but tenacious ailment of which they'd been unaware. Rested, well looked-after, like children on an extended holiday pampered by adults, they were invigorated, enjoying the power and poise of contentment. Audie had even stopped teasing the waiters about the food, calling the uttapam 'shit on a shingle'.

Everyone was pleasant to them, the staff always pausing to say hello or *namaskar*; always smiling, deferential without groveling, they waited on the Blundens, devoted servants, prescient too, anticipating their desires. 'Carrot juice again, sir?' 'Green tea sorbet again, madam?' And when the Blundens skipped meals the waiters would say, 'We missed you last night, sir,' as though their absence mattered and was a diminishment.

The Blundens were, to their surprise, grateful and patient. What Mr Blunden said about owning 'a bunch of businesses' wasn't a hollow boast – it was true. They were wealthy, they owned four homes, in four different states, and they knew all about employees and servants. They had gardeners, housekeepers, caretakers, odd-job men, but all of them were so well paid and so used to them as to be unafraid and presumptuous. *You need us*, seemed to show in their resentful eyes. Indian workers were different, neither presumptuous nor servile; well-spoken, even educated, and skilled, they were like people from another planet, whose belief was, *We need you*.

'I should start a company here,' Audie said. 'Or do what everyone else is doing, outsource here.'

They had arrived in the dark smoky midnight at Mumbai Airport and had been driven swiftly past lamp-lit shacks – a vision of fires, of torches – on the way to the brilliantly lit hotel, where they stayed in the Elephanta Suite – Audie intoned the name printed over the carved doorway. They had slept well, waking at dawn to be driven to the airport for the one-hour flight, and they had been met by a driver in a white uniform holding a signboard lettered *Balondon* in one hand and a platter of chilled face towels with the other.

What the Blundens had seen of India, the populous and chaotic India they'd been warned about, the India that made you sick and fearful and impatient, was that one-hour drive from the airport to the top of Monkey Hill, the ayurvedic spa known as Agni. Mr Blunden thought of the drive as a long panning shot, the sort you'd get in a documentary with a jumping camera, the very first image a woman with no hands, begging at a stop light just outside the airport, raising her stumps to Audie's window ('Don't look, honey'), then the over-loaded lopsided trucks with *Horn Please* lettered on the bumper, the ox-carts piled high with bulging sacks sharing the road with crammed buses painted blue and red, the sight of women slapping clothes onto boulders in a dirty stream ('laundering' the driver said), others threshing grain on mats. Wooden scaffolding on brick buildings that already looked like ruins, whitewashed temples, mosques with minarets like pencils, gated houses, hovels, the lean-tos and tents of squatters. 'Gypsies – many here, sir.' Small girls in clean white dresses, boys in shorts, men in business suits on bicycles, youths on motorbikes, skinny cows chewing at trash heaps, a man pissing against a tree ('Without a pot to piss in,' Audie said), another squatting at the edge of a field, the whole country on the road. Every few miles huge billboards showing movie posters of bug-eyed fatties in tight clothes. This India had no smell and hardly had a sound: the windows of the car were closed, the air conditioner on. Whenever the subject of India came up, the Blundens referred to their drive from the airport, through the small city and along the road and up Monkey Hill to Agni, that one hour of India.

'They've got zip,' Audie said, his face to the car window. And to various Indian guests at Agni in conversation, peering at them closely, 'Sure, I saw the Indian miracle.'

The miracle to them was that India was not a country but a creature, like a monstrous body crawling with smaller creatures, pestilential with people – a big, horrific creature, sometimes angry and loud, sometimes passive and stinking, always hostile, even dangerous. And another miracle was that they'd found a remote part of it that was safe.

Agni seemed to be in the heart of India, yet India seemed far away. Perhaps that was the secret to experiencing India, to bury yourself deeply in it to avoid suffering it. The few times at Agni they'd seen something exotic or strange – like the monkeys staring at the sunset, or had they been looking at the town? – it was not anything they'd anticipated, not the India of stereotype, and that was so disconcerting they withdrew into the Agni gate and shut India out.

They had been surprised to hear the old man say he lived 'just here' in the town, Hanuman Nagar. Where was this? They had believed they were on a rugged foothill of the Himalayas, an empty hill. Where was the town? They had no idea there was a settlement anywhere near Agni. And the 'venerable temple' was news to them too. They suspected that the old man, a fantasist and yarn-spinner, was indulging in hyperbole, another Indian trait, for how could there be a village nearby? Agni – the spa and maharaja's residence – occupied the serene top of Monkey Hill, at the end of a road that wound around the steep slope. Had there been a village they would have spotted it on the drive up that first day. Instead, they had seen a yellow forest of trees with dusty leaves, the staggering cows and glossy big-beaked crows, a few people on foot, and that was all.

The Blundens had woken refreshed in the silence of their suite, a powdery dawn at the window, of pink dust and diffused light. They stretched, they bathed, they put on their white suits, like pairs of elegant pajamas, and they went downstairs and across the lawn to yoga.

But here was something new. On this morning

following their encounter with the old man they looked down the hill and saw, from the direction where he had pointed with his skinny hand, ropes of smoke untangling in the sky. There was an earthen smell of damp flowers but also a smell of that distant smoke.

They crossed the lawn to the yoga pavilion. Half a dozen others had preceded them and sat on rush mats, in lotus postures. Some of them had their eyes shut in meditation, others greeted them softly; all were wearing the same white suits. The Blundens took their places. Vikram, the yoga teacher, sat on a raised platform at the pavilion, his hands clasped under his chin.

'Om,' Vikram intoned, *auuummm*, three times. Then, 'Rub your hands, massage your eyes, feel the energy, feel the vibration. Open your eyes slowly, listen to the birds singing.'

The Blundens, without communicating this thought, each smelled the smoke they'd seen earlier, and another smell penetrating it, something sharp, like burned toast.

They stood, they stretched, they did 'the tree', balancing on one foot, then the other; they raised their arms, locked their hands and stood on tiptoe. They felt like children, faltering in an exercise they barely understood and, like children, not caring.

'For *tadasana*, mountain pose. Think, "This is Hanuman mountain." Find something to concentrate on,' Vikram said. 'A brick. A leaf.'

Audie saw a crack on a pillar of the pavilion. He stared hard at it. It held him up; he balanced on the crack, and it turned from a flaw to a distinct profile, a coastline, something with symmetry and meaning.

23

'Now, slowly, lay on mat with feet apart. Inhaling breath, raise legs twenty degrees and slowly let out breath.'

They did this, lifting their legs higher, feeling their stomachs twist. They then knelt, extended one leg, did more poses and counter-poses. Their arms and legs were tingling.

'Feel the energy,' Vikram said. 'Breathe in, raise your arms as you inhale, bend to the left as you exhale and hold the posture. Very good for kidneys, for spine, for pancreas, for blood circulation. Five regular breaths.'

No one except Vikram spoke. They assumed the posture of the archer – pulling a bow; the cat, the dog, and resting with their hands on their chins, the crocodile.

Without remarking on it to each other, feeling quietly strengthened, the Blundens knew they were improving. Beth, who had gripped her calves on the first day, could now touch the mat with her fingertips; Audie, who had trembled with his legs aloft, could now hold the position until Vikram said, 'Exhale slowly and lower your legs. Prepare for *pranayama*.'

The breathing exercises cleared their heads, first the sequence of explosive breaths, expelling air through the nose; and then using the thumb and ring fingers, closing one nostril and drawing a breath through the other, exhaling through the first nostril.

'This finger is earth. This is fire. This is sky. Use earth and sky.'

All this time, Audie felt buoyant, vitalized, refreshed, serene; and Beth was enlivened, discovering new muscles, her arms and legs awakened. The end of the session came sooner and sooner, Vikram saying, 'Now *om* and *shantih* three times,' and taking a breath, '*Auuuumm.*'

Afterwards they lay for a minute or so, stretched flat on the mat, the cool air on their dampened faces, all the drowsiness of deep sleep wrung from their bodies.

But lying there with their eyes shut, they were aware of the subtle smoke-smell, not burned toast anymore, but something fouler, a whiff of excrement.

'I am limp,' Audie said. 'I feel wonderful.'

Not limp, Beth thought. She felt a heightened awareness, a keener sense of smell and touch. She was not soothed so much as set on edge.

'Just floating,' Mr Blunden said.

No, she was alert, something quickening within her, nevertheless she hummed as though agreeing with him.

'It's like an out-of-body experience.'

She felt it was the opposite, an intensification of the flesh, not the buoyancy he was describing to her as they walked past the clocking bamboo grove to breakfast. She had felt – still felt – a density in her body and a control over that density. Certain of her muscles were attached to her active mind: she was aware that she inhabited a whole live body in which she had been buried.

'With each breath,' Audie was saying, 'I was sort of inhaling peacefulness through my nose, calming myself and getting lighter.'

Beth smiled at him and said, 'It's lovely – I want to go on doing this when we get home,' yet nothing that Audie described was familiar to her. When she had lain on her mat she had felt energy pulsing out of the solid earth into her back and up her spine. Raising her eyes, tipping her head backwards, she had sensed more energy pouring from the sky into her. Her fingers were limber, her grip was tested; she received power through her bare feet.

'Like I'd slipped out of my body,' Mr Blunden said.

Not at all – Beth had felt naked, and she was soothed, as though a lover's hands had touched her, not erotically but as a caress.

Audie had always spoken for her, expressing what she felt. That had been the case since before they were married, and it accounted for the happiness in their marriage. They were happier than ever, but these days at Agni he would say something and she would smile not because she agreed, but in disbelief.

Even at breakfast this was subtly so: they chose the Indian options, but she saw that they each selected something different from the stainless-steel containers at the buffet – he took a plate of idlis and sambar and curry soup, she chose the rotis and spiced beans, the sprouted lentils, the yogurt. She did not comment on this; he did not seem to notice. They ate without feeling full, they drank green tea, and they compared their re-actions to the yoga session – that is, Mr Blunden enlarged on what he called his lightness of soul, while Beth nodded in agreement, yet feeling distinctly that she had been affected not just in her arms and legs but in the pit of her stomach and in every inch of her spine.

'Like I've had a lube job, an oil change, all the fluids checked,' Audie said. 'This is the nearest I've ever come to religion.'

'Yes,' Beth said. That part was true. She had felt

touched in a particular sense – light fingers on her body.

'And I want more of it.'

'Yes,' she said with conviction.

'Meet you at the pool,' he said. 'I'm going up to the lobby to sign on for another week.'

Beth was reading by the pool when her husband returned. He peered at her book – a hefty volume – and raised his head queryingly, to which Beth made a face. She was wearing earphones and listening to her iPod and so she spoke very loudly.

'One of these novels by an Indian! About India! Not a lot of jokes! I don't think I ever want to go there!'

But she went on turning pages and vowing to leave the book in the library of the residence, where there was also a billiards table and a smoking room. Audie had a book on yoga, mostly pictures, which he smiled at.

'Check this out. The Scorpion. Is that one of the Flying Wallendas?'

As they were reading under the sun shade, they became aware of a stirring just behind them – Audie hearing a rustle of feet in dry leaves and a thicker flutter of leaves in the shake of branches; while for Beth it was less a sound than a prickling of her skin, a brushing of the hair on her head, and a distinct phys-icality like a change in temperature, a sudden hotness, and a sense that she was being watched and that the air around her was being somehow stroked.

They both turned, Beth first, Audie a second after-wards. They saw nothing but a swaying tree limb.

'Thought I heard something,' he said.

She had heard nothing at all, but said, 'Yes.'

'Look at the time,' he said twisting his wrist. 'I've got a treatment.'

'Which one?'

'*Abhiyanga.*'

He did not say that on his way back from the lobby of the residence he had stopped by the spa and requested this treatment, specifying that his massage therapist for this ayurvedic massage would be Anna, whom he had met the previous evening working in the restaurant.

He scuffed on Agni sandals to the spa lobby, where he was given a key to a locker in the men's section. He changed into a robe and on returning to the spa lobby he saw Anna, her hands clasped before her, her head bowed in greeting.

'This way, sir,' she said, leading him up the marble stairs and past the gushing fountain to the massage room. A small dark girl awaited them there. She too bowed her head and greeted them.

'This is Sarita,' Anna said.

Sarita washed his feet in a bowl of cool water and smooth stones. They murmured prayers, they chanted, they rang a brass bell, while Audie stood sniffing. And delicately they tied a loincloth on him, for modesty's sake.

The two women helped him onto the dark wooden table, where he lay on his stomach, his face on a folded towel. His first sensation was of hot oil drizzled on the small of his back, fingers stirring it, spreading it, squeezing it into his spine. Anna was on one side, Sarita on the other; he was massaged, his muscles chafed and pressed. From time to time, more hot oil was poured on his shoulders and limbs, the warmth of it penetrating his body as it was worked into him by the four active hands and insistent fingers.

Without effort, Mr Blunden sank into a reverie of women he had known. He did not orchestrate the reverie – he let it wash over him. He could not say why he always had the same reverie, why it began whenever he was massaged. He guessed it was his reaction to being touched by a strange woman's hands.

'I must check,' he was told by the Indian clerk when he requested a woman to massage him, and he learned that in India it was uncommon, though at Agni it was acceptable.

He learned to relax and receive the treatment, the two young women pressing on his oiled back and working their way from his shoulders and down his arms, to his legs, to his feet. As this happened his mind locked onto the thought he'd suspended when the massage had ended the day before.

The women in his reverie, mainly faces, soulful ones, were lovers he'd had in his life, the ones he'd remembered for the desire he'd felt for them, not casual sex or one-night stands, but affairs that had exhausted him with the pleasure and pain of love. Yet what he recalled in the course of the massage was the last day he'd seen them, when he'd told them it was over, he could not see them anymore, after his desire had died and his guilt at deceiving Beth overcame him.

Only with great difficulty could he recall the moment of their first meeting, and the succeeding days, but it was no effort at all for him to remember the day they parted, usually after making love – saying what he had rehearsed, 'I won't be able to see you anymore' – the expression on their faces of shock, indignation, sadness, anger. And he averted his eyes from the woman's body, fearing to be attracted by his pity, and watched her get dressed, the awkwardness of it, sometimes sad and slow, sometimes spitefully hurried, the expression, the eyes, the moment that Audie called 'the last look'.

Even as he stood there in the room, usually a bedroom, they seemed to recede, grow smaller, losing significance. They were affronted, abandoned, just as though they were standing on a railway platform, and he was at the window of a train, pulling away, waving goodbye.

Each parting that had caused him pain, had caused them greater pain, anguish. But he was always able to say, 'What did you expect? I'm a married man. I have obligations. What about my wife?'

The mention of his wife, just the word, had maddened some of them. But anger had usually given way to tears. The opposite of sexual desire was not indifference; it was tears. Tears made him impotent, clumsy, just a big pointless jug-eared man with enormous and futile hands, incoherent in his consolation.

The endings of love affairs were tableaux in his mind, nearly always enacted in hotel bedrooms, the room going colder and dimmer, and then just cheerless with white wrathful voices.

'I hate you' and 'How could you?' and 'You led me on' and 'I wish you ill, I really do, I hope something bad happens to you.'

Each parting was a moment of crisis that he relived as he was being massaged. He could not say why this was so, why the occasion of his nakedness in the presence of strangers who were pressing upon his body revived these memories, yet it was so. And there was something new today, the memory of a woman he'd ended an affair with, who had turned to him in fury to insist that he make love to her one last time. He went through the motions, hating himself, feeling that she was made of clay. She seemed to be testing him, perhaps even trying to humiliate him. He believed he had brought it off but at the end she'd said, 'That was horrible.'

'Sorry.'

'You're right-handed?'

'Yes.'

She adjusted herself in the bed and parted her legs and said, 'Use that, then.'

On the days of these break-ups he'd buy something for Beth – an expensive charm for her bracelet, some flowers, a scarf, a pair of earrings – and offered her the present, saying, 'I love you, Tugar. I could never love anyone else.'

She had told him that, as a child, unable to pronounce sugar, she had said, 'Tugar', and the name had stuck. He used it only on these moments of grateful tenderness, as on similar moments of gratitude she called him 'Butch'.

His love for Beth was sincere. He had said he'd loved these women but the word never got out of the bedroom. He had desired them and could spend an entire afternoon in a hotel room with them, but it was

31

an evaporating passion – he shrank at the thought of sitting across a table from them for an hour to have a meal. In his life, though he had searched, he had never met a woman who felt the same, who could separate desire from love. The women he'd known combined these feelings. For them, desire was love and it was also the promise of a future. Desire was hope, a house, children, a car, a vacation, new shoes, even grandchildren. But for him desire had a beginning and an end – no middle, no future, only its ungraspable evaporation. The end that seemed so natural to him was seen by the women as a betrayal. But worse than 'I hate you' was that rejected face, that abandoned posture, the disappointment, the tears.

Then it was over and he heard, 'Be careful, sir.'

Anna was wiping the oil from one of his feet, Sarita wiping the other.

They helped him off the massage table and guided him to the shower, where he scrubbed himself clean, and he left the room swaying slightly, fatigued and stunned by the experience.

At lunch, Beth said, 'How was it?'

'The treatment? Very nice.'

He had no way of describing the turmoil of it, the women's hands, the drenching of hot oil, the reverie of sifted memories, the exhaustion, his sense of peace, and he regretted that this seemed like a deception.

They were sitting outside, the sun-speckled shade falling across their table.

'Carrot juice?' the waiter asked.

'Please.'

'Did you swim?' Audie asked.

Beth shook her head. 'I wasn't in the mood.'

That was not the reason, and she pitied this man who, in thirty years, she had never deceived. After her husband had left to go to his treatment she'd felt that someone had crept up behind her from the trees, a child, or a small sinister man; she could sense that creature's presence on her skin – the prickling of its hovering just out of sight, waiting for her to relax her vigilance, so that he – it was male, and damp – could snatch her Birkin bag. Everything she needed was in the bag – her money, her picture ID, her passport and credit cards, her best charm bracelet, her perfume and make-up, her keys and (not that either of them worked in India) her cellphone and BlackBerry. She knew that had she been foolish enough to jump into the swimming pool she would have returned to her chaise longue and found she'd been robbed, her bag gone.

'I might take a dip,' he said.

He was a man, the indispensable person in her life who always said to her, 'Let me handle it' or 'I'll take care of it', and for that alone she loved him. He looked after her. He knew how to look after himself. He kept all his valuables in the room safe. She didn't trust the safe, but hardly trusted herself with her bag either. She wondered why she was here in India with thoughts of being stalked and violated, and for him the subject never seemed to occur, which was another reason she didn't bring it up.

'I've got a treatment,' she said, setting her soup spoon down, patting her lips with her napkin.

They kissed, brushing cheeks, puckering, a sound like tasting air.

As Beth walked through the bamboo grove to the spa lobby she passed the gift shop. A woman in an Agni sari standing at the door to the gift shop stepped aside and said, 'Please. You are welcome.'

'I'm running late but I wanted to know if you have any shatooshes.'

'We can obtain,' the woman said, a sweep of her head indicating her complete cooperation. 'But it is not easy.'

'In what way not easy?'

'It is contraband item.'

'I had thought of looking in the town. I didn't even know there was a town!'

'Hanuman Nagar. Not available. Not hygienic.'

'But there's the monkey temple?'

'Shrine, yes, but not temple. Disputed temple, so to say.'

'I'm sure it's interesting,' Beth said, because the woman was agitated, as some Indians at Agni seemed to be when they were flatly contradicted, or even questioned.

'There is such confusion, madam. Even hullabaloo,' the woman said, widening her eyes, swishing the drape of her sari over her shoulder. 'Please, you desire shatoosh, we will obtain full range of shatoosh for you, with discretion.'

Beth was given a locker key at the spa, she changed into a robe, and when she went upstairs she was met by a young girl in a white uniform, in a posture of greeting, hands clasped, head bowed. '*Namaskar*. I am Prithi.'

On the way to the massage suite, Prithi complimented

Beth on her lovely bag ('It is smart, madam') and on her clear skin. Beth thanked her but thought, Why not? I take care of myself. I eat right. I exercise. I'm only fifty. She was fifty-three but what was the difference? Her big birthday was far off and unthinkable.

Prithi sat her down and washed her feet and said, 'We believe that guests come from God,' and the solemnity of this ritual, with the antiphonal music playing on a plant-stand, the warm water on her feet and Prithi's gentle hands, brought Beth to the verge of tears.

She found she could not speak – her throat ached with emotion. Prithi helped her onto the table and lifted the large towel and Beth slipped off her robe and lay down, as the towel was tucked around her.

'Thai massage, mam.'

'Yes,' Beth murmured into the cushion under her face.

She was tugged, first her shoulders and back, her legs pushed and pulled, Prithi's elbows and palms working her muscles, stretching her arms, tucking them behind her and applying pressure to them.

And at each touch Beth was reminded of her strength, the legs that were toned from tennis, the limber calves and ankles, as her heels were pressed into her buttocks, the buttocks themselves trim from her exercise, even her hands responded when they were manipulated – she was proud of the strength in her fingers and wrists.

Each part of her body proved its elasticity in the massage; the physicality of the treatment was like an acknowledgement that she was fully alive. And something else – that no man apart from Audie had ever

35

seen her like this. How odd that an Indian girl, hardly twenty, was caressing her this way. But the rhythm of the massage, the moving hands, the sense of blood being expressed through her muscle bundles, induced in her a dream state of being embraced and warmed by another body. She did not mind that the other person was a woman – was in fact reassured to know that only another woman would understand.

Yet in this dream state at the edge of reverie she made Prithi a man, made those massage movements into caresses, the breathing of the young girl into a man's endearments. It worked. She was aroused, as though enclosed in the intimacy of a private bower in which she was exhausting herself in the throes of a passionate embrace.

The music helped too, she felt it resonating within her, the vibrating fibers of the Indian strings clutching at her vitals. Even the massage oil, its fragrance, had an aroma of sensuality, not a perfume but a musky heaviness that soaked her body and soothed it. Every bit of her body was awakened, sweetened by the pain of the massage, the attentive fingers, and before she knew it – before she was ready – it was over.

'Here is some water, mam. I will await you outside. Take your time, mam.'

Audie was peering into the fishpond outside the dining-room lobby, seeming to stare at the white and orange koi thrashing back and forth, darting, gulping at bubbles; but he was only killing time, looking side-ways at Anna who had changed into her restaurant uniform, the cream and gold sari. And where was Beth?

'Good treatment, sir?' Anna said, creeping behind him.

'The best,' he said.

'Thank you, sir.'

He turned to size her up, wondering if she knew that she sounded like a coquette, looking for a nuance on her lips, a lingering light in her eyes, the posture as well, the signs of *Take me*.

'They are lucky fish,' Anna said. He was sometimes unable to understand what she said, yet she made this assertion briskly. Indians could sound so confident even in their mispronunciations.

'Lucky in what way?'

'One Japanese guest tell me so, sir. Lucky fish.'

The fish were fat, their fins like wings, their big purse-like mouths gasping.

'Jesus Christ is a fish, sir.'

Audie dipped his head sideways as he did when he heard something unexpected.

'The sign of fish is in all church, sir. Is a symbol you can say, sir.'

Do I know this? Audie wondered, yet he was muddled, pondering the odd fact, distracted by Anna's doll-like face, her clear skin, her slightly slanted eyes in puffy sockets, her pulled-back hair, her small sticking-out ears, her fleshy lips. She was lovely, and although she was still talking about Jesus the fish, Audie was fascinated. He could take her so easily into his arms, could scoop her up and possess her.

His mind raced ahead, imagining Anna saying, *But what about my mother?*

I will buy her a house.

What about my brother's schooling?

He can live with us. I'll send him to school, and: *You are the prettiest thing I've seen in India.*

'In the Greek language "fish" means Jesus,' Anna said. 'And it was a secret word, sir. Even in my church, sir, fish picture on the wall.'

He was baffled and fascinated by the certainty of the Indian doll lecturing him on Jesus the fish symbol, but only half-listening to this talk, hardly following it, while devouring her with his eyes.

'Is that on the menu?' Beth said, stepping through the door, seeing her husband and the employee at the rail of the fishpond.

Audie was not embarrassed by his reverie of possessing Anna. He was pleased with himself. He was someone who seldom craved anything. He'd had everything he ever wanted, he was content, he could not imagine wanting more. And here he was, experiencing desire – a rare emotion for him these days.

Anna stepped back and became formal, deferring to a superior in the Indian way, as Dr Nagaraj approached and greeted them.

'We were discussing the fish,' Audie said.

'Ah, yes. Fish.' He said *peesh*, making it sound inedible.

'The Christian symbolism. Jesus is represented as a fish.'

Dr Nagaraj waggled his head; he was saying yes, but didn't have a clue.

Anna, self-conscious, perhaps suspecting that she would be referred to as the bringer of this news, sidled back to the table of menus and the brass dish of seeds.

38

'Will you join us for dinner?' Beth asked.

As the doctor waggled his head again, Audie said, 'Just pineapple juice for me. I'm not eating after six.'

'Avoid sour juices,' Dr Nagaraj said. 'You are *kappa* body type.'

Beth said, 'I'm hungry, I'm eating.'

The massage had given her an appetite, made her thirsty, tired her and reminded her that she had a body – her hunger she took to be a sign of health. She loved her body after it had been stroked by the young girl whom she had trouble simplifying in the word therapist.

'Hinduism predates Christianity by many centuries,' Dr Nagaraj said at the table, without prompting. 'You can find god Agni in Rig-Veda – more than three thousand of years back. It is our path, our way of seeing the world, our consolation and salvation. Multiple functions and essential to ayurveda.'

Audie asked himself again, Is he a real doctor? Is he a quack? And, Does it matter?

Dr Nagaraj was still speaking, perhaps answering one of Beth's questions. He had the Indian habit of monologuing, which was a gift for rumbling on, past all obstacles, deaf to any interruptions, indifferent to anyone's boredom, as though no one present had anything worthwhile to say – which, Audie reflected, was probably so, since neither he nor Beth had much to add. Beth was intent on what had become one of Dr Nagaraj's stories, or was it the same story?

'Elephants,' he was saying, 'bearing down on my friend Sanjeev.'

Surely he had told this story before?

'But Sanjeev could not swim. He sank to his knees, as big bull elephant approached. And elephant, too, fell to knees and enclosed poor Sanjeev between his great tusks.'

His teeth gleamed on the word tusks.

'And protected him from the other elephants,' Beth said.

'In beginning, yes, protection was there. Tusks were there,' Dr Nagaraj said. 'But elephant rose to his feet and withdrew. Sanjeev remained on his knees, head down. When coast was clear I went down to that side and found that my friend was dead.'

Surely this was the same story, with a different ending?

'He had not been crushed,' Dr Nagaraj said. 'He somehow died of heart failure. I could not help him, yet I had brought the poor man to this place. Of course, I was devastated.'

'Did he have a family?'

'No wife, no children. But parents are there.'

'Life's so short,' Beth said.

Dr Nagaraj smiled, 'No, no. Life continues. It flows. There is no end.'

3

Mr and Mrs Blunden, Audie and Beth, lay in bed, side by side but apart, sinking into sleep by tumbling and bumping in the narrowing cave of consciousness, along the flowing stream of their vagrant thoughts. Sometimes they stirred in the shallows of embarrassed memory, often slowed and heavy in the eddies of the darker past, but always going down deeper, wishing for the gulping light to cease as they vanished into slumber and different images, twisting in the underground river of darkness, sleeping. Yet they were both awake.

They had said good night and 'Love ya,' enacting their bedtime ritual, and kissed with dry lips like siblings. Some minutes later they were still wakeful but numbed by the night, breathing slowly, buoyed by their reveries, foundering, going under, but not deep enough.

The specter of death hung at the periphery of Audie's wakefulness, pressing a bony finger to his lipless grin in admonition. The dead could seem like scolds, never mind whether they were right or wrong, you couldn't answer back, they had the last word, which was *Told you so*. Audie was thinking of the things he owned, his mind roving over his many rooms in his four residences, the accumulation of so many objects, having turned his fortune into the valuable clutter that filled his house. He imagined collapsing, falling face forward into the middle of it, like someone stifled in a closet of expensive furs, or tipped off an expensive but wobbly chair to expire on the floor, blood leaking from his head. Thinking of what he owned, he was appalled, for all he had was that sagging face that looked back at him in the mirror, the jug ears, the thinning hair. He was no more than his breath.

Not even the poor are more cynical than the rich, he thought.

Something more, something only a man of sixty would know but a girl of twenty smiling at a school of fish in a fishtank would not know, sustained him and kept him calm: that the life force was the push and pull of repetition; a novelty at first, you were easily deceived into thinking that the next phase would be something new. And so it seemed to the young, but growing wasn't progress, all aging was decline. Audie had gone from a belief in experience to a realization that it was downhill all the way. His whole life he had been dying. Time passed and the something new, looked at closely, was something he'd seen before; then it repeated, and occurring again it seemed trivial, even seedier, a mockery of his hopes. Feelings repeated and shamed him; glittering objects appeared, and when he reached for them he was embarrassed by his gesture, for it was all a repetition – perhaps a new chair, possibly bigger, better upholstered, gilt or chrome, lumbar support, an original design, but no more than another chair; and he had more than he needed. And it, too, was one he could fall from and break his neck and after his death the mute thing would still be there, to be auctioned for ready money by someone he hardly knew.

He wondered, Have I lived too long?

For if you live long enough, you see everything, and if you go on living, everything happens over again, just the same, even the women – or especially the women. Earlier in his life he'd understood: a young woman wanted to be married, or a married woman wanted a nicer or richer husband, many women wanted to try again for something better. Who could blame them for looking at the future? But he like most men wallowed in the present and did not see farther than the foot of the bed. The women he'd known were, each of them, different, but what made them sisters was their same question, always spoken in the darkness, at a moment when he felt fulfilled and complete. *Where is this going?*

He kept the answer to himself, because it was devastating. He'd had what he wanted and now he wanted to go home. They wanted more. He hoped for a night – not even a night, hardly a few hours; they wanted a life.

He did not know if he was like other men. That didn't matter, a comparison was futile. But he knew his past and how his life of accumulation had deluded him. He had years more to live but knew in advance that there was nothing new for him. An older man looking for novelty was fooling himself, and was even more ridiculous than he knew. He was just a clown, a bumbler in a circus.

The remorseless symmetry of his life had become apparent to him since his arrival in India, his life of

43

repetition, and anything that appeared new was what Dr Nagaraj had told him was *maya*, illusion. Without putting the disturbing thought into words, keeping it an emotion that penetrated to the core of his body like the shiver of a taboo, he had the feeling that there was no point in being wealthy if you could still be deceived. To him, money represented privacy and comfort, but more than that – if it did not also allow access to the truth then it was nothing but a deception. A rich man who was conned by a lie had no one to blame but himself. And there was no greater fool than a rich man who was self-deceived.

And here was the irony – the man who ran a great company, who hired the best people and ruthlessly fired employees who were perceived as weak in their jobs; who took a faltering firm and whipped it into shape, cutting costs here, eliminating a whole department there, walking into offices of old timers and saying, 'I'm sorry but I'm letting you go – clear out your desk' – getting rid of them in a day so that they didn't linger and stink the place up with their aggrieved indignation – that same scary CEO who nuked entire floors of their workers would meet a young ambitious woman, greedy to be married, swift as a raptor, and that man would offer himself to be snatched. Men who could spot an unreliable employee a mile away were possessed by the most transparent upstarts. Not that they weren't presentable; they might indeed be beautiful, but that was all, and it was only afterwards that the men saw how they had been fooled, how they had fooled themselves. The big swaggering toughie from the boardroom found himself snared by someone he would not have hired to work the photocopier. Then the woman had a child and either said, 'I want stock options for junior' or else, 'I don't love you anymore,' and she got the penthouse, the plane, child support, and a meal ticket for life. Didn't any of these men ever say to themselves, 'Uh-oh, look out.'

In the hour or so before he finally subsided into sleep, Audie Blunden saw this with his Indian clarity. Because India was a land of repetition, a land of nothing new. You couldn't say anything in India that hadn't been said before, and if you succumbed to India's vivid temptation to generalize, all you could do was utter a platitude so obvious it looked like a lie – 'The poverty's a problem' or 'All these cows in the street' or 'It's real dirty.'

Like a living, billion-strong festival of futility, India was the proof that you could not do anything here that hadn't been done before. India was a reminder of the extravagance of human self-deception, and the fundamental lesson of Indian life was that people and even animals have previous existences, other lives, past incarnations; they'd lived on earth before, they'd been through all this – they had to have done so, for otherwise how could they stand it? Nothing was new, and even the illusions were hackneyed, the deceptions old hat.

I've lived enough, he thought, entering the mind of someone about to be reincarnated. Had everything I've wanted.

On this thinning note, at the vanishing point of consciousness, seeing so little ahead of him, out of hope, but weary of the process of perceiving it, Audie fell uncertainly into sleep, at the end of that subterranean river that flowed into oblivion, as though he were no more than a pebble smoothed by the current and dropped into the dark.

Beth Blunden was still awake. She sensed the ripple of resigned certitude pass through her husband's body, relaxing it until he sank and breathed differently, something innocent in the air that entered his nose and mouth, as he lay defenseless in sleep.

At moments like this, Beth felt like a sentinel. And the sense of her being his protector made her feel vulnerable and misunderstood, keeping guard over him and wishing to be concealed. She had spent most of her adult life standing by her husband, or waiting for him to appear; and sometimes he was not there as she stood, or did not return when he said he would. Sometimes she had the feeling she had passed this time in suspense, being a woman, being a wife, being a house cleaner, a cook, a waiter. This trip to India had been her idea, yet they had not been able to leave until he had given the word. The demeaning sense of needing permission wearied her by confining her to a world he occasionally visited and was often absent from. Maybe he had misgivings about what India would do to them? She didn't know; as Audie Blunden's wife she felt she didn't know much. The decisions, the money, the activity, the gusto, the opinions were all his; she was his companion.

Krishna had gopis – milkmaids. She wondered if Krishna represented most men, because most men, like the blue god of power, had women attending to them.

Have I lived at all? was a question that had occurred

to her only now, in India. The whole of India was visible in its chaotic streets, as big as its movie posters, the agonies of life and the flaming deaths; in the streets the big questions were asked and no answers were available, which was why she was so excited and frightened. She had been woken, she had been challenged, the challenge was physical – the sight out the car window on their ride to Agni, the greasy water in sacred tanks, the skinny animals, the tortured-looking trees, the women washing dirty clothes in a dirty stream. She was not disgusted. She accepted these as facts of life.

And that afternoon in the massage room, with the gong music and the chanting, and the young woman working on her, the pressure of the fingers did not soothe her. She was roused again, excited as she had been riding through the towns and villages along the Indian road, seeing the market stalls and the shouting men, the jostling pushcarts and the faces of beggars and postcard sellers and curious children and owlish men at the window. Women in scarves, men in turbans and waistcoats, the thick jerkins of cotton and silk. Naked men too, the ones in diapers, with holy splotches on their foreheads, and the women forever showing the bareness of their soft bellies. She saw the faces now, especially the pretty faces and white teeth of the children, their big glossy eyes and long lashes, their downy arms and their pale fingernails; faces at the window.

Here at Agni, the sensation had been keener: I have not lived, I have known only my husband, I have spent my whole life waiting; this is my life.

And she yearned to be touched again by the fingers of the masseuse – 'Massage therapist,' the girl had said, correcting her.

What was it like to be loved the way men were loved, casually, recklessly, never having to explain it? Men never needed to know all the implications of love. Men took a woman as though taking a drink and moved on.

Audie had smiled at the mobs. He was not daunted. He believed he was invisible to these people, and perhaps he was, behind the tinted windows of the car. But she had feared suffocation – you could drown, you could sink and die in the middle of all these indifferent people. The crush of them was not exotic to her but rather like an intensification of her life. In India, even in this car, she was outdoors, in the world, confronted, as though being asked whether to live or not. In the car, Audie had seen the people struggling on bicycles or driving yoked buffalos or standing like anonymous victims and casualties and he'd said, 'Will you look at that?'

India was as near to life and death as it was possible to be on earth. But it was not one or the other: here was life in death and death in life.

Still wondering whether she had ever lived at all and smiling sadly she tilted herself into sleep.

In the morning, exhausted by their dreams, they woke like campers in a wilderness and prepared themselves for the routines of the day, yoga, breakfast, treatments, the pool, lunch, all the rest of it, not even talking. They had come to like the program of un-demanding events, finding serenity in the ordinari-ness of the routine.

But walking to yoga that day, each of them saw the

smoke rising from beyond the perimeter of Monkey Hill, funneling up the slope where they'd been told that Hanuman Nagar was located. They smelled it too, as sulfurous, the sharpness of scorched dirt, that tang of burned excrement; but neither of them mentioned it, each thinking, *It's smoke, it will be blown away*, and they continued in their routine.

But when, around noon, there was a break in their routine, they were disturbed.

Dr Nagaraj left a message tucked under their door requesting a meeting at one o'clock in his office. He had never written before; his handwriting was black and severe and intimidating; and one o'clock was their lunch hour.

'What's this all about?' Audie asked.

They met him together, feeling importuned, but Beth was sheepish when it turned out that Dr Nagaraj was only being helpful. Somehow he had discovered – obviously from someone at the front desk – that she had been looking to buy a shatoosh, perhaps more than one. Dr Nagaraj said that he knew a certain man, but that it was not possible for this shatoosh seller to enter Agni. It was not permitted.

'He is just a common hawker, you see. From the town.'

'The town we keep hearing about,' Beth said.

'Hanuman Nagar,' Dr Nagaraj said. 'His shop is that side.'

That name again, of the invisible place.

'How will we get there?'

'I will request a vehicle – a motor car.'

They did not meet the car at the residence in the

circular drive but in a more circumspect way, at the Agni entrance, near the signs, *Right of Entry Prohibited Except by Registered Guests* and *No Trespassing* and *Authorized Vehicles Only*. The white old-fashioned sedan was waiting, curtains on its windows, tassels dangling on the curtains. The Blundens got into the rear seat, Dr Nagaraj in the front with the driver ('This is Deepak') and they left Agni for only the second time in more than three weeks, descending the hill.

Passing the lookout at the bend in the road where they had seen the monkeys, Beth said, 'This man, the shatoosh seller, is he a friend?'

'I know him,' Dr Nagaraj said in a tone that suggested: I am a doctor, how could a mere shatoosh-seller be a friend?

Walking to the main gateway, Audie had said, 'The doc gets a kickback. That's how these things work. The driver will get something, too. Everyone's on commission here.'

The road leveled off at an intersection, the wider road continuing to descend, the narrower one traversing the slope. The car turned into this narrower road, into the glaring afternoon sun which dazzled them. They averted their eyes and when they were in shadow again it was the shadow of a row of roadside huts and shops, where there were plodding cows and two boys kicking a dusty blue ball.

This was the talked-about town, the town they had smelled and heard, the town of the smoke. And now that they were in it they could match the sounds – not just the laboring buses and trucks, but the wailing of music, shrieking songs.

Dr Nagaraj said nothing. The Blundens sat horrified, as they had been on the way from the airport, at the squalor, the crowds of people. They drew level with a bus stop where people had gathered near a rusty Tata bus that was shuddering and letting off passengers. Beyond it the road became the main street of a town of one-story shops set shoulder to shoulder above storm drains.

'What's that?' Beth asked.

Up ahead there was a pile of soot-blackened rubble inside the sort of walled courtyard she associated with holy places and private villas.

'Eshrine,' Dr Nagaraj said.

'Are they tearing it down?'

'No. Building it up.'

Audie smiled at the confusion, that it was impossible to tell whether the place was in the process of being destroyed or put up.

'Formerly it was mosque. Before mosque it was Hindu temple. Back to Hindu temple now.'

Smoke swirled behind the fortified gates.

'Who are those people?'

'*Yatris*. Pilgrims. Holy people. They are venerating the site. Also some people protecting the site.'

'Protecting it against who?'

'*Goondas*. Rascals, and Muslims. *Badmashes*, you know?'

Now they could see occupiers and protestors, both sides carrying signs, all of them shouting. Few noises were more frightening to the Blundens in India than these human voices, barking in anger.

'How can you tell they're Muslims?'

'Beards are there.'

'Is this a problem?'

'It is situation,' Dr Nagaraj said.

'What if it gets out of hand?'

'Not possible. Though this is a Muslim area, so to say, Muslim people are outnumbered in this town. This is historic town. This town is mentioned favorably in Atharvaveda. This is Hanuman town, where he seized mountain of medicinal herbals to heal the sickly Lakshman.'

As he lectured them, Beth saw that a detachment of uniformed policemen had lined up and were holding four-foot sticks against a crowd of men – the men shouting and shaking their fists at the men inside the enclosure, where a bonfire blazed, sending smoke into the air high above the town.

'I think I mentioned how I led my friend among the elephants,' Dr Nagaraj said, hardly seeming to notice the people peering into the car, the motorcycles and handcarts vying for space in the road, their own furiously honking driver whom Beth hated for drawing the attention of bystanders to their car.

'I seem to recall it,' Audie said, but he thought: which version?

Beth was only half listening. She could feel the tension of the town in her body like a cramp, she could smell it and taste it. It was dreadful and disorderly, yet she was roused by its truth, as the revelation of something which had lain hidden from her, but was hidden no longer – no one hiding, no one groveling, the sight of smoke and fire and open conflict. She was shocked and excited by it. It was India with the gilt scraped off, hungry India, the India of struggle, India at odds with itself. She had seen Indians at Agni but they didn't live there. This is where Indians lived, in the smoke and flames of Hanuman Nagar.

'I was devastated,' Dr Nagaraj said. He was still talking about his friend, dead among the elephants. 'I could not stop sobbing at his funeral.'

They had come to the shop. Beth could see the stack of shatooshes on the counter, the welcoming shopkeeper pushing people aside so that they could alight. They entered the shop and were shown to plastic chairs. The shopkeeper then pulled a wooden shutter, as though to conceal the transaction. With some ceremony he unfolded a shatoosh and presented it to Beth to admire. Before she could register her pleasure, he gave her another one.

'His grandmother took me aside. She said, "Do you know the story of Vishnu, who rode on the great bird Garuda to the House of the Gods?"'

'Feel, *chiru*,' the shatoosh seller was saying, unfolding one piece after another and draping some of them on the counter and thrusting others into Beth's hands.

'As Vishnu and Garuda entered the House of the Gods they saw a small bird at the gateway. The Lord of Death also entered, and he smiled at the little bird. Garuda was so shocked at this he seized the little bird in his beak and took him fifty kilometers away, to save him from the Lord of Death. And by the way,' Dr Nagaraj said, 'these are first-quality shatoosh. Made from chin hairs of very rare Tibetan antelope. Woven in Kashmir. This man is Kashmiri himself.'

Audie said, 'Is that the end of the story? The little bird was saved, right?'

In their experience Dr Nagaraj never said yes or no. He considered Audie's question and said, 'When ultimately they left the House of the Gods, Vishnu said, "Where is the little bird?"'

Beth turned to him and saw that he had kicked off his sandals, that though he was still speaking he was admiring the stacks of unfolded shatooshes. He had turned his back on the Blundens yet speaking into the shadows of the shop, where a naked child was slapping the tiles with a plastic drinking cup, he sounded more composed and oracular.

'Before Garuda could reply, Lord of Death said, "I smiled to see little bird here, because he was supposed to be fifty kilometers away, to meet his death."'

Hearing this, Beth was stricken, as though Dr Nagaraj had pinched her, and without thinking she said, 'We must be going.' She was overcome by the mustiness of the shop, the incense that seemed a mingling of perfume and cowshit, the imploring shatoosh seller – the illegality of what he was doing – and within earshot the yells of the men at the shrine, the smell of its smoky fires. She picked up two scarves and said, 'I'll take these two.'

'I told him you are not tourists, you are *yatris* yourselves, doing puja at Agni.'

'That's us,' Audie said.

'I will deal with money. You know it is some thousands of dollars?' Dr Nagaraj said. 'You can pay me later. I will find you in the car.'

They made their way to the car through the crowd

that had gathered at the shop to gape at them. Dr Nagaraj got into the front seat and they were soon driving down the main street again of the cracked and littered town. It was a whole town, spread as though broken and scattered on the side of Monkey Hill, out of sight of Agni. Dirty, busy, poorly lit, shops selling shoes and saris, one shop with barred windows selling beer and whiskey, chaotic, so full of life it suggested death, too.

'Monkey temple?' Audie said as they passed the shouters, the fire, the sign-carriers, the policemen.

'Hanuman temple,' Dr Nagaraj said.

'How long has this mob scene been going on?'

'Some years now.'

Beth sat stunned and heard Audie inquire in a reasonable voice, 'Would you mind explaining your story? Maybe I'm stupid. But I don't get it.'

'Listen, my friend. Grandmother of Sanjeev said to me, "Don't be sad. Garuda guided the little bird to his death, unknowingly, as you guided Sanjeev. You were meant to deliver him."'

They continued the rest of the way to Agni in silence, and at each curve in the road a little of Hanuman Nagar was lost, first the sight of it, then the sound of it, and at last even its smoke, until at last when they entered the Agni gate, it was gone.

'"Maybe this is your purpose in world," she said.' As soon as the car slowed down Dr Nagaraj began speaking. '"To guide people to their fate. You are wee-ickle." Better we stop here.'

After Dr Nagaraj dismissed the driver the three walked the rest up the hill. On the way, Audie asked the cost of the scarves. Dr Nagaraj seemed relieved and mentioned the price and smiled as five thousand dollars was counted into his hand.

'A great bargain, sir. And you are so lucky. This antelope is almost extinct.'

4

The shock of the day, and her excited fear, gave her perfect recall. At yoga the next morning, during a massage – hot oil, slippery fingers – inside the pavilion, by the pool, she remembered everything. She was not able to rid herself of the images of the town of Hanuman Nagar – the cows, the bus stop, the shops, the cracks in the old walls, the paper advertisements peeling from the walls, the thick bars on the windows of the liquor store, the mocking boys like little fearless old men, the overworked women, the secretive shatoosh seller, the whole weary town held together by rusty wire and wooden braces. One oblong pothole in the street had looked to her like an open grave – she could have fitted in.

Most of all the confusion at the monkey temple. Audie had explained it over breakfast. A mosque had been built centuries ago on the site of an ancient Hindu temple, and protestors had besieged it and reclaimed it – torn the mosque apart and built a shrine to the monkey god. The Muslims were angry, they were protesting the occupation, but the Hindus were defiant, chanting and stoking their fire.

She remembered details she had only glimpsed at the time, chief among them the sight of monkeys scampering among occupiers and protestors, snatching at bags, biting each other, swinging up the trees and onto the parapets of the shrine itself.

Now in the stillness of Agni she believed that she could hear the loud voices from the town, the straining of car engines, music, fugitive laughter, the pinching smell of smoke; or was that sense of life from the other world, the sounds from the hidden place, another illusion?

'Amazing story, eh?' Audie said.

She stared at him. *What story?* was in her smile.

'About that guy Sanjeev. The Lord of Death. Kind of an *Appointment in Samarra* thing.'

Beth said, 'I didn't know what he was talking about. Anyway, didn't you say he was a quack?'

'It doesn't really matter if he's a quack. He makes me feel better.'

'You said his story keeps changing.'

'I like that he could talk a dog off a meat wagon,' Audie said. 'And I sometimes think I'm a quack. When I was on a board, I never wanted to admit when I was wrong. Lots of times I thought – I'm a phony.'

She stared at him again, distancing herself with a smile.

He said, 'Don't you ever think that?'

'About you?'

'About yourself.' Normally he became hot and impatient when he needed to clarify something obvious to her – she could be so slow sometimes. But he wasn't impatient now, he was sympathetic and mild.

'Never,' she said. And she thought: I have never believed I was a phony. If anything, I felt more real than anyone ever took me for. There was more to me than they realized or cared about. To those people who looked at her and thought *wife* or *woman*, she wanted to say, *I am more than anything you see.*

Now it was early afternoon, she was reading by the pool, on the platform under the trees, hidden by a hedge from anyone who happened to be in the chaises longues – but there was no one there, or at the pool. And Audie was at a treatment. She had ordered a lemonade and grilled vegetable sandwich, but had only sipped at the drink and eaten just a bite of the sandwich.

With an accompanying thump, something landed behind her, the sandwich was snatched, and she flinched, raising her arms, and saw the monkey bound away. In her instant memory it was a monkey; at the moment of muddled confrontation she had seen the thing as a hairy, hostile child – like one of the mocking boys she'd seen at Hanuman Nagar – and she was too panicked to scream, though still her hands were raised to protect her face and breasts.

After leaping into the biggest of the trees the monkey found a branch, grasped it with his feet and began to gnaw at the sandwich, scattering vegetables. These were seized by other monkeys – six or seven – no, more, maybe a dozen, big and small, more insolent than afraid, with a malevolent patience, a defiance that she identified – just a hunch, something about the set of their jaws, the biting faces – as the courage of hunger.

They moved towards her without a sound, scarcely seeming to touch the deck boards in their tumbling, noiseless, flowing at her, their wicked faces twitching.

She opened her mouth to shout but could not make a sound.

Their hair prickled on her body, the dampness itched as it scraped at her legs. They had pinched more of the loose vegetables that had been lying on the deck, poked them into their mouths, yet kept their eyes on her.

She knew they wanted to eat her face, push her legs apart and knock her over, squat on her breasts and stink. The stink was in the air, preceding them as they pushed towards her.

She covered her face with one arm, flung her other arm across her breasts and went numb from the waist down, as in a dream where she found her legs so slow as to be crippled. She wished she could scream as she saw that the monkeys, perhaps twenty of them now, were about to overwhelm her with their dirty paws and wet teeth.

The crack of something landing in their midst – a heavy clattering stick – startled her, and the monkeys fell back. Then another stick with a thump, as a man hurried past Beth shouting, 'Shoo! Shoo!' Holding his sandals in his hands the man waved his arms, still shouting, physically thrusting the creatures away, into the trees, finally picking up the sticks he had thrown and flinging them again, until at last the monkeys retreated and were out of sight.

As the man had advanced, Beth had stepped back, recovered her strength, and climbed the stairs to the apron of the pool. She found that she was out of breath, her chest tight, and panting from the simple effort of backing up. But she was still afraid.

'Don't worry, madam,' the man said – he was young,

hardly man, in white pants and a white smock, barefoot. He looked beautiful.

Beth was choking with anxiety, unable to speak, her upper body rocking for balance.

'They are very bold,' the man said. He retrieved his sandals and slipped them on. He was smiling – lovely teeth, great confidence, not even breathing hard, not fazed at all. Audie would have been gasping.

She made a grateful, approving sound, meant to be 'thank you,' but it was just a nervous exhalation.

'You see, they have been around humans for so long they have lost their fear. They are used to being fed by hand, and others – at the temple in town – they are like little gods, spoiled children you can say. Are you all right, madam?'

Because she hadn't said a word.

'Where did you come from?' Beth said, with difficulty.

'Hanuman Nagar.'

'No, no,' she said – he had misunderstood, thinking she'd asked him where he lived. She rephrased the question. 'Were you watching them?'

'I was watching you, madam.'

He faced her squarely, not smiling, looking intently at her.

'Thank you.'

He did not blink. He said, 'Since you arrived at Agni, I have not stopped watching you.'

That made her pause. She was at a loss to reply, she had felt giddy, joyous at having been rescued from the monkeys. But now she felt awkward – unaware of the young man's gaze, she had been observed. He was forcing her to concentrate, as though this episode was not over yet – something more was required, he was hovering.

'I don't know how to thank you,' she said. 'Please take this,' and she went back to her bag by the chair and took out some rupees. They felt like cloth in her hand they were so worn.

'Oh, no, madam,' the young man said, and put his hands behind his back in a prim gesture, complete with a show of dimples.

'Isn't there anything?'

'Yes.' He was quick, already he had control of the situation. 'You can request me.'

'Request you?'

'For treatment,' he said. 'Ask for Satish.'

The slow drip of hot oil on Audie's back, the pressure and heat, suggested her fingertips, and when she drizzled the oil in widening circles it was as though she was caressing him. The brass pot was set down on the heater with a click and then he felt her hands. She did not say much, had only greeted him, and she hardly spoke unless he asked a direct question. Yet the confident intelligence in her hands moved down his back, a wise inquiry in the motion of her fingers. She was able by touching him to find parts of his body that, until that moment, were unknown to him, and so her insinuating hands awakened a knotted muscle, rested her thumb on it and pushed, giving it life.

'That's nice.'

Anna paired her thumbs and pushed again, swiveling downward along the meat of his spine, gliding through the oil to the small of his back.

'You are having this in America, sir?'

'Doubt it.'

She went silent. Perhaps she hadn't understood his grunt. She worked harder, still on the bundles of muscles next to his spine.

'I would like to go to America. Where is your home, sir?'

He did not say, *That's a hard question. We've got a place in Florida, an apartment in New York, a house in Maine.*

'I'm from Boston,' he said. 'Near Boston.'

'Boston Tea Party. Boston Red Sox. Boston beans.'

He laughed into his towel, then raised his head and asked, 'Ever been outside of India?'

'Only to Delhi, sir. School trip, sir.'

That reminded him of how young she was. He said, 'You could probably make a lot of money in the States. Doing massages.'

'But also to meet people, sir. To be happy, sir. To be free, sir.'

'You're free here, aren't you?'

'No, sir. Not free. It is very hard here for me. As I mentioned, I am Christian, sir.'

She was now working on his right arm. She had begun on his shoulder, squeezed and pressed her way to his wrist, and was now massaging his palm and, one by one, his fingers. Her manipulating his fingers he found like an act of the purest friendship, more sensual, more intimate, as she pushed and pulled, than her touch on any other part of his body. Take my hand, he thought. It meant everything.

'Wouldn't you be afraid to be in the United States alone?'

'Oh?' she was holding his fingers with one hand and kneading his palm with the thumb of her other hand. The way she touched him told him she was thinking. 'Maybe I will find someone to look after me.'

'Give you money, you mean?'

'I will earn it, sir.'

His throat thickened at the implications of what she said. He asked, 'What would you do?'

'I can do so many things, sir.'

'What makes you so sure?'

'I have training, sir.'

'Lots of girls have training.'

'But my training, sir, is not in school.'

'Experience?'

'Experience, sir. Best teacher, sir.'

'That feels nice,' he said. 'But can you do the hardest thing of all?'

'What is that, sir?'

'Keep a secret?'

She had begun to stroke his other arm. She held it as though it were detached from his body; she weighed it and traced her fingers down his forearm to his wrist as though evaluating it. Then she caught his fingers and brushed them against her body, he could not tell where, her softness, her warmth, perhaps her breast or her smooth cheek.

'Oh, yes, sir. I can do that, sir.'

He was aware that he had had this conversation many times in his life, the flirting, the allusion, the euphemism, his earliest talks with girls, as a boy of twelve or thirteen, and almost fifty years on, the same innuendo, the same themes – like a language he'd learned early in life, a second language that was used exclusively between a man and woman, the language of suggestion, never quite coming to the point yet always knowing what the point was. He delighted in this inexplicit talk.

'Sir?'

'Yup?'

'Please turn over, sir.'

'Not just now.'

She sighed in approval. She knew he was aroused and embarrassed. He could not turn over without exposing himself, bulging against the covering, lifting it at an angle, his conspicuous desire.

'That is all right, sir.' She was trying to be serious.

'Give me a minute. I'm happy.'

'I want to please you, sir.'

'You're doing fine.'

'Thank you, sir.' She leaned against his back, as though embracing him, but using her elbow, her forearm, her fists on his packed muscles. She was canted over him, resting on him, her breath warming his shoulders and his neck. Because he was faced away from her she seemed bolder, and what aroused him again was his suspicion that she knew the effect she was having on him.

'Did you learn that in school?'

She did not hesitate, she pressed harder, her whole body upon him.

'No, sir.' He could tell she was smiling. 'In life, sir.'

For a few days, Audie and Beth found reasons to be busy, to remain apart at the very time when, a week earlier, they would have been punctually together, looking at Agni and its people – guests and staff – and agreeing with each other: at the pool, in the restaurant, in their suite, at yoga, awaiting a treatment, poking golf balls across the putting green, side by side.

Now, 'I guess I just missed you,' Beth would say, as a way of explaining her all-afternoon absence.

'That's okay,' Audie would reply. 'I was tied up longer than I'd expected.'

Each was grateful for the other's casualness, since in the past they'd seemed to agree that solitude was selfish. But their absences were an unexpected relief, and the fact that they did not need to explain them to each other left the absences ambiguous, almost without meaning, as in other years when, late home from the office, Audie had said, 'I was held up.' On many of those occasions he'd been with a woman, his secretary, someone from the company, the wife of an employee.

Beth somehow knew but hadn't asked, since asking would have made it real, more serious than she imagined it to be. And Audie, in the wrong, was thankful to her for giving him the benefit of the doubt. Because he did not examine these affairs, kept them in the dark where they were enacted, they vanished, and apart from some moments, the bitterness mainly, even the memory of them was gone. Only in the reveries of the treatment room, being massaged, flirting obliquely with the therapist, did he remember. And in the week when Beth had begun to say that she'd been held up – 'Just missed you' – he was calm. He owed her that much.

As for Anna, he had never felt so attracted and yet so resistant to a woman. All his memories had welled up in him, and though he was aroused the feeling was like a farewell. He was delighted that he still felt it as a throbbing in his ears, a swilling of blood; but he knew that it led nowhere. Knowing that he could have the woman so easily made him generous; and the knowledge calmed him. He saw Anna one evening with a young man walking through the grove of bamboos, and he smiled, even as she was flustered – he knew that she did not want him to draw any conclusions, for everything in her demeanor said, *I am waiting for you*.

Still he saw her every day. He wondered where she lived, what her room was like, what she wore on her day off, the details of her real life when she was not in a uniform and working. Seeing her in an Agni sari, or in the white pajamas of a spa therapist, gave her an anonymity that prevented him from seeing her any other way. It was not physical desire he felt, hardly any compulsion at all, but only simple curiosity. He thought, Who are you when you're at home?

Beth, in her absences, which were most of them treatments, wanted to be touched. And in the hours in between she needed to be alone, to reflect on being touched, being held, caressed, dripped with hot oil, and at last whispered to, even if the words were only 'Please relax your arm' or 'Please turn over for me' or 'Is it too hard, madam?'

She found that she could not pass easily from the intimacy of a treatment room, the fatigue following a massage, to a meal or a drink with Audie. She wanted enough privacy and solitude to reflect on what had just happened.

I feel like a schoolgirl, she thought afterwards, lying in a chair by the pool, out of sight, near where the monkeys had snatched her food. Had she been with Audie she would have felt vulnerable and slightly ridiculous. But being alone there was something delicious in her reverie – no one to judge it, nothing to measure it by, like the fantasy of a virgin almost, easy for her to recapture, since in her life she had been intimate with one man, whose absence now seemed like a kindness.

And each of them, husband and wife, remembered what they had seen of Hanuman Nagar, the other world down the slope, on a dusty ledge of Monkey Hill, its disorder and its ragged shadows.

5

Someone breathing hard was waiting for her, someone's wet face watching her, eager for her to join him – all this was new and it made her happy. And as long as she was apart from Audie she did not have to examine any of it. Unexamined, the thing held no blame: you could call it anything. It was a pulse, nothing more, like a sudden chord in a passage of music, notes played from that other world, the music that she'd been hearing ever since she'd come here. None of it had a name.

Only when she picked something apart with self-conscious fingers, or was made conspicuous by someone familiar, a pair of scrutinizing eyes on her, did a tremble of guilt cause her to hesitate. Otherwise, what did it matter? She had done nothing wrong.

If Audie's contentment was a plus it was also a puzzle. He was too kind, too beneficent; he left her to herself, he did not inquire as to her whereabouts. His benign absence made her uneasy, for her thoughts were complicated and whenever she saw him – at meals, in the suite, glimpsed in the half spinal twist at yoga – she felt, without any reason, that she was deceiving him; that her heart was halfway down the mountain in the dusty and littered bazaar of Hanuman Nagar.

Still she did nothing to encourage Satish – in fact she resisted him. With the sort of impatient clumsiness that he'd used against the wild monkeys, he'd offered her all sorts of invitations. She had first pretended not to understand; then had flatly refused. She stopped short of telling him that he was breaking the Agni rules – that seemed overbearing. Yet why had her refusals made her flush with guilt? Perhaps because she knew they were her secret, and when had she ever had a secret from Audie? None of her refusals had been so strong as to discourage the boy. As the days passed he had become more familiar, which was his way of being persistent.

One day before a massage, while she stood in her robe, the blinds half drawn, the music playing – ragas, chants of Ganesha – he'd raised his hands and said, 'Moment, madam.'

Satish assumed the lotus position and then, twining his legs and falling backwards, hauled himself up in a series of specific but fluid moves, tipping forward onto his forearms, supporting his head and whole body and raising his legs until they were vertical. Finally, he lowered his legs over his back and lifted his neck, so that his feet touched his face.

'*Vrischikasana*,' he grunted through his wiggling toes.

'I've seen that in circuses,' Beth said.

'Scorpion pose.'

He was, she realized, trying to impress her, and his effort made her smile. She was happy merely being with him, in the incense-filled room, the music playing, anticipating his hands on her, the hot oil, the sounds of his breath as he touched her. But he was young: he felt the need to perform.

'You see this watch?' he said another day.

She looked, she could not tell the make; it was plump, it seemed absurdly technical.

'Chronometer,' he said, pressing the protrusions at its edges. 'Timer, digital read-out. Twistable bezel. Totally waterproof. Immersible for two hundred meters. Self-winding.'

'I thought it was a bracelet.'

'Is also jewelry. Valuable!'

Wide-eyed, blowing bubbles with his boasting. *Walubloo!*

'You're not supposed to wear that when you do massages, are you?'

Beth took him by the hand and turned his wrist over and squeezed the watchband, plucking open its fastener, slipping it off.

'Isn't that better?' She had touched him for the first time.

He looked chastened, as he ducked outside to allow her the privacy to slide beneath the sheet on the massage table. But in the half-dark of the room on his return he was confident again, working on her shoulders, breathing softly against her neck.

'Have a nice night,' he said to her the following afternoon when the massage had ended.

It seemed like an inquiry. She said, 'What do you do at night?'

'I repair to my house. Reading to improve education. Yoga to improve body and mind. Also painting.'

'You paint pictures?'

'Classic painting,' he said. 'Indian gods and goddesses.'

What made her feel awkward was that she knew,

before he said another word, where this entire conversation was going, the next elements of it, her questions, his responses, and how in a matter of minutes
it would end. And she had started it.

'Lovely,' she found herself saying. 'It sounds lovely.'

'Painting with brush. Making pictures for puja.' He
wobbled his head, a misleading movement she now
understood as affirmative. 'Classic.'

'You're a man of many talents.'

She was hardly speaking her own mind; she was
glad no one could hear these predictable phrases and
clichés. It was as though she was reciting dialogue that
someone else had prepared for her, that other people
had practiced. Or perhaps all love affairs began like
this, as repetition, as mimicry, as passionate clichés. Yet
she wanted to believe that the feeling was real and
originated within her.

It was better not to say anything, better just to smile,
to let his hands work on her, to give nothing a name.

In spite of this, another whole unthought-out line
came to her. 'I'd like to see them.'

'Yes, please.'

'Maybe sometime.'

'Madam, tonight.'

Against her will she found herself agreeing, and just
afterwards, avoiding Audie at the pool, she felt excited,
thrilled and yet jittery, like a girl.

Satish had said he'd meet her below the laundry
building, which lay on the path that wound down the
Monkey Hill to the main road into Hanuman Nagar.
She told Audie she was going up to the spa – 'A treat-

ment.' He smiled, he said, 'Have a good one.' But instead of climbing up the road, she ducked through the bamboo grove, and walked quickly through the thick flowering trees into the smoky air that rose from the town.

She felt on her face the sourness of walking down the path into a thickening smell, plunging towards shadows, ducking beneath the silken daylight of dusk in this upper world into the fugitive and divided lamplight of the town below.

A person thrusting a broomstick at her rose up on the road and caused her to gasp.

'Moddom.'

'Who are you?'

'Chowkidar, moddom.'

'What do you want?'

Fright made her severe, and her severity made the man deferential.

He said, 'Protection only, moddom.'

His mildness calmed her. She found some rupees in her pocket – in the darkness she could not tell how much – and handed the notes to the watchman. He touched them to his forehead, he bowed to let her pass.

The downward path was so narrow her shoulders brushed the bushes on either side of it, and she imagined that at that time of day there might be monkeys, crouching to observe the setting sun, like the ones she'd seen with Audie almost two weeks ago, when they'd heard the name Hanuman Nagar from the spectral old man.

The sense that she was leaving one world for another

was palpable: in the rising dust and the sound of impatient voices, the men shouting at the monkey temple, the smell of smoke, and other voices, the sharp Indian yell, meant to be heard at a distance and to make the hearer submit to it. The grating of traffic, too – heavy trucks, the laboring bus, all shuddering metal and hisses. And, farther from the clear air and the tidy gardens of Agni, the stink of the town – dirt, dung, smoke, oil, mingled with cooking odors and scorched oil. Disorder was also a stew of smells.

Where she thought she saw a monkey squatting on its heels, a man stood up. Too startled to scream, her hands flew up to protect her throat and her face. She saw it was Satish.

'Not to worry,' he said.

She hoped he wouldn't touch her. Rattled from her uneasy descent from Agni on the filthy path, she said, 'I can't stay long.'

'It is near,' he said, placing a finger on her elbow to steer her, and when she reacted, he said, 'Sorry!'

His touch made her stumble; the path here was littered with loose trodden stones. He was still apologizing as they passed behind a shop, a wall that reeked of urine and was scribbled on, and came out onto the road. In the distance, at the curve in the road, she saw the shop fronts of Hanuman Nagar, merchandise hanging in doorways, and the fires at the monkey temple – men waving torches, some men chanting, the line of policemen holding sticks.

'Cart road,' Satish said, blocking her way as a truck went slowly past in gusts of diesel fumes.

'That temple,' Beth said.

'Hanuman shrine. Long ago, Mughal time, Muslim ruler put mosque in its place. Now it is restored to Hindu. Now everyone so happy.'

'Why are those people shouting?'

'Muslim people,' Satish said, hurrying ahead, away from the center of town.

She followed him, her head down, walking just above the gutter and the storm drain, by the roadside, thinking, *This is insane.*

'I have to go back' – and felt even more like a girl, but a foolish one.

'It is just here,' he said, fluttering his fingers into the middle distance.

All she saw were small yellow windows, like lanterns hanging in darkness, faces at some of the windows, the blue flicker of TV sets, and the woof-woofing of dogs somewhere. At one doorway, she smelled meat grilling, the sputter and hiss, the pucker and bust of hot snapping fat.

Satish must have smelled it too. He said, 'Muslim people. Many here. This we are calling' – he was pointing at Monkey Hill but the sweep of his arm seemed to take in the whole province – 'Muslim belt.'

She said, 'I can't go any further.'

'We have arrived,' he said and led her up a path of broken paving stones that rolled under her feet, past a small astonished girl in a bright pink dress dawdling by a lighted doorway, past a padlocked shed, to a door latch which Satish manipulated, pushing the door open. Beth stepped inside quickly, fearing to be seen, and was at once suffocated by the smell of cooked food, steaming on a low table.

'Bhaji,' Satish said, lifting the lid of a tin pot. Then more lids up and down, 'Mung dhal. Uttapam. Bindi. Naan bread. Rice.'

'Very nice,' Beth said, overcome by the heat, the stifling aromas and a distinct smell of turpentine.

'Gurd,' Satish said, offering her a dish of curded yogurt.

'I really must go back,' she said.

'Madam,' he said. 'Take some food.'

'I'm not hungry,' she said, and remembered from a book on India that it was considered offensive to refuse food in an Indian household, but that a small symbolic mouthful was all that was necessary. She said, 'But some of that curd would be delicious. Just a touch.'

He spooned some into a bowl and handed it to her, saying, 'Sit, please madam. A drink. Hot tea. Juices. Cool water.'

She was rechecking the position of the door, preparing her exit, when she saw an assortment of foot-high paintings propped on a shelf, under a bare light bulb.

'No thank you. Are those your pictures?'

She was still standing, eyeing the door. He went to the paintings and selected a highly colored one of a fat naked baby attended by a smiling chubby-cheeked woman in a yellow sari.

'Bal Krishna,' he said. 'Krishna baby. Mother Yashoda.'

Moving closer to the shelf, she saw other pictures she had taken to be animals, yet some of them had human features in spite of their snouts and multiple arms.

'Ganesh. Hanuman. Durga. I do with brush. Classical.'

'Superb. Thank you. Now I must go.'

'Madam.'

But as soon as she turned and found the latch and got the door ajar he was next to her, embracing her, pressing himself against her, whinnying. *Madam. Madam.*

'I don't feel at all well,' she said.

'I have aspirin, madam.' His hands and fingers flexed on her waist as though testing its pliability.

But now she had gotten the door fully open, and the night air had a chilly smell of dirt and wood smoke in it that clung like grime to the bare skin of her face and arms.

Just a few feet down the path the small girl in the pink dress gaped at her, the light from the open door falling across her face, brightening her wide staring eyes. Satish had pursued Beth but when he saw the little girl he hesitated, seemingly overcome, and he dropped his arms to his sides, gathering his hands into his pajama top as though in a reflex of shame.

Without a word, moving efficiently in fear, Beth stepped along the walkway, those same uneven paving stones, and fled into the road, keeping her head down when car headlights passed her. She looked back several times, to make sure she was not being followed.

She slipped into the suite with all the stealth of a burglar, called out 'Audie?' but there was no reply. The suite was empty.

In the darkness outside the Agni enclosure, the smell was more apparent. Audie had stood just at nightfall, watching the sun drop as though dissolving into the depths of dust and haze that lay in thick bars above the horizon, obliterating the mountains – and the mountains were the Himalayas. And rising around him in the gathering dusk the sharpness of dry trees, the stray grit in the air, the dander of grubby monkey fur, and boiled beans, burned meat, wood smoke, foul water, until the darkness itself seemed to stifle him.

Had Beth not announced that she was getting an evening treatment, he would not have come. But impulsively he had called Anna's cellphone and, as though expecting his call, she'd given him explicit directions, saying that she would meet him. *Six-thirty, sharp*. She'd chosen sundown, but even at sundown there was left-over light, and this was the reason he gave for her being late.

'Excuse me, sir.'

Her voice came out of the darkness. She was walking towards him, and she emerged as though materializing before him like a phantom.

'I didn't see you coming. Don't you have a flashlight?'

'A torch, sir, yes. But not necessary now.'

She did not want to be seen. That was a sign of her seriousness. And so Audie summed her up quickly: she is meeting me secretly. She thinks she knows what I want. She is willing to cooperate – all this was obvious in her unwillingness to use a light. Artful, he thought, but even I don't know what I want.

'Your cellphone works pretty well on the hill.'

'My mobile, sir. Guest Services provides. Sometimes we are on call for night treatments.'

'Is that what this is?'

Anna laughed, snuffling nervously. 'I don't know, sir.'

'Where's your flashlight, honey?'

'Here, sir.'

He groped for it, found her warm hand, took the flashlight and switched it on, hoping that the light would drive away the smell. It seemed to work; as soon as he could see the stony path the whiffy shadow dispersed, and he could breathe more easily.

'Where are we going?'

'My friend's flat, sir.'

'In the woods?'

'Not woods, sir. Residential Civil Lines.'

'Where do you live, Anna?'

'Staff block, sir. Hostel, sir.'

'You keep saying "sir".'

'Yes, sir,' and she giggled, her hand over her mouth.

Only the path just ahead was lit, but farther down the hill there was the glow that he now knew was the town of Hanuman Nagar and from that distant glow a chattering and shouting.

'What's that noise?'

'Temple, sir.'

'Monkey temple?'

'Hanuman temple, sir.'

Audie was careful not to touch her, though she was walking just in front of him, on the steep downward path towards the sound of a coughing vehicle and the glare of some sulfurous lights. He saw a three-story squarish building, a smell of rotting clothes lingering near it.

'Is that it?'

'It is, sir.'

But he had stopped. He'd lost the momentum he'd had in the darkness on the path above.

'In here, sir.'

He took a step towards her. He reached and put his arm around her, and he could tell in his embrace that she was breathing hard. She was tense, she seemed to quail, holding her face away from him yet presenting her hips to him. Her bare belly was soft like a cushion of bread dough in his hand.

'Are you all right?'

'Yes, sir. I am all right, sir.' He could tell she was willing; he could also tell that she was terrified. 'Let we go inside, sir?'

Audie took a deep breath and, expelling it, he slackened his grip on her. Aware that he was holding her lightly he became self-conscious and let go. He felt in his pocket for his wallet that was fat with rupees and without looking at the denominations – he carried only 500 rupee notes – he took out a thickness of them and pressed them into her hand.

'This is for you.'

'Thank you, sir.'

Not only did she accept them, she seemed relieved. Her whole body relaxed as she breathed more easily.

'You're a good girl. I want you to stay that way.'

'Thank you, sir. Bless you, sir.'

She giggled a bit in relief, and drew another deep breath as she watched him back away, up the path.

Beth was in the room when Audie returned. He was so sheepish from his errand he did not notice how Beth held the book to shield her face; did not see her apprehension, he was himself so apprehensive.

'I wasn't very hungry,' he said.

'I just had a snack.'

'Love ya,' he said.

Waiting in the woods, standing in the lowering darkness had tired him; walking all that way down the path to the isolated apartment block had wearied him too. He thought, I don't have the energy anymore to walk in darkness. And he was ashamed of himself – of the power he had over the girl to make her obey. She had been afraid. He hated himself for putting her in that position, her obvious horror at the prospect of sex yet willing to sacrifice herself to him, for the money. In the exhaustion brought on by his shame he fell asleep, his mouth open, his harsh breath rising and falling.

He did not hear Beth slip out of her bed and dress quickly; did not hear her pad out of the room, carrying her sandals in her hand; did not hear the door click shut.

Beth hurried from their suite to the stairwell, moving carefully, out the front door, past the porte cochère and across the night-damp lawn to the grove of bamboos. Guided by the risen moon, she found the path to the laundry, and behind it the path to Hanuman Nagar.

'Moddom! Chowkidar, modom.'

The night watchman was on his feet, saluting with one hand, his flashlight in the other showing her the way.

Everything seemed easier, now that it was an exercise of her will and not a stumbling in the darkness.

The downward path lit by the fluorescence of the moon seemed much shorter, and ahead the main street of the town was empty. Two or three men hunkered on their heels, warming their hands at a flaring brazier; some others she passed slept on the sagging rope beds they'd been squatting on earlier in the evening. The monkey temple at the curve in the road was silent, just a few torches burning.

She had been this way before: it was simpler the second time. She found the alley, stepped over the monsoon drain, smiled at the doorway where the little girl had been and was no more; and at the latched door in the whitewashed wall she tapped lightly.

A murmur came from inside, a word – but not an English word. She was aware of the twitching of curtains at the window next to the door. Then the sliding of a rusty bolt, the door snatched open, the now familiar smell of food.

'Oh, thank you,' he said.

6

They were up early for yoga, seated on their mats on the shelf of the pavilion before anyone else had arrived, even Vikram, the instructor; seated with their legs stiffly folded, an almost achieved lotus position. Their eyes were closed, they were listening to the slight breeze brushing at the willow boughs, the twitter of birds, distant voices, feeling – as Vikram had urged every morning – the peaceful vibrations.

Hearing 'Namaskar', they opened their eyes and saw that Vikram had already taken his place on the pavilion and was holding his hands clasped. They were surrounded by other people sitting on mats. Without their realizing – for no one had spoken – the rest of the yoga class had gathered on the platform, eyes closed, waiting to begin.

Audie leaned towards the couple next to him. They did not turn away, but neither did they acknowledge him.

He was thinking: Everything has a past, especially in India, all the roots, the context, the history, the significance of the slightest thing – every name, every gesture, every morsel of food, every note of music; bend your knee or touch two fingers and it has meaning. But nothing I have ever done or said, no family name, or meal I've eaten, has any past or present, no meaning beyond its ordinariness: it is only what it looks like. Which is better, he wondered, the primary colors of my American life, or the subtleties of Monkey Hill? I am what I appear to be, and the Indian never is.

Distracted, he had not noticed that the class had been bidden to rise and were engaged in stretching, first the arms, hands clasped high above the head, and then an elongated posture, on tiptoe.

'This asana is good for blood circulation. For back. For bowels. Tadasana. Mountain.'

Even this has a name, he was thinking; every gesture. He smiled at Beth, impressed that so great was her concentration, she held her posture.

Beth's mind was traveling backwards, tugged by her uprightness and her lengthened arms, clasped hands aloft. His hands had held her tighter than this in an unnecessary grip, even after she'd said, *I'm not going anywhere.* He was repeating, *Thank you, thank you,* and soon after he had led her somewhat roughly – perhaps it was just his impatience – to the corner of the room, onto the mat, and was pushing at her clothes and seeming to sob with urgency.

She had been at a loss – had no idea what was expected of her, was relieved simply to allow him his freedom to lift her clothes, to stroke her body, was even prepared to say, *Take me.* But in his frenzy any talk was unnecessary. After fumbling with her clothes, and it was as though he'd never touched buttons before, he snatched them off her and knelt to embrace her. She was surprised by his furious impatience.

'And down for crocodile posture,' the yoga instructor was saying.

He had lain upon her just like this, lengthwise, his whole weight pressing her, one knee forcing her legs apart. His jaw was clenched, he was fierce, his breath sucked between his teeth.

'I am bad, I am wicious,' he said, still sucking his breath. 'I love you.'

She twisted under him, feeling the bumping of his hips, and wanted to say, *It hurts.*

None of it was printed on her body now. She was pure; she had washed herself clean.

After his frenzy, almost sobbing to get his breath, he had said, 'Sorry, madam,' and rolled to the side, leaving her naked and unsatisfied and feeling assaulted – not seriously hurt but chafed and subtly bruised. But when she looked over at him his hands were over his face and she felt sorry for him in his shame. He had all at once deflated.

'*Ardha matsyendrasana.* Named for holy man. Spinal twist, don't exert, gently stretch,' Vikram said, leading them in a posture of sideways body twisting. 'Good for blood pressure. For estomach. For espine. Compresses intestines and kidneys.'

Stretching, Beth remembered how Satish had recovered. At the door he had said, 'What about present, madam? Some few rupees.'

The encounter – briefer than she'd expected, one-sided, more like a humiliating shove or a mild spanking – had left her lucid and a bit rueful. It had not been an act of possession, more one of rejection.

'Haven't I just given you something?' she said.

His voice going smoky and dark, he said, 'I will see you tomorrow.'

But she was thinking now, I don't want to see you again.

Beside Beth, on his mat, stretching and bending, breathing in gusts through his nostrils, Audie was preoccupied with a vivid glimpse of holding Anna, the memory of her bare skin on his hand, and how he had let go, given her money and, seizing her last look, had gone away. He thought: I could have had anything – she would have given me whatever I'd asked for. It unsettled him to remember how he had kissed her on the cheek and walked up the dark path to Agni and his suite. But he also thought how virtuous he'd been – faithful to Beth, after so many years of cheating. He could face her now.

'Now, for rest, Savasana,' Vikram said. 'Corpse pose.'

Audie lay in a zone of sleep and did not waken until the chanting ended, *Shantih, shantih, shantih*. He squirmed to a kneeling position, to roll up his mat, but by then the yoga class had dispersed, all of them, mostly Indians, walking away from the pavilion and across the lawn as the sun rising above the distant ridge struck through the trees and dazzled him.

They breakfasted as usual, choosing the Indian option, filling their plates with beans and curried vegetables and yogurt, while the waiters held the lids of the tureens open.

'Everyone's so polite.'

'I'm going to miss that,' Beth said.

'Who said we're leaving?'

The staff was more polite than usual this morning, but that seemed the Indian way. Instead of becoming more familiar, friendlier, loosening in conversation and growing chattier, Indians became more formal, more solemn, coming to attention like drilled foot soldiers facing generals; more respectful, straighter, heels together. Or was it just here at Agni?

'As you wish, madam,' one of the waiters said, bowing that morning – but it was only a request for more tea.

'It is my pleasure,' another one said to Audie.

'They make you feel important,' Audie said, yet he also sensed more distance than warmth in the politeness, and no one was smiling. 'You going for a treatment?'

'I think I'll pass.'

But Audie was eager – most of all eager to see what sort of reception he'd get from Anna, who owed him, he felt, unlimited gratitude. For hadn't he let her off the hook? He wanted to experience her grateful hands.

At the spa lobby, three of the staff, like male nurses in white uniforms, stood to attention as Audie approached. Audie smiled, thinking that if they had worn shoes instead of sandals their heels would have clicked.

'I'm here for my treatment.'

'Have you booked, sir?'

'I'll take anything you've got.'

'Nothing available, sir.'

What struck Audie was that the young man had not even glanced at the register of appointments, the thick bound book that lay open on the desk.

'What do you mean, nothing?'

'Nothing, sir.'

Anna had told him that she would be free in the

morning. She said it, as she usually did, like the promise of a romantic assignation, an eagerness lighting her eyes.

He said, 'Anna – is she free?'

'Not here, sir.'

'When will she get here?'

'Not at all. Not employed here anymore, sir.'

Only this one man had done the talking – stonewalling, was more like it. The other two, he sensed, were watching closely for his reaction, but Audie did not smile until he turned away, thinking, That's it – take the money and run.

Later in the morning, curious about the route she'd taken the previous night – proud of her initiative, two times down the path to Hanuman Nagar: when in her life had she ever struck out alone like this? – Beth wandered through the bamboo grove and the trees above the laundry, just to see where she'd been. Pretending to admire the jasmine that edged the walkway, she worked her way to the path and saw the raw wood of a new fence, with a gate crudely wired to it.

'No entry, madam.'

A man in the khaki uniform of the grounds staff had stepped from behind a bush to block her way. He held a shiny truncheon.

'I was just looking.'

'Needing chit for passage. Having chit, madam?'

'Who are you?'

'Chowkidar, madam.'

'This fence wasn't here yesterday.'

'No, madam. Put up today morning.'

Testing him, she said, 'What if I want to go to the laundry?'

'Not available.' The man, still holding his truncheon, folded his arms over his chest.

'I gave you money yesterday.'

'No, madam. You gave to Kumar.'

'Where is Kumar?'

'Gone, madam. His willage, madam.' He gestured with the truncheon then dinged it on the boards of the new gate. 'Hanuman Nagar side.'

She could see that the watchman was adamant, that her arguing with him would only give him a greater victory, something he clearly relished. His eyes were glittering with defiance, his posture – skinny though he was – that of stubborn authority.

On her way back to the pool, rattled by the encounter – but why should this flunkey rattle me? she thought – she passed the spa to get a glimpse into the lobby. Instead of the usual boy in the chair who received people for treatments, she saw three men dressed in white, standing like sentries. Noticing her, one of them came to the door.

'Yes, madam?'

Beth smiled. 'Lovely day, isn't it?'

'You have booking for treatment?' He hadn't smiled back.

'Not today.' She peered behind him. 'Is that Satish?'

'No, madam.'

'You didn't even turn around. How are you so sure?'

'Satish is gone.'

'What do you mean?'

'Charge-sheeted, madam.'

She smiled again, as though she'd understood. 'Actually, I was just going to the pool.'

Gone? All that she could think was that he had somehow slipped away; that he was guilty of some sort of thieving. He had asked her for money. With money on his mind he had probably stolen something from the spa strongbox – some guests paid for their treatments in cash; she had seen the stacks of rupees.

Beth looked at the big blue pool, remembering the monkeys – how they'd crept around her, snatched her food, frightened her until Satish had appeared with his stick to scatter them. *I have not stopped watching you*.

Slipping off her smock, she kicked her sandals to the side of a chaise longue and walked to the edge of the pool, the sun on her face.

'Take shower first!'

The voice was so sharp, such a screech, Beth's whole body jerked as though pushed. She saw at her feet a floppy bathing cap – rubber, with a mass of pink plastic petals attached to it, enclosing a fierce-faced Indian woman she had never seen before.

'Excuse me?'

'You cannot use pool without shower!'

The force of the woman's utterance was shocking – even her big teeth were frightening – but she was not just angry, she also seemed panicky, as though fearful of contamination.

'Who said I was using the pool?'

'Foot is in water!'

It was true, Beth was standing in the gutter that ran around the pool to receive and drain the overflow.

The woman was probably insane. Indians could

seem mentally unbalanced, especially when they didn't get their way. Contamination was always on their tiny paranoid minds. Beth kicked at the water in spite and left.

Over lunch, Audie and Beth sat hardly speaking, except to remark on the pleasant weather, the sun-flecked veranda, the flowering trees, the bolder birds raiding the leftovers at just-vacated tables.

'Lovely place,' Audie said.

He was feeling virtuous again for having resisted the girl, virtuous for having given her money. He had assured her safety. He told himself that he had come all this way and done the right thing.

'You look happy,' he said.

Beth nodded, swallowed her mouthful of food, and said, 'Never better.'

All her questions had been answered. She had braved the risk. She had nothing to compare it to – she did not want to think that it had been brutal, though Satish had been briefly fierce. Food on his breath, his soapy-smelling skin, his teeth reddened by the betel nut he chewed. *I am bad, I am wicious.* His harshness. She played it all in her mind, until *What about present, madam?*

'What's wrong?'

Had she frowned? She said, 'Nothing.'

The waiters came and went, refilling the water glasses, using tongs to put warm naan bread into the basket, and finally slipping the bill to be signed into a plastic wallet and placing it near Audie's plate.

'So polite,' Audie said.

He found himself whispering, because everyone else

was whispering. The angry woman Beth had seen in the pool was hunched over her food, avoiding eye contact, and there were some people eating on the veranda whom Beth and Audie had never seen before at lunchtime.

That large table near the far rail, for example, was occupied by two men in suits and ties, looking out of place, one of them talking to the man Audie knew to be the manager, a man with an unpronounceable name whom he spoke to every Friday, to renew their booking for another week. Today was Friday – he'd be seeing the man later.

When the waiter approached Audie to pick up the wallet with the signed lunch bill, Audie put his hand over it to detain him.

'Who's that?'

'Mr Shah, sir. Owner of Agni, sir. And his managing partner. Also, as you know, Mr Rajagalopalachari, manager.'

Audie smiled in the direction of the owner, this Mr Shah, as businessman to businessman, wishing for eye contact. But the man was still speaking, using the back of his hand, tapping on the table with his gold ring for emphasis.

'I want to tell him he's got a great little place here,' Audie said. He kept looking. 'He's got things on his mind. He's working. I recognize that. Taking a meeting.'

'Coffee, sir? Madam?'

'I'm going to do without the toxins,' Beth said.

'Good idea.'

They left the veranda restaurant, holding hands,

feeling grateful – to have each other, to be in India, to be staying in this wonderful place.

'Another week, Tugar?'

They walked through the gardens and up the slope to the lobby of the main building, to signal their intention to stay another week.

The clerk they spoke to stood up at his desk and faced them. 'You must see the manager, sir.'

'He's at the restaurant,' Audie said.

'Yes, sir.'

'So what do we do?'

'Come back later, sir.'

They had a nap by the pool, in the shade of the overhanging trees, and at four, yawning, they made their way back up the slope, for the formality of requesting another week.

A man they had never seen before met them on the stairs of the main building, greeting them but also obstructing their way. He was smiling broadly though his eyes had a glaze of unblinking vigilance.

'You're not the manager,' Audie said.

'Acting manager.'

'Where's the manager?'

'He has been put on indefinite leave,' the man said. 'How may I help you?'

'It's just, here we are again. We're staying another week.'

There was a head wagging that meant yes, a wobble that meant certainly; but this man's head did not move, and he went on staring. Then his mouth tightened. He said, 'Sorry, sir.'

Audie said, 'What do you mean?'

'Fully booked, sir. From tomorrow, sir.'

'We've been doing this week to week. We've never had a problem. You can fix us up.'

Beth added, 'We'll take anything you've got.'

'Nothing available, sir.' He had begun to smile, which made his intransigence the more baffling.

'The place is practically empty,' Audie said. 'What are we going to do?'

'Departure time tomorrow morning-time is eleven, sir. Bags will be picked up. Car will be waiting.'

'What about Dr Nagaraj? He might be able to help,' Beth said. 'We hate to leave.'

'Yes, madam.'

'Maybe we can get another treatment,' Audie said.

Though he had spoken to Beth, the man said, 'Spa is closed until further notice, sir.'

'What are we going to do?'

'Settle bill, sir. Paperwork, sir. All charges to date.'

'You mean now?'

'If you please.'

Their excessive politeness now seemed to the Blundens like a form of excessive rudeness of an old-fashioned kind. Audie handed him his credit card, and then sat with Beth in the garden among the hibiscus bushes, listening to the Indian musicians who played in a corner of the garden, seated in an open pavilion.

From here, above the music, they heard loud voices, scolding, possibly the owner – it was a tone they had never heard before at peaceful Agni. There were sounds of scurrying, the whirr of golf carts coming and going, the important slamming of car doors. It was a suggestion of turbulence, turmoil anyway, the sort of thing they'd seen in the lower world of Hanuman Nagar.

'Someone's getting his nose bitten off,' Audie said. 'Glad it's not me.'

He took Beth's hand, and from the pressure of his fingers she knew he was rueful. He didn't want to leave, nor did she. Yet Audie, who hated not getting his way, seemed content. They sat, feeling relaxed, with a glow of health, the harmony that they had hoped for penetrated by the light of peace that made them feel almost buoyant, loving each other.

'I don't really want to see anything more of India,' Beth said, still holding his hand, as though answering a question he was asking with his fingers.

They skipped dinner and went to bed early – too early perhaps, because neither of them could sleep. Beth kept seeing Satish's toothy face saying, 'I will see you tomorrow,' and now it sounded like a threat. Audie wondered what Anna was going to do with the money and regretted giving her so much. He had made that mistake before. They lay in bed wakeful, face-saving, too chagrinned to confide their feelings – yet they knew, without conferring, that they had been rebuffed. *Nothing available* was just a lie, like one of those obvious lies intended to humiliate you. But they were not sorry to leave. It was India, after all – at least the lower slopes of Monkey Hill counted as India – and they were headed home. They were dimly aware that they were being cast out, banished from Agni – sent below.

The morning was smokier than usual, a haze

hanging over Agni, seeming to rise from the town. Sniffing it they decided that they were glad to leave. When they put their bags out to be picked up, they saw the golf cart parked at the entrance, the porter standing beside it. So they rode with their bags to the main building.

They had expected one of the white Mercedes from the Agni fleet to be waiting, but instead saw a tubby black Ambassador parked in the porte cochère. The car's hood was secured with a piece of rope that dangled over the radiator. No driver in sight, nor was there anyone from Agni to see them off. After more than a month of Indian effusiveness and thanks they were leaving in silence. They were used to a send-off in luxury hotels. *Please do come back and see us again.* But there was nothing, and even the golf-cart driver had gone after putting the Blundens' luggage in the trunk of the Ambassador.

As Audie began to complain, he heard Beth say, 'Hello, stranger,' in a grateful way.

Dr Nagaraj had approached the car and was opening doors for them. Now Audie noticed that the car had side curtains, a flourish that made it look older and somehow grubbier.

'My wee-ickle,' Dr Nagaraj said.

'You're taking us?'

'Why not?'

'Where's the driver?'

'Not available.'

Yesterday's lame excuse. And though Beth had already gotten into the back seat, Audie was puzzled. 'I don't get it. Why no drivers?'

'They were lodging complaints about road conditions.'

All these uncooperative people, and the sense of being banished, made Audie cross; he showed it by seating himself next to Beth and slamming the door hard.

'I will drive you to the airport for the first Delhi flight.'

They could see, from the way he clutched the steering wheel and labored with his forearms, that Dr Nagaraj was a terrible driver, stamping on the brake, thumping the clutch, and mashing the gears. Audie mumbled 'Grind me a pound.'

Down the drive, through the gate, past the sign *Right of Entry Prohibited Except by Registered Guests*. Audie winked at Beth and knew what was in her mind: who cares?

Now Dr Nagaraj was taking the curves amateurishly, veering too far over at each bend, cutting into the oncoming lane. Audie was going to tell him to be careful but realized he didn't have to, because when he spoke to him, Dr Nagaraj slowed down to reply.

'Anyway, what's wrong with the road conditions?'

'Main road is closed,' Dr Nagaraj said, riding the brake. 'Blockage and stoppage. *Rasta roko*, we say.'

'Is that unusual?'

'It is usual. People are angry because of Hanuman temple. Muslim people. That is the snag. The blockage is on the main road.'

'Which way will you go?'

They were approaching the junction, where the main road continued downhill and the road to Hanuman Nagar turned to the right, leveling off.

'Just here. Cart Road.'

Beth recognized the name. 'That's the road that goes past the temple. If there's a mob there won't it be dangerous?'

'I will guide you,' Dr Nagaraj said.

Audie smiled at Beth and said, 'Tugar, you actually know the name of this road?'

As he spoke, the road constricted and India seemed to shrivel around them, the stony slopes rushing up to the windows of the car, not just a pair of stray cows and the poorer shops at the edge of the town but a family of monkeys looking up from where they were picking through a garbage pile. This sense of walls closing in was made weirder by the absence of any people – not a single soul on a road that had been crowded with bikes and buses the last time they'd been on it, heading to the shatoosh seller.

'Where is everybody?'

This empty road in India had the familiar desolation of a road in an absurd dream you woke from sweating.

Dr Nagaraj, snatching at the steering wheel, rounded another curve and spoke in Hindi, slowing down. A multicolored barrier lay in the distance, a head-high barricade.

No, it was a solid mass of men jammed together like a wall across the narrow road. They were waving sticks, perhaps the men were shouting too, but there was no sound. The windows of the car were shut and what the Blundens saw resembled the India they had seen from the car on their first day. But these men were bearded and angry, and the sunlight made it all much worse.

'Turn around!' Audie shouted.

Shocked into his own language Dr Nagaraj was yapping with fear. He slowed the car, he struggled with the steering wheel, attempting a U-turn. But the road was too narrow, and seeing he could go no farther he began to jiggle the loose gearshift. When he looked back to reverse the car, his face was close to the Blundens, gleaming in terror.

'Get us the hell out of here!'

'Oh, God.' Dr Nagaraj winced at the pock-pock of stones hitting the car, the sound on its metal as of teeth and claws.

The Gateway of India

I

On these stifling days in Bombay, when a meeting dragged on, Dwight hitched himself slightly in his chair and looked at the spot where his life had changed. From the height of the boardroom on the top floor of Jeejeebhoy Towers, where Mahatma Gandhi crossed Church Gate, he could see down the long table and out the window, to marvel at it and to reflect on how far he'd come. He loved the Gateway of India for its three portals, open to the sea on one side, land on the other; regarded it as something personal, a monumental souvenir, an imperial archway, attracting a crowd – the ice-cream sellers, the nut vendors, the balloon hawkers, the beggars, and the girls looking for men.

Eight Indians sat at the gleaming conference table, four on either side, and he, Dwight Huntsinger, visiting American, lawyer and moneyman, was at the head of it.

'You are a necessary evil,' M. V. Desai the industrialist had joked.

Objecting to the preening boldness of the man, Dwight smiled, saying, 'You bet your sweet ass I am.'

The man was worth millions, everyone at the table winced, but Dwight's remark was calculated: they would never forget it.

An assortment of roof tiles were scattered on the table – the samples, to be manufactured somewhere in Maharashtra. Also a bottle of water and a glass with a paper cap at each place, a yellow pad, pencils, dishes of – what? – some sort of food, hard salty peas, yellow potato lumps, spicy garbanzos, something that looked like wood shavings, something else like twigs, bundles of cheese straws.

'It's all nuts and cheese balls at this table,' Dwight had said the first day, another way of responding to M. V. Desai, another calculation. They stared at him, as though they'd just heard bad news. None of the food looked edible. Although it was his second trip to India he had not so far touched any Indian food, he did not think of it as food; all of it looked lethal.

Get me out of here had been his constant thought. India had been an ordeal for him, but he had chosen it in a willful way, knowing it was reckless. It was deliberate. Recently divorced, he had said to his ex-wife in their last phone call, 'Maureen, listen carefully, I'm going to India' – as though jumping off a bridge. It was the day he received her engagement ring back – no note, just the diamond ring FedExed to him at the office – and he was hoping she'd feel bad. But as though to spite him she said, 'It'll probably change your life,' and he thought, *Bitch!*

That was the first trip, a week of Indian hell – a secular hallucinatory underworld of actual grinning demons and foul unbreathable air. He had dreaded it and it had exceeded even his fearful expectations – dirtier, smellier, more chaotic and unforgiving than anywhere he'd ever been. 'Hideous' did not describe it; there were no words for it. It was like an experience of grief, leaving you mute and small.

The worst of it was that Indians never ceased to praise it, gloating over it, saying how much they loved it. But it was a horror, and here was his discovery: the horror didn't stop, it went on repeating, he turned a corner and went down a new street and his senses were assaulted again, the sidewalks like freak shows.

'You seem a good deal disappointed,' Mr Shah said. Shah the point man was his guide in everything.

'Not disappointed,' Dwight said. 'I'm disgusted. I'm frightened. I am appalled. Don't you see I want to go home?'

In this world of anguish he felt physically hurt by what he saw. But it continued for the days he was there and did not stop until he had gotten back on the plane and left the smell of failure, of futility, of death and disease, returning to Boston with another discovery, that in all that misery there was money.

'I can't believe we closed the deal,' he said to Shah. 'My clients are very happy.'

Shah smiled and said, 'I am at your service, sir.'

They're either at my throat or at my feet, he'd emailed to Kohut back at the office, after the deal had been made. *And then they're biting each others' ankles.*

But there was another deal to be done. After two days of fighting the misery he'd stopped going out. He stayed in his hotel until it was time to meet the car; went to Jeejeebhoy Towers and the meeting, ate nothing, and returned to his hotel in the car. He ate bananas in his room – bananas were safe. But a diet of bananas and bottled water blocked him solid. There's a headline, he told himself. But it was something to report.

'You get sick?' It was the usual response to his saying he'd just been to India.

'I was constipated.'

Second trip, the life-changing one. At first he had refused. He had taken his risk, Maureen didn't care. He had pleaded with Sheely to take the assignment. Sheely had been to India once and was allowed to say 'Never again' because he was a senior partner, but he didn't stop there.

'Go to India?' Sheely raged. The very name could set him off. 'Why should I go to India? Indians don't even want to go to India! Everyone's leaving India, or else wants to leave, and I don't blame them. I understand why – I'd want to leave, too, if I lived there, which I don't, nor do I ever want to go to that shitty place ever again. Don't talk to me about India!'

Kohut too had seniority. Instead of pleading, Dwight thought: extreme measures. He brought a supply of tuna fish, the small cans with pop-off lids, and crackers, and Gatorade. It was like a prison diet but it would be bearable and appropriate for his seven days of captivity in Bombay. These he would spend in the best room, in the best hotel – the Elephanta Suite at the Taj Mahal Hotel, just across from the Gateway.

Yet he was ashamed of himself, standing in his hotel bathroom of polished marble and gilt fittings, leaning over the sink, eating tuna fish out of the can with a plastic fork. Three days of that, three days of Shah saying, 'You must see Crawford Market and Chor Bazaar. Perhaps Elephanta Caves, perhaps side trip to Agra to see Taj? What you want to see?'

'The Gateway of India.'

'Very nice. Three portal arches. Tripulia of Gujarati design. Not old, put up by British in 1927. But . . .' Shah widened his mouth, grinning in confusion.

'What?'

'You can see it from here.'

'That's what I like about it.'

India was a foreign country where he'd been assigned to find outsourcing deals, not a place to enjoy, but one to endure, like going down a dark hole to find jewels. He worked in the boardroom, wrangling manufacturers, he sat in his suite and watched CNN. His grimmest pleasure was looking through the classifieds of the *Hindustan Times*, the pages headed 'Matrimonials', and he smiled in disbelief at the willingness in the details, the eagerness of the girls desperate to be brides, the boys to be grooms. His disillusionment with marriage was compounded by his misery in India. He suffered, and the firm was grateful, for India proved to be outsourcing heaven.

'I had a query from a potential client at a hotel near Rishikesh, my brother's place,' Shah said. 'One Mr Audie Blunden. He owns a mail-order housewares catalog. He wants prices on power tools.'

'The question is whether they'd meet the codes.'

'Meet and surpass codes,' Shah said, insistently. 'You can make anything in India.'

They were in the boardroom, waiting for Mr Desai and his entourage.

'Kinda wood is this table?' Dwight asked.

'Deek,' said Manoj Verma. 'You want some? I can arrange consignment.'

'That some kinda Indian wood?'

'Deek? You don't have in Estates?'

'Never heard of it.'

But *You can make anything in India*, he remembered. He was thinking of it now as he looked past portly confident Mr M. V. Desai, his assistant Miss Bhatia, their lawyer Mr R. R. K. Prakashnarayan in a thick cotton knot-textured jacket, Manoj Verma the product analyst, Ravi Ramachandran on the right-hand side munching wood shavings, Taljinder Singh in his tightly wound helmet-like turban, Miss Sheela Chakravarty keeping notes, and lastly Mr J. J. Shah – indispensable Shah – also a lawyer, who was a master of postures and faces, scowling in disbelief, distrust, his defiant smile saying, *No. Never. Prove it.* Shah always had the right answer. He said, enigmatically, 'I am Jain, sir.' Dwight, trying another joke, said, 'And I'm Tarzan.' And past the end of the table, the empty chair, out the window, below the level of the stained rooftops, the rusted propped-up water tanks, to the Gateway of India, where he could see the people milling around, promenading, as Indians seemed inclined to do at the end of the day, near the harbor, the gray soupy water, the people just splotches of colored clothing but he knew that each of them was there for a purpose.

'Do you not agree, Mr Hund?' Shah asked. In a country where anyone could say Vijayanagar and Subramaniam, 'Huntsinger' was unpronounceable. So he said, 'Call me Hunt. All my friends do.' But 'Hund' made him smile.

The way the question was framed was a kind of

code, meaning that Shah approved of the terms of the deal and the answer had to be yes.

'Absolutely,' Dwight said, but his gaze returned to the window, the stone arch far below, the shuffling people.

He had stopped following the negotiation. He had a stomach for details but not Indian details – minutiae, escape clauses, fine print, subsections of clauses. His presence was important to the meeting but not his participation. In fact, he had discovered that his saying little added to his mystique and gave him more power for his seeming enigmatic. He had learned early on in Indian business deals that the power brokers were men of few words, well known and even revered for their silences. Underlings could be talkers, chatterers, hand-wringers, anguished in their bowing and nodding. He had seen a man in a diving attempt to touch Mr M. V. Desai's foot in a show of respect, which was another reason for his saying, 'You bet your sweet ass I am.' Touching his foot!

Anyway, the deal was apparently done. They had found a supplier, they had agreed to a price structure, they had approved the samples – the ribbed, composite roof tiles of fibrous plastic that looked so odd on the lovely table, identical to the ones made in Rhode Island at eight times the price, same quality, no liabilities, no restrictions on the noxious fumes such plastic-making produced – a class-action law-suit was pending in Providence. The idea was to encourage the Indian tile-maker to build inventory, to keep this supplier desperate and backed up and hungry, one or two payments in arrears. Shah would handle that.

Dwight's attention had drifted from the boardroom to the promenade at the Gateway of India, where he'd been walking off his three days of jet lag, enjoying the late afternoon coolness, the breeze from the harbor, and a bit fearful, away from his suite.

'Ess crim. Ess – ess.'

He almost bought an ice cream, then he remembered that he might poison himself. Instead he bought a soda, something called Thums-Up. As he'd paid for it a woman had approached him.

'Sir,' the woman said. She clasped her hands and bowed.

He was moved by her politeness, her submissiveness. He half-expected her to touch his foot. Yet he resisted her. She was smiling – seeing into his suspicious eyes.

She saw that he was looking past her at the lovely building and she seemed to read a question in his mind.

'Taj Mahal Hotel, sir. Best hotel. It is dop of line.'

Walking to the rail at the harbor's edge he saw that she was following him. What struck him was that the woman was stout and gray haired, not destitute-looking, decently dressed in a blue sari and shawl, carrying a tidy straw basket. She was not a beggar but someone's granny. An echo in his head, something to do with the woman saying *dop*, made him think, *Deek – Verma was saying 'teak'.*

He said, 'I can't give you anything.'

'Sir!' the woman exclaimed. 'I am wanting nothing.'

But that put him on his guard. In business here, in business generally, someone who said he wanted nothing was suspect. Who wanted nothing? Always someone who was untruthful, who had a plan, who wanted to negotiate for something specific. Never say what you want, was a tactic he had learned from Shah on his first morning in India.

He was still walking, while eyeing the woman sideways.

'What is matter, sir?'

'Nothing,' he said; but he knew he was lying. He was wary of this big confident woman.

'Your first time in India, sir?'

'Second,' he said.

'Second! We are honored. You have made return journey.'

'Thank you.'

Now he didn't look at her. He was walking along the perimeter of the railing, honking traffic on one side, bobbing boats in the harbor on the other, and also uncomfortably aware that the woman was keeping pace with him. Why hadn't he brushed her off, why had he thanked her? Because she wasn't a beggar. She was a plump housewife, a granny maybe; not indigent. She wore gold bangles.

Probably an evangelist, he thought. She's going to hand me a religious pamphlet. If not Hindu then something Christian, with Bible quotations. One of those busybodies. *Are you saved?* And when he said no, she would set about to save him.

Without slackening his pace he said, 'What do you want?'

She laughed a bit breathlessly because he was walking fast and she was trying to keep up and failing. 'Only to bid you welcome, sir.'

'I appreciate it.'

'You are a kind man, I can see.'

That was another giveaway: only someone who was angling for something would say that.

'I'm a very busy man,' he said.

But if I were so busy why would I be swigging a Thums-Up and sauntering along this seafront, yapping to this woman at four in the afternoon, he thought; and he knew she had detected the same idleness in him.

'As you wish, sir. I will not detain you further.'

She dropped behind. He kept walking to the end of the promenade, where there was no shade, and the only people were some boys fishing with bamboo poles at the revetment below the rail.

He glanced over his shoulder and saw that the woman had stopped walking and was sitting on a bench, though was still watching him, perhaps to give him his privacy, having abandoned any thought of talking to him. Had he been rude to her?

Continuing to the end of the promenade he was startled by a commotion ahead, some children being loudly threatened by an Indian man in a white suit. The man was old, white-haired and fierce, waving a cane at them, swiping the air just above their heads and shouting.

Dwight summed it up. The children, gypsy-looking, had obviously asked him for money – a young boy in shorts, a small girl in a red dress, a taller girl in colorful skirts. But they were skinny and poor and probably persistent – the man had taken offense and was screeching at them to go away. The stick looked wicked in the man's furious grip, and he struck with it again, just missing the taller girl, who seemed terrified.

'Hey!' Dwight called out. 'You!'

The man swung around, and seeing Dwight he stepped back, looking chastened. Dwight saw just where he could snatch the cane and disarm the man, and maybe an elbow in the gut. But the man's anger left him and as he dropped his guard, Dwight went nearer.

'Leave those kids alone!'

The man made a conciliatory gesture with his hands and backed away.

'*Acha. Acha.*' And still muttering he moved quickly, now using the cane to propel himself into the street and among the traffic.

'Thank you, sir,' the tall girl said, and she quickly knelt and touched Dwight's shoe as the underling had attempted to do with M. V. Desai.

The girl had large famished eyes, and though she was child-sized he could see she was the eldest, probably sixteen, not wearing a sari but rather a white blouse with long sleeves and traced with embroidered flowers, a thickness of red slightly tattered skirts, and gold satin shoes, like dancing pumps. She did not wear gold jewelry, but instead colored bangles and orange beads, and a marigold pinned in her hair.

All this Dwight took in because the smaller children seemed so drab and fearful, the girl in the dress, the boy in shorts, both of them twelve or so. But who could tell the ages of hungry children? They might have been older, but stunted.

'Be careful,' Dwight said. 'That old man could have hurt you.'

But at that point the children had begun looking past him and he turned to see the old woman in the blue sari hurrying forward, her basket bumping against her side.

'You are a good man,' she said. 'You have protected my children from wrath of that wicked person.'

'These are your kids?'

'I am their auntie. I have come to meet them.' She had taken the small boy's hand, the small girl pressed herself against her, the gypsy girl smiled and seemed to skip. The woman was walking, and still talking, not looking back. 'Now you will come and have cup of tea with us.'

Dwight followed them into the traffic to the other side of the street, and past the Taj Mahal Hotel into narrower streets and sudden, reeking lanes. All the while he was thinking of how he had reacted – his anger, defending the children, defying the man, and had never doubted that he could have snatched the stick and used it to beat the man. He imagined the gratitude of a woman who had just witnessed her children being rescued.

A ten-minute walk took them through crowded streets and more smelly lanes and a recumbent cow near a row of parked motorbikes. Ahead, he saw the woman entering a seedy porch at what looked like a shop front. Yet it was not a shop, nor did it seem to be a café. The porch led to the vestibule of an old building near the dead end of a lane.

'Cup of hot tea, sir,' the old woman said.

Dwight took a seat at the table that was just inside the door. He said, 'Got any coffee?'

'Indeed.'

The children sat at the table, with their cups of tea. Dwight's coffee was instant, but it was scalding hot, it had to be safe. He sipped it and marveled. Just a little while ago he had been alone at the Gateway of India and now he was sitting with this strange little family on this dead end, the children watching him, the old woman fussing. The taller girl had sat herself next to him. She had thin downy arms and chipped pink polish on her fingernails, and yellowish eyes.

'Thank you, sir,' she said when she saw he was staring.

'What's your name?'

'Sumitra.'

The old woman said, 'Tell uncle what is your speciality.'

The girl pressed her lips together, took a nervous breath, and said, 'I am dance.'

Now he saw not starvation in her but a dancer's skinny build, and a dancer's delicate hands, and a dancer's upright neck.

'That's nice,' Dwight said. 'Who taught you?'

'Auntie.'

'She want to make dance for you,' the old woman said.

Dwight folded his arms and sat back on his chair and thought: I can leave now, and that will be the end. I will be the same man. Or I can stay, and follow the old woman's suggestions, and see it through, and something will happen that can't be undone.

He drank his coffee, which had cooled a bit, and tasted weak and muddy. He knew he was being watched. For a reason he could not explain he thought of the Elephanta Suite, the bathroom shelf of pop-open cans of tuna fish, and he disliked the idea of going to that empty place and hiding himself.

The old woman was talking. Had she been talking all this time?

'Because you saved these children from harm,' she was saying.

He thought, *Dance*? He looked at the children again and around the small vestibule and was relieved that no one was watching him; that he was hidden from the people who were walking past the porch on this narrow lane.

'Where?' he said, hardly knowing what he was asking.

'Upstairs. Second floor, back. Last door on right.'

The woman was precise, but he must have made a face.

'It is clean, sir.'

'How much?'

'No charge, sir. You have helped us, sir.'

Now the girl reached beneath the table and put her hand on his knee. She had to slump in her chair and lean awkwardly to do this, and that made her seem small. But still she kept her gaze on him, and he was fascinated by the glint of her yellowish eyes.

'Name a price,' he said, because he feared the ambiguity of her gratitude and a shakedown afterwards.

'One thousand rupees only,' the old woman said and as she spoke the number, for the first time since he met her he felt he understood her. In naming the price he heard her true voice and he knew her: shrewd, firm, a bit impatient, a practical pimp attaching a fluttering price tag to the girl.

'Let's go.'

He followed the girl up the stairs, losing count of the flights, until she led him to a landing and down a hall. He was fearful of meeting someone; but the building was empty and hot and stifling. The girl found a key on a dirty string somewhere within her skirts and turned it in a locked door. He saw a window that was almost opaque from its film of dust, a couple of chairs, a mattress on the floor, a large framed picture of a Hindu god, and on the floor with a trailing cord what looked like a radio. It was an old tape deck. The girl snapped a cassette into it and switched it on. Music filled the room and made it more bearable.

Gesturing for Dwight to sit, the girl went through a door. He heard water running. He went to the window and drew the curtains. When the girl re-entered the room Dwight was sitting in the chair. He could see that she was wearing fresh lipstick, she had powdered her face, she looked doll-like and delicate, and then she raised her arms, sending her bangles sliding to her elbows, and she cocked one leg. She began to dance in the shadowy room, to the aching music.

2

That night in the Elephanta Suite he had lain on his bed, staring at nothing, feeling fragile; the slightest sound jarred his ears. He was exhausted and empty – sorrowful, but why? Perhaps for the young submissive girl, who had shocked him by being so deft, for understanding so much, for her gift of anticipation. How could she know all that?

Her dancing had held him with its formality and precision, the way she lifted her knees and crooked her arms and made fans of her fingers; the way she twirled her skirts. Without hesitating, she had looped her thumb under one shoulder strap and slipped it sideways, and then the other; and soon she was dancing bare breasted, barefoot, lifting her gauzy red skirts with her knees. At certain points in the music she seemed to move in a trance-like state, oblivious of him, her yellow eyes upturned to the portrait of a fierce and blackish Hindu god, whose legs were similarly crooked, and who wore a necklace of human skulls.

Unhurried, pacing, turning, reaching upwards with her skinny arms, she had danced to the music that twanged in the hot dusty room. Her face was a powdery mask, her cheeks rouged, her lips red. She had brought him to the room like a servant girl, but re-entered with her make-up, the white powder that made her face purplish, her lips larger and sticky red, bangles clattering at her wrists, silver earrings, and some sort of bells tinkling on anklets. Soon she was half naked, with small breasts, with sallow skin, and she was not a servant girl anymore but an object of desire, with flashing eyes, stamping feet, twirling and skipping, until the music stopped.

He lay in his suite in the same posture as on the mattress in the upstairs room, watching the girl Sumitra kneeling beside him.

'Can you take this off?' he whispered, touching the thickness of her full skirts, and now he could see they'd been sewn with sequins, tiny round mirrors of mica.

She had stood and unfastened her skirts with a cord and stepped out of them. Then she'd folded them, placed them on a chair, and returned to him naked, kneeling, as he lay watching her, her long eyelashes, her lips, her arms, the powder clinging to her hair. But when he touched her, trying to encourage her, she resisted.

She reached beneath the mattress. 'Condom,' she said, and tore the small package open with her teeth.

He lay back and closed his eyes, and from time to time she released him and leaned aside and spat.

He did not want to remember the rest, but there was more, his shame like sorrow, the bold conspiratorial woman who bantered with him afterwards, asking him for baksheesh. And at last, as he left the place, pausing in the coolness of the lane to get his bearings, he'd seen the old man from the promenade, still in his white cotton suit, carrying his cane. The man who had been shouting at the children looked so mild and elderly now. He didn't smile, hardly acknowledged Dwight, probably resented him for being a debauched white man in India, though (Dwight was walking quickly away) hadn't the old man schemed with the pimping woman?

On his way to his hotel the word came to him again. He was debauched. He had been aroused, he had held the Indian girl in his arms in that dusty room. Without being able to put the emotion into words he felt he belonged here and could not remember how long he'd been in Bombay or when he was supposed to leave, and didn't care.

He was debauched, that was the word for how he felt – a corrupt man trifling with a teenaged whore. It was bad enough that she was so young, somehow much worse that she could actually dance expertly – she knew the steps, she could have performed in a dance troupe, becoming brilliant. Instead, she danced to titillate and seduce the greedy American who'd given her money.

It had been a colossal set-up – the older, over-familiar woman, the children he'd happened upon, seemingly by chance, the old man playing his role as an indignant and self-righteous pedestrian. Dwight, who thought of himself and his lawyer's skills as shrewd, had been snared, fooled by this cheap trick, this ragged band, and he had gone the rest of the way, allowed himself to be lured into the room.

He was ashamed, but his shame did not overcome his wish to see the girl again. He felt sick with a need for her. He told himself she was poor, desperate, helpless and that the only way he could help her was by seeing her, letting her dance, making love to her, giving her money. The money mattered most, it was a kind of philanthropy – gift-giving, anyway – and might save her. If she had some money she'd be able to give up the sex trade and be a dancer. He would tell her this.

'You are looking fit,' Shah said at the meeting the next day, but Shah peered a little too long and inquiringly.

They took their places at the table, and that was the first time Dwight raised himself from his chair and glanced down from Jeejeebhoy Towers to the Gateway of India for a look at the people milling around it.

The meeting with Shah and the suppliers was like an interruption of the day. Dwight endured it, approved the terms as quickly as they were set out, glanced over the draft contracts, and sighed when Shah began to quibble over the sub-section of a clause.

'I would like to invite you to dine at my home,' Shah said. 'It will be a simple meal, but you will understand better the custom of my people, the Jain.'

'I'm sorry. I've got some paperwork to attend to.'

He wished Shah had not invited him, because when he went in search of the old woman and the children later that day he kept thinking of the purity and innocence of Shah's earnest invitation. *A simple meal.* And here he was pursuing a pimping old hag and those corrupted children, not her own but obviously kept by her to make money, and he was as corrupt as they were.

He waited until almost sunset before he began to stroll past the Gateway of India and the drink sellers, the peanut vendors, the ice-cream men, the people hawking children's toys, the balloon sellers. He knew that he would not find the woman – it was she who'd find him. And so it happened.

'Hello, my friend.'

She winked at him. She knew why he was there. She didn't even ask him to follow her. She kept walking and he was a step behind her. He hated himself, hated the thought that she knew him so well, but he told himself that it was necessary. He did not want to speak to her, and it was not until they reached the lane and stepped onto the porch of the stone house that she said, 'Sumitra.'

'But no dancing.'

'As you wish.'

The girl's dancing, the singularity of it, the glow of her soul in her whitened face, had upset him. He had not expected such seriousness, such concentration, such formality. The whole performance and the piercing notes of the music broke his heart and made her seem hopeless, using this brilliant skill to attract him for sex and money.

He gave the old woman a thousand rupees in an envelope, reminded himself that it was twenty dollars, and let her show him upstairs. As she left him at the door, he tried to read her face. He suspected that she despised him, but she gave nothing away.

The room was the same, the mattress, the tape player plugged into the wall under the portrait of the fierce, toothy, blackish-faced deity. Dwight waited, shuffling, too nervous to sit, and then the far door opened and Sumitra appeared and stepped forward.

She did not smile. She looked summoned, a little reluctant, like someone sent on an errand, which

Dwight thought was exactly the case. But this time she wore a headdress, a sort of lacy veil, and her make-up was more carefully applied. She was barefoot and her anklets jingled as she came over to him. He leaned to kiss her.

'No,' she said, and averted her eyes, moved her head sideways with a pinched face, as though reacting to a bad smell.

She started the music and stood, one leg crooked, her arms upraised, to begin her dance.

'What are you doing?'

'I am dance,' she said.

'No dance.' He took her by the hand and set her down at the edge of the mattress, wishing that her anklets had not sounded so merry. He had another envelope of money ready. He placed it into her hand.

Sumitra stared at him and tucked it into a fold of her thick skirt where there must have been a pocket.

No 'thank you', hardly an acknowledgment, just a sullen blinking of her yellow eyes within a shadow of mascara, and a little nod of her head; how many other men had sat here and done this?

He had planned to give her the money and leave, but with her sitting next to him, her knees drawn up, her head bowed, the powder of her make-up prickling on his arm, she was like a cat in his lap. He could not get up, could not bear to abandon her.

The warmth of her body warmed his hands, the slightness of her figure aroused him; he fumbled with her clothes, to hold her. She squirmed slightly, and he guessed that she was resisting him, and almost apologized; then he saw that she was letting down the shoulder straps of her bodice, baring her small breasts for him. After that, he felt her hands on him, in a routinely practiced way, like someone feeling an obscure parcel, squeezing it to reveal what's inside. Even though he recognized how mechanical an act this was, and despised himself for sitting through it, he was aroused. He let her do what she did well; she was intent, and silent, and then she spat on the floor.

'See you again,' the old woman said, when he went downstairs.

The other children were staring at him in the vestibule. He said nothing, he was too ashamed, he thought, *Never again*, and was nauseated by the stinging reek of urine and cow dung in the narrow lane.

All through the following day he reminded himself that he was corrupt and weak. He felt sorrowful whenever he thought of Sumitra, her yellow eyes and small shoulders and thin fingers with the chipped polish on her fingernails. This sad and sentimental feeling penetrated him with the sense that he belonged in India and nowhere else, that he had begun to live there in a way that he could not explain to anyone.

'That man Blunden,' Shah said.

What man Blunden? Dwight thought. He had paid no attention to business these past few days. The name rang no bell.

Seeing his vagueness, Shah explained, 'American man. He wanted information on outsourcing for his housewares catalog. Pricings for commodities and products.'

'Yes?'

'He was Rishikesh side.'

'And?'

'A happenstance has occurred.'

'Can't we do something?'

'He has met with accident.'

'Serious?'

'He has left his body.'

That was the Indian surprise. India attracted you, fooled you, subverted you, then, if it did not succeed in destroying you with the unexpected, it left you so changed as to be unrecognizable. Or it ignited a fury in you, as it had in Sheely, who hated the very name of the place, and spat when he said it. Or it roused your pity and left you with a sadness that clung like a fever. Even the simplest sight of it. He had watched an American woman entering the Taj lobby weeping after the drive from Mumbai airport, her first experience of India, those five or so miles of shanties that had once shocked Dwight.

I'd like to leave my body, Dwight thought. He was a lost soul, but he was also reminded that for the past two days he had conquered his fear of India – in fact, felt possessed by it, weirdly vitalized, with something bordering on obsession, his body was a stranger he inhabited, but a risk-taking stranger.

I can't help myself, he wanted to tell Shah; but Shah was pious, he would be shocked, as a family man, a Jain, someone who had never allowed himself to be led into a dingy room for sex with a skinny girl.

But what did Shah know of passion? Dwight could not explain how he was both attracted and repelled, like a drunkard with a bottle, sick from the pleasure of it, knowing the thrill, knowing the consequences; but no consequences could outweigh the ecstasy of the drink; no anticipated shame could prevent him from seeing the girl again. So there was shame in his desire, but his desire was stronger.

He couldn't help himself; he drifted back to the Gateway of India at nightfall, and he loitered, with the peculiarly unhurried walk of someone trawling for a woman, someone going nowhere. The old woman was not there. He felt sick at the idea that she'd found another man, yet that had to be the case. He was disgusted and gloomy, his vision clouded by his distress. He felt sorry for himself, and for the girl Sumitra. He almost said aloud, 'I should have given her more money.'

A young woman was staring at him. She wore a white dress, knee length, like a nurse's, with a white belt and white shoes and knee socks. She did not look away when he stared back at her; she came nearer.

Instinctively he clapped his hands to his pocket where he kept his money, suspecting a thief. They worked in pairs, he knew that; and he knew how elaborate their scams were – some threw shit, some carried razors. Where was this one's pimp, what was her ruse? The lump of his wallet on one side, the diamond wedding ring in its purse on the other – there was a safe for valuables in his suite, but he had not broken the habit of carrying the rejected ring.

He bought a bottle of Thums-Up, so that he could delay and have a look at the girl. The soda wallah seemed to recognize him, greeted him heartily, and then hissed at the girl. But she shrugged, and though she walked a few steps away Dwight could see that she was lingering.

Using the bottle as a prop, he carried it to the edge of the walkway beyond the Gateway and pretended to be interested in the boats in the sea, their bows to the wind. He sipped and was calmed by the setting sun, the light breeze, the smells of roasted nuts on braziers, the sight of strolling families, the popcorn trolley, the energy of the boys jumping from the parapet into the frothy water. Lost in the rhythms of this activity, his need for Sumitra was leaving him.

'Please, sir.'

The girl in the white nurse's uniform was next to him, putting on a pained pleading face. Why was she wearing this white dress and not a sari? Her hair was plaited into a long braid that lay against her back.

'Give me money, sir.'

She was neither a girl nor a woman, seventeen maybe, older than Sumitra anyway, attractive and primly dressed, an unlikely beggar, more like a hospital worker or a dental assistant in her knee socks and white shoes.

'What is your country, sir?'

Dwight turned away, feeling self-conscious. He wanted her to keep walking, so that he could examine his diminishing ardor for Sumitra. He had come to search for her, and now he had concluded that the old woman had found someone else.

'I am hungry, sir.'

'What's your name?'

'Indru, sir.'

'Do you work at a hospital?'

'Hair-and-nail salon, sir. But my money is gone.'

'Here,' Dwight said, and handed his bottle of Thums-Up to her.

As though disgusted, she stepped back and shook her head.

'Why not?'

'You have taken some, sir. I cannot take from self-same bottle.'

He was not offended but impressed that she would not share the same bottle: she was both a beggar and a chooser!

'I must have my own bottle,' she said.

'If I buy you a drink, what will you give me?'

He said it without thinking, without knowing what he meant. It was reckless, but he was in India. Who cared? On fine days, walking to the office, he had often encountered panhandlers on Boston Common, sometimes women, now and then young and attractive, if a bit grubby. He would never have dared to engage one in conversation or ask for something.

Indru smoothed her dress and said, 'What is it you want, sir?'

'Think about it.'

He gave her some money for a bottle of soda, a hundred-rupee note – he had nothing smaller. Handing it over, seeing her become submissive and polite, bowing to him, he felt powerful, and at the same time annoyed with himself for even caring.

Yet he sat on a bench and watched Indru buy a bottle of soda, and he was not surprised when she returned and sat next to him.

'Where do you live?'

'Far from here.'

'Where are your parents?'

'In village, sir.'

'Why is everyone always asking for money?'

'No work, sir.'

'But you work in a salon?'

'Casual work, sir. Not enough.'

'What kind of work can you do?'

'I can do anything, sir. What you like?'

He knew he had gone too far. As he raised his bottle and prepared to toss it into a trash barrel, the soda wallah hurried over – he must have been watching – and lifted it from Dwight's hand. Just then, looking up, he saw across the road four floors up, his Elephanta Suite, and at a distance, looming above the other buildings, the big bright windows on the top floor of Jeejeebhoy Towers. He got up and started to walk away.

'Where are you going, sir?'

'Got work to do.'

He walked quickly past the Gateway crowd, through the taxi rank and the traffic, then onto the sidewalk where there was a guardrail. People plucked at his sleeve, not just beggars but shopkeepers – 'In here, sir. All kinds of electronics' – but he kept walking. He passed a movie theater displaying a big colored poster of a fat woman with stupendous breasts and purple talons for fingernails. He was thinking, It wasn't me. She was the one who'd asked.

'What is it you want, sir? Come inside,' a man in shirtsleeves demanded at the doorway of a curio shop.

Crossing a busy rotary of honking traffic, he began to notice the heat. He was perspiring now, but he would not let it slow him: he needed to go on walking. The sights, the shops, the churches made it easier for him – and wasn't this a Christian church, in the English style? He thought of going inside but he saw a padlocked hasp on the front door.

Farther on he saw an emptier street, less traffic, just a few pedestrians, and heading there he found himself among lanes leading to another part of the harbor. He saw warehouses, a market with empty stone tables, the stalls vacated at this time of day.

Its emptiness looked attractive in this overcrowded city. He turned into the lane. He could see to the end, another warehouse, and water. Sensing movement he looked down, he saw a rat. He kicked at it, but the rat was unperturbed, big as a cat, nibbling at the husk of a coconut.

While he had been walking the sun had gone down. He walked under the afterglow in the sky, where there were streaks of pink and gold. At the far end of the covered market was the warehouse, shuttered and dark, and stacked against it were great coils of rope and a partly rubbed-away sign, on which he could read the words, *Jute Mills*.

He was near enough to the water to see the glimmer of the sea. He found a place to sit and drew a breath, thinking how odd it was in such a populous city to be here where there were no people.

Then he heard another rat. He stamped his foot and turned to frighten it.

'Sir.'

Indru – her dress and shoes so white in these shadows.

'How did you find me?'

'I follow, sir.'

She bowed to him. She looked older with the shadows on her face, her white cotton dress glowing. Her stillness alarmed him, and her accent seemed stronger in the twilight.

'May I be seated, sir?'

He was seated on a coil of rope on a giant spool the size and shape of a tractor tire. Still, he was impressed by her formality.

'Go ahead.'

'Thank you, sir.'

Was it her formality, the mode of her politeness that made him feel if not powerful then dominant – in charge in this lonely place?

'Indru,' he said.

'You did not forget my name.'

'What do you want?'

'I am so hungry, sir.'

It was a terrifying statement. He put his hand into hers. Her hand lay open on her lap, small, though her palm was hard, almost coarse, and her skin like that of a scaly little animal. She said she worked in a salon but perhaps she also did some sort of hard work? Her stiff stubby fingers closed on his hand – she was trying to show him some affection.

'You're a nice girl, Indru.'

'Thank you, sir.'

With his free hand he touched her thigh through her loose dress, hiking it up slightly. He felt her skin just above her knee, and slipped his fingers around her thigh, where she was warm, as though holding a fresh piece of meat, even sensing that this smoothness would taste good.

She did not resist, yet she made a sound in her throat, swallowing, as though bracing herself; the sort of sucking breath a person draws just before taking a risk.

Hearing a rustling sound, he saw in the dim light a rat nibbling a broken blossom that was easily visible because of its white petals. But everywhere else it was dark in the alley. The only available light was the patch of sky above the lane, and the twilit harbor framed by the end of the warehouse.

'Can I kiss you?'

'Why not, sir?'

Her willingness to kiss seemed like the proof she wasn't a whore.

He kissed her lips, loving their softness, and he marveled at the risk he was taking. But she had followed him here, the way a homeless animal seeks comfort. He remembered, *I am so hungry, sir*, and he dug in his pocket for the small soft pouch and the ring that he often fingered, hating the memory of it.

He had to do it now, before anything happened. It was a gift, not a fee. He put it into her hand. She took it without looking, slipped it into her pocket.

'Do you like me?'

She seemed to hesitate. Was it his searching hand that disturbed her? After a reflex of resistance, she allowed it.

'Yes, sir.'

3

Now, looking down at the Gateway of India from the boardroom at the top of Jeejeebhoy Towers, he saw the warehouses, the docks, the rope works, Apollo Bunder, the Taj Hotel, even the corner window of his suite, the steamy streets he had hurried through afterwards, hot with exhausted desire. He could even see beyond the promenade, where the old woman had led him, and a rooftop that might have been part of her house. Laid out before him was the map of his last three days – transforming days. He did not know what to make of it except that he was not afraid of India anymore. He was anxious about what he had discovered in himself, but he did not want to look any deeper. He didn't want to feel ashamed for something that he regarded as a kind of victory.

Someone – Miss Bhatia? – was passing him a dish of curried potato. He scooped some onto his plate. Three days ago he would have refused it. He passed the dish to Shah.

'I am not taking potato,' Shah said.

'Allergic?'

'They are having germs,' Shah said. 'Also fungus. And little growths.'

'Afraid of getting sick?'

'Oh, no. As I mentioned to you. I am Jain. We do not kill.'

'You mean' – and Dwight began to smile – 'you're trying to avoid killing the germs?'

'That is correct.'

'And the fungus in the potatoes?'

'I will take some nuts and pulses,' Shah said. And turning to Mr Desai, 'Shall we now discuss payment schedule?'

That was the second, the transformative, trip. He left that night, or rather at two the next morning, a changed man. Or was he changed? Perhaps these impulses had always slumbered in him, and India had wakened them, allowing him to act.

'I can't wait to come back,' he told Shah, who was pleased.

How shocked Shah would have been if he had explained why, and described his encounters – the dancer Sumitra, the waif Indru. He could not stop thinking about them, solitary Indru most of all. The whole of India looked different to him now – brighter, livelier; but more, he was himself changed. I am a different man here, he thought, as the plane roared down the runway and lifted above the billion lights of Bombay. I want to come back and be that man again.

His fears were gone, he was a new man, he was happier than he could remember. The image of the Gateway of India came to him, and he thought: I have passed through it.

Back in Boston, at his desk, the partners stopped in to convey their routine greetings – 'Nice to see you, Dwight' – and the repeated note was that they admired him for having gone to India, regarded him as a real traveler and a risk taker, gave him credit for enduring the discomfort, talked only of illness and misery, and said he was a kind of hero. All the senior partners congratulated him on the deals he'd done – such simple things, if only they knew. He could have said that Indians were hungry, and they helped him because they were helping themselves.

On the first trip, and for part of the second, he had seen India as hostile, a thronged and poisoned land where a riot might break out at any moment, triggered by the slightest event, the simplest word, the sight of an American. And he would be overwhelmed by an advancing tide of boisterous humans, rising and drowning him among their angry bodies.

'Did you get sick?'

India was germ-laden. Sheely had ended up dehydrated and confined to his hotel room with an IV drip in his arm; and he swore he would never go back to that food and that filth.

Dwight too had been anxious. That was why he needed Shah. But giving Shah all that responsibility had released Dwight from the tedium of negotiating the outsourcing deals. Shah had the respect of the businessmen, he could handle them, and Dwight's silences had been taken to be enigmatic and knowing. Not talking too much, indeed hardly talking at all, had been a good thing. His silences made him seem powerful. How could he explain that to his talkative and bullying partners?

He had feared and hated India. He had gone nonetheless because as a young, recently divorced man with no children he had been the logical choice. He had said, 'I'll hold my nose.'

On the first trip, he had not eaten Indian food, he had not gone out at night, he had seen the deals to their conclusion and then ached to be home. He had been welcomed home as though he had been in the jungle, returned from the ends of the earth, escaped the savages, the terrorists, a war zone. India represented everything negative – chaos and night. And so on his return from this second visit he understood what the partners were saying; he had once said them himself.

'Human life means nothing to those people,' Sheely had said. And because he'd been to India – and gotten sick – his word was taken to be the truth.

'It's teeming, right?' Kohut said. 'I saw a program about it on the Discovery Channel.'

Ralph Picard, whose area was copyright infringement, said, 'I've got to hand it to you, Dwight. I could never do anything like that.'

The Elephanta Suite was one of the best in the hotel. He had a driver, always; and he seldom opened a door – doors were snatched open for him to pass through. Yet, even knowing that these praising remarks were undeserved, he accepted them and was strengthened by them; after the fiasco of his brief marriage it was nice to be thought of as brave, and he liked being regarded as a kind of conqueror – it was how a success in India was seen by the Boston office. It was unexpectedly pleasant to be thought of as a hero.

And so, although he was seldom inconvenienced in India, and lived in luxury, he played up the discomfort – the heat, the dirt, the rats, the beggars, the sidewalks so filled with people you couldn't walk down them, the sight of fierce bearded Muslims and their shrouded women, the sludgy buttery food that looked inedible, the water that wasn't drinkable, people sleeping by the side of the road and pissing against trees. He said nothing about his suite, or the man-servant who came with it – 'I will be your butler, sir.'

'Pretty grim,' he said.

But those characterizations of India, though containing a measure of truth, did not say it all, nor did they matter much to him. They merely described the stereotype of India; and it was always a relief for people to hear a stereotype confirmed.

He couldn't say: I've broken through it all. He couldn't say: It was the girl.

In small ways he'd known it in the past, this feeling of a place altered by a single person. How often a landscape was charged and sweetened for him because he had been in love; because he'd somehow managed to succeed with a woman. He had her and everything was different – he had a reason to be there, and more, a reason to return. It was not just the sex; it was a human connection that made a place important to him.

This discovery in India, of a desire in him that had found release – and also to be thought of as a hero, suffering a week of meetings and clouds of germs, when the fact was that India could be bliss – had happened so simply, because Indru had pursued him.

'I'm coming back,' he said.

'I wait you.'

Who in the States, in his whole life, had ever said those words to him with such a tremor of emotion? He wanted Maureen to call, to ask him how he was,

137

so he could say, 'Fine – and, by the way, I gave the diamond ring away, to a girl I met in an alley in India.'

He felt happier without the diamond in his pocket. But maybe it was better that Maureen didn't call. He didn't want to tell her he was happy. She'd say, 'See? I told you it would change your life', and he didn't want her to be so complacently right about him.

He was strengthened by believing that India was the land of yes. And for the five months he remained in Boston he felt he was like the exiled king of a glittering country that was full of possibilities and pleasures. What made this sense of exile even more satisfying was the knowledge that his colleagues regarded his having gone there as an enormous sacrifice, a trip fraught with danger and difficulty.

He lobbied to return, first with Kohut, who was the most senior partner; then with Sheely, who was terrified of being sent back. But his lobbying took the form of casual questions rather than an outright offer to go. If he looked too eager, they'd take him less seriously and would be less inclined to offer him a hardship allowance.

'We've got a couple of clients pending,' Kohut said. 'It's great of you to ask. We'd like to send you back with three or four deals, not so much to maximize the hours as to make it simpler for you.'

'I'm just saying I could probably help. I know the terrain a bit better.'

'It might mean two weeks of back-to-back meetings.'

'Make it three. Less pressure.' And Dwight spoke of strategy.

'Hunt, you're amazing.'

'That I've developed some contacts?'

'That you'd go there at all. To me, it's a black hole.'

'There's money in that hole.'

But even as he spoke about the potential deals and the money to be made, he was thinking of Indru and how she had followed him in her white dress and white shoes; how she had said, *I wait you.*

Not just Indru, but she seemed to speak for thousands of others who were waiting, like the willing girls in the ads in the newspaper section headed 'Matrimonials'. Something within him had been liberated and released, perhaps something as simple as his fear. He was a new man, he had discovered an India he had never heard about; all he'd been told about was the misery.

So this was what true travelers knew, and maybe some lawyers too! You said, 'Poor guy, so far away in that awful place,' never guessing that he was someone you didn't know at all, a happy person, in a distant place that allowed him to be himself – girls saying *Whatever you want, sir,* and, *What you like,* or the most powerful word in the language of desire, *Yes.*

He realized that he had discovered what other travelers knew but weren't telling, that India could also be pleasurable. He was one of those men, just as smitten, just as cagey. He didn't say to Kohut, *Please send me back*; instead, he let the client list accumulate and he waited for Kohut to summon him.

And then he left, going to India as to a waiting lover, a patient mistress.

*

'We have meetings tomorrow,' Shah said. He had met him at the airport, behind a man in a uniform carrying a sign lettered HUNTSINGHA. They were sitting in the back of his car.

'It's already tomorrow,' Dwight said.

It was two in the morning. He was thinking: this odor of dust and diesel, wood smoke, decay, industrial fumes and flowers, and the odor of humans, the complex smell of India – he had never been anywhere that smelled like this. This dense cloud contained the hum of India's history, too – conquerors, burnings, blood, the incense of religion, it was less a whiff than a wall of smell.

'Back-to-back meetings,' Shah said. Kohut's expression – they must have been talking. Shah was an element of the firm now.

'When's the first one?'

'Eight-thirty, and so on into the day,' Shah said.

'Okay.' Dwight thought: At least I'm here.

'Hit ground running, so to say.'

'But I'm free tomorrow night?'

'Tomorrow night we have fundraiser at the Oberoi, main ballroom. Two of potential clients will be attendees.'

This 'we' was new, along with Shah's brisker manner.

Shah dropped him at his hotel, saying, 'See you shortly.'

It was a bad joke. It kept Dwight awake, wide-eyed in the darkness of the Elephanta Suite, his alertness reminding him that it was late afternoon in Boston. He lay sleepless in his bed, dozing, and did not begin to slumber deeply until it was time to wake up.

Being weary and irritable at the meeting had the effect of cowing the manufacturers – the textile man with his order of leisurewear, the plastic man and his patio furniture, the team from nearby Mylapore who made rolls of nylon webbing, and at the end of the day, the hardest negotiation of all, the techies from Hyderabad whose company made components for mobile phones.

Kohut had provided the client list, Shah had lined up the product people. As always there were costs to be assessed, samples to be examined and evaluated, quality-control clauses, shipping costs. The contracts were like architectural plans, each stage of the discussion a new set of elevations, a sheet of specs, going deeper into the descriptions. But Shah had taken care of that, too. Dwight sat while Shah went through the contracts, turning pages slowly, always drawn to a detail, as though to wear the manufacturer down.

'Item four, subsection B, paragraph two, under "definitions",' Shah said. 'We suggest inserting "piece goods", do we not, Mr Hund?'

'Gotta have it.'

But, frowning for effect, he was thinking of Indru. He was impatient to see her and, because he had not heard from her, he knew he would have to go looking for her. He couldn't marry her. He fantasized adopting her. *This is my daughter*. Could he get away with it? Give her piano lessons, find her a tutor, get her some grooming, teach her French, move to Sudbury and buy her a pony.

After the meeting, alone with Shah in the board-room, he said, 'I'm wiped out. I can't face this fundraiser.'

'Gala dinner and dance for charity,' Shah said.

'Whatever.'

'It is necessary.'

This finicky urgency, this tenacity, set Shah apart – perhaps set Indians apart. It was another aspect of the obsession with detail. Dwight had arrived at 2 a.m., he'd hardly slept, the meetings had gone on all day; now it was almost six in the evening and Shah was insisting on this further event.

'Give me a reason.'

Shah said, 'Reason is that sociability is highly prized by Mumbai people. You will be noticed. You will get big points for attending. And Oberoi is important venue.'

Dwight was shaking his head.

Shah said, 'And major client will be there, software developer Gopinathan. You must meet him in a social setting in the first instance. It is critical. We are seated at his table.'

'What's the dress code?'

'Suits for gents.'

But half the men at the gala wore black tie. In the hotel lobby a large placard propped on an easel was lettered, *Shrinaji Gala Dinner Dance to Aid Women in Crisis.* Glamorous couples chatted in the busy ball-room, where tables had been elaborately set, three wine glasses at each place. Dwight noticed that many of the beautiful women were being escorted by their much shorter, much older, much fatter husbands. It was a genial and noisy crowd, people loudly greeting each other, some with *namastes*, some with kisses.

Wine was being served by waiters in white suits and

red turbans. A tray of filled champagne flutes was offered to Shah.

'I do not take,' Shah said.

Another waiter slid a platter of hors d'oeuvres towards Shah.

'I do not take.'

A gong was rung, no one paid any attention; but after it was rung three or four more times, the guests drifted to their assigned tables.

'Mr Gopinathan, I have the pleasure to introduce you to my colleague . . .'

Before Shah could mispronounce his name, he said, 'Dwight Huntsinger. And I want you to know that although I arrived at two this morning and put in a whole day's work, I would not have missed this for anything.'

'Good cause,' Mr Gopinathan said. 'Women in crisis. Battered, abused, that sort of thing.'

'And meeting you,' Dwight said. 'I am looking forward to learning from you.'

'You are too kind,' Mr Gopinathan said. 'Please be seated.'

Dwight sat next to Mr Gopinathan's wife, whose stoutness made her seem friendlier, easier company than the woman on his other side, a golden-skinned beauty in a bottle-green sari. During the meal he concentrated on Mrs Gopinathan.

'I am co-chair of the charity,' she said. 'It is a heavy burden.'

'You're doing good work,' Dwight said. He wondered if his weariness was making him slur his words.

'And it is not just women. It is young girls – schoolgirls, abducted and abused. You cannot believe. Treated like property. And the health issues!'

He was glad for the woman's volubility. After he had listened to two courses of this he turned to the woman on his right, the beauty, and said, 'Tell me your story.'

'Perhaps when we have more time,' she said, and because she had said it coquettishly Dwight looked past her, expecting to see her husband, but only saw Shah, spooning orange paste from a small bowl.

'It is *choley*,' Shah said, startled in his eating.

'Have you lodged any bids in the silent auction?' the woman asked.

'No, but I'd like to lodge some,' Dwight said. 'Maybe you can advise me.'

Glad for any excuse to leave the table, and wishing to stretch his legs – his fatigue was beginning to tell – he excused himself and went with the woman to the foyer, where auction items were set out on long tables, each item with a numbered pad next to it showing the bidders' names.

'These are exquisite,' the woman said, lifting up a velvet-covered box in which a pair of hoop earrings lay on a satin cushion.

When a woman said *exquisite* like that it meant *I want them*.

'I don't know much about this stuff,' Dwight said, to see her reaction.

'It's South Indian style,' the woman said. 'Perhaps something for your wife.'

She was sharp-faced, her green eyes set off by her honey-colored skin, a necklace like a draping of golden chain mail, and her green sari was edged with gold highlights. She was the loveliest woman Dwight had seen in India.

'If I had a wife,' Dwight said. 'Which I don't.'

'Pity. Any woman would love to have that piece.'

On the pad next to it was its number and a list of names, the last one showing a bid of twenty-two thousand rupees.

'How much is that in real money?'

'In dollars, about' – the woman pursed her lips and swallowed hard, looking even more beautiful in this moment of concentration and greed – 'six hundred. Even twice that would be a bargain.'

'So I'll improve on it.' Dwight added five thousand rupees to the bid and as he was signing his name, a woman passed by, waited for him to finish, and lifted the pad.

'Bidding is closed,' she called to the room.

'You're in luck,' the lovely woman said. 'You're the last bidder, so you'll get the earrings.' She smiled at him. 'What will you do with them?'

He leaned towards her and said softly, 'Maybe you can help me decide.'

'It would be my great pleasure.' Saying this, she drew a small card from the silk purse at her wrist and slipped it into his hand. Then she dropped her voice to a whisper and said, 'My mobile number is on it.'

'Thanks.'

The woman was still talking. 'It would be better if we did not leave together. The dinner is over in any case. Call me in thirty minutes and I will give you directions.' She turned to go, and then remembered something else. 'You can pay for that at the table over there, where a queue is forming.'

Shah saw him in the payment line. He said, 'Ah, you succeeded in a bid. What did you win?'

'Just a bauble.'

'You succeeded with Gopinathan, too. His wife said you are a great listener.'

It had been his weariness, his inertia, yet now he felt wired, hyper-alert, as though drugged. He wondered if it was the woman who had wakened him.

'Want a lift?'

'I'll get a taxi.'

All day he had thought of Indru. At the dinner, especially seeing the expensive food and wine, he had tried to imagine what Indru might be eating at that moment. And having stayed up so late he had thought of perhaps strolling past the Gateway of India, just to see whether she might be out strolling herself.

But, instead, here he was in a corner of the Oberoi lobby, looking at the name on the woman's card – it was Surekha Shankar Vellore – and dialing the number on his cellphone.

'Hello.'

'Is that Miss Vellore?'

'Yes. Where are you?'

'Still in the lobby.'

'Step outside. Have the doorman hail a taxi. Show the card to the driver and he will take you to my address. It's not far.'

Blind to the progress of the taxi, Dwight had looked out the window, hoping for a glimpse of the Gateway of India. He saw nothing. Yet he felt unfaithful – where was he going, and why? The last part of the brief taxi ride was a steep hill lined with tall, whitish apartment blocks.

'Shall I wait, sir?'

'Not necessary.'

Dwight pressed the bell labeled *Vellore*, and the door latch buzzed open. He heard her voice in the speaker: 'Eighth floor.' Dwight saw his haggard face in the elevator mirror and said, 'What are you doing here?'

Her apartment, the door ajar, was diagonally across from the elevator, and she stood just inside. She had changed from the green sari into one that was crimson and gold. She had done something to her hair, unbraided it, combed it out. There was more of it than he had seen at dinner. She was barefoot.

'You're Surekha.'

'Please call me Winky. Come in. What will you drink?'

He asked for water, and when she brought it, filling his glass with a pitcher, he said, 'Um, Winky. You're not married?'

'Divorced. ' She sipped at a glass of white wine. 'My husband left me for a more up-to-date model. The latest model. That's how he was in life, in business, and cars. Always competitive, but blessed with taste. Always he had to have the best of everything.'

She seemed to be praising the man who had dumped her for a younger woman. Dwight said, 'People like that are never happy.'

'He was supremely happy,' Winky said, contradicting him. 'Arun had exquisite taste. It rubbed off on me, I'm afraid. When we used to travel to London together on holiday we always stayed at the Connaught. One shopped at Harrods, and we had many posh friends nearby, in Ovington Gardens. They were delightful and highly educated but London can be so, how does one put it?'

She spoke slowly but deliberately, so Dwight could not interrupt, as he wanted to at this point, to tell her about his trips to London.

'So damnably trying. Masses of these colored people, Hubshis from Africa, who go there just to get welfare, all these lazy people on the dole. One can't bear looking at them. Knightsbridge and Kensington are fine, but parts of London are absolutely filthy. Arun used to say, "All these welfare people should be given a broom!"'

Dwight said, 'But Bombay is . . .'

'Vibrant,' Winky said. 'One has lived here one's whole life. Oh, yes, visitors complain about the crowds. But look closely at these so-called crowds – everyone has something to do, something to make. It is a hive of activity. We Indians manufacture everything under the sun. Arun said that it was only a matter of time before we'd be making jet aircraft. We make cars, buses, lorries, even ships. We have a great navy – my father was in the military. Arun told me that China has no navy, did you know that? It's true! And it's not just the broad range of manufacturing but of course we make quality too. Go to Jodhpur and you will see they are producing fine linens and silks for the high fashion houses and the designer labels of New York. Go up and down New York and virtually everything you see in the best shops is made in India – women's handbags, fine coats, silk scarves, lingerie, garments of all sorts, even shoes, though all one's own shoes are made in Italy. But Americans hardly know the difference.'

Shut up! The throbbing in his temples was battling his desire – and yet the easy way she sat on the sofa, leaning slightly forward, caused her heavy breasts to sway as she spoke, and kept him attentive.

'Um.' Sipping from her wine glass, she couldn't utter a word, yet she was making a droning sound in her nose, as though to signal that she was about to start speaking again.

'Where do you stay in New York?' Dwight asked.

'Gracious me, one would never go to America. It's far too violent. Everyone has a gun, and it's far too dirty. The fast life! Arun's brother had business there, somewhere in California. Electronics. He had so many stories about drugs and gangs – one was quite terrified, just listening. An employee of his was killed, some sort of mugging. No, thank you. One has no plans to go to America. One's London holiday suits one nicely. One used to buy jewelry in Bond Street but it's all got so predictable – all the shops in London cater to American tourists, so the pieces are nothing special and the prices are absurd. I think the piece you picked up at the charity auction was quite acceptable, was it not?'

Was this a question? Dwight could not remember ever being subjected to such a barrage at short notice. In the woman's confidence was a weird honesty. Awful as it was to endure, he was almost grateful to her for this monologue, because in it she gave everything away: she was a snob, she was materialistic, a boaster, a bigot.

Now he was too tired to respond, her talk had tired him the more, and so he sat on his plush chair in the over-decorated apartment watching her breasts move in counterpoint to her complaints. He also sensed that her talk might not be the idle chatter it seemed but rather a way of wearing him down, a way of dominating him. She was still talking but when at last she stopped his willpower would be gone and he would be hers.

If her talk was like a test – of his patience and his own opinions – it also allowed him plenty of time to sit and stare. She was lovely, even if her chatter and her opinions were obnoxious. He smiled to think that the woman was desirable. Her golden skin, her lovely eyes flashing in indignation; her lips were full, her face fox-like, beaky, imposing. Her heavy breasts swayed in her sari but such was the odd wrap of the sari that he could gaze at a great expanse of her pale belly, and in his fatigued state he imagined nuzzling its warmth and pillowing his face upon that softness.

Repelled by her talk, attracted by her body, aroused by being in the seclusion of her apartment late on this Bombay night, he watched for the wine to take effect – and she was still talking! Now it was about her ex-husband, and what was strange about that was her frankness, her fondness for the man, the way she talked about his bad-boy side, in the way that Indian women – Miss Bhatia and Miss Chakravarty anyway – talked about men, always in motherly tones.

'What about children?' he managed to ask, reminding himself that in situations like this (but it usually involved a nervous client) he felt like an interviewer.

'Thank goodness, we didn't have any, so there were no entanglements. Aren't there enough unhappy children in the world without adding to their number? Though one sometimes thinks, wouldn't it be nice to have a little girl to take shopping and to spoil rotten with all sorts of delicious treats? One can see her on a pony – riding lessons at the Gymkhana Club. Arun wanted a son. Well, maybe his new woman will provide him with one, and jolly good luck to them. He was a good provider. He found me this flat and he still keeps in touch. He knows that it's not easy for one. A divorced woman in India is damaged goods.'

At the back of his throat he was gargling, blah-blah-blah, and was so intent that he did not notice, until a few moments had passed, that she had stopped speaking. What had she just said? He asked her to repeat it.

'You don't look it,' he said.

'I assure you one is.'

She laughed because she knew she was attractive and liked the conceit of calling herself damaged. Smiling, she looked even prettier; she tossed her hair, she laughed, she patted her hair into place. Her pale belly was dimpled and only when she leaned over to refill her glass did a fold of flesh press against the silk. Now, sipping, she looked over the rim of her glass at him.

'What about you?'

She did not know his name and after – what? – maybe half an hour of yapping, her first question.

'Me? Damaged goods.'

'Not at all,' she said. 'You wouldn't have been at

that charity ball, and at Gopi's table, if you didn't have some standing. All Bombay was there, the best sort of people, and – hey, presto – you came up trumps with your bid.'

Her tone annoyed him, but he was still so dazzled by her glamour he tried to change the subject. 'What kind of wine are you drinking?'

'Indian made. A vineyard in Karnataka. Quite drinkable, actually,' she said. 'Do you have them with you?'

'The earrings? I think so.' He took the silk pouch out of his pocket. It reminded him of the pouch in which he'd carried his rejected wedding ring. That thought created an after-image of Indru, who now possessed the diamond ring.

As he handled the silk pouch, Winky extended her arm, dark and slender and articulated – delicately jointed like the limb of a spider – and Dwight shook the earrings into the palm of her hand.

Deftly, she slipped off the earrings she was wearing and in a set of movements like a dancer's gestures, more like touching her ears than attaching earrings, she hooked them, one and then the other, and turning to face him made them swing and glitter.

'They suit me, don't you think?'

Dwight said yes, realizing what was happening, but could not say anymore.

'They catch the highlights of my sari,' she said and twitched her sash where it was trimmed with gold piping.

'Let me see,' Dwight said. He placed his glass of water onto the marble-topped table and went over to the sofa and sat heavily next to her. He lifted her hair and smoothed it, then touched the earrings, poked one with his finger, and peered closely. 'I guess they're a good fit.'

'I'm delighted you approve.'

He saw that this, like her rambling talk, was another test. He did not like her but he was fascinated by how obvious she was and he longed to weigh her breasts in his hands.

'Look at me,' he said – because she was looking away, at a cabinet where there was a mirror.

She turned her head and lifted it slightly with a kind of hauteur that the earrings framed and accentuated.

He kissed her then, just leaned over and put his mouth on hers as though lapping an ice cream. She did not part her lips; she remained as she was, like a big doll, and as she did not even purse her lips to receive his kiss they seemed to bump his, almost to resist. The first awkward kiss he had ever bestowed on a girl – at the age of twelve: Linda Keith, behind the First Baptist Church – had been something like this.

'What's wrong?'

'Isn't that a little sudden? A little previous?' She turned back to look at the mirror, as though to assess whether she had been injured by the kiss, and her earrings danced.

'I guess I had the wrong idea.'

'You're a very nice man. A generous man' – still she was looking at her reflection, the earrings trembling on her ears.

'What's the plan, then?'

'The plan,' she said, repeating it his way as though to mock him. 'Perhaps we can meet for lunch some time. Perhaps you can take me shopping.'

Another test, another hoop.

'Perhaps,' he said, using her tone as she had used his. She did not know that when Dwight said 'perhaps' it meant never. At this moment he had finally concluded that he disliked her and almost said: I hope I never see you again. He got up and looked at his watch and put on an expression of surprise, and said again, with finality, 'Perhaps.'

She seemed startled that he was leaving. She touched the earrings with her beautiful fingers. She said, 'Well, then, cheerio.'

'By the way, my name is Dwight Huntsinger.'

'I'm terrible at names. Will you email me? My address is on that card.'

'Perhaps,' he said.

In the street he was rueful but not unhappy. He mocked himself, replaying some of what she had said. Tingling, yawning with exhaustion, he felt giddy as he walked down the hill to the main road to hail a taxi. And in the taxi he reflected on how for the hour or more he'd been in Winky Vellore's apartment he had not once objected to India. He had forgotten the stink, the noise, the crowds. Now on the main road he was back in India and he was surprised by his reaction: he was glad.

He was forty-three, he believed he had made many mistakes in his life, but his pride had saved him from more. He'd married late, the marriage had lasted less than a year, an expensive mistake, but necessary. He knew men who, rebuffed by a woman, pursued her until she submitted; men who were energized by *Isn't that a little sudden?* and *Perhaps we can meet for lunch some time. You can take me shopping*, when they had asked for a simple yes or no to sex. He was not one of them. Meeting resistance, Dwight shrugged and accepted it as final; was in fact slightly ashamed at having met resistance – ashamed of having requested a favor to which the answer was no. The word *no* did not rouse him. He did not pursue the woman, he had never pursued a woman, never tried to woo one without at least a smile of encouragement. He was literal-minded in sexual matters, and so *Perhaps we can meet for lunch some time* he translated as *No dice*. The process of wooing he found discouraging and at times humiliating.

Because of this, his experiences of women were few and, since his divorce, the only women he'd had were Sumitra and Indru – essentially streetwalkers, who had pursued him; offered themselves to him in the dark.

Now he thought only of Indru, and after the evening with Winky Vellore – those shattering hours, like a whole relationship, beginning, middle and end – he had never felt more tender towards Indru. That evening with Winky helped him understand Indru. He knew that Winky would have despised her – but that was a measure of Indru's worth.

At the Taj, he paid the taxi and was saluted by the doorman and he stood in the stew of odors, strong here even on the marble stairs of the expensive hotel. He remembered his first trip, his solemnly worded thought 'the smell of failure'. But there was vitality in it, not only death but life too.

Meetings the next day kept him in the boardroom late. Shah did most of the negotiating, yet he needed to observe the process and approve the wording of the contracts. Indian lawyers, their passion for redrafting, their love of wording: they could sound in the middle of it all like astrologers. Manoj Verma had not married (and this was just idle water-cooler chat at the top of Jeejeebhoy Towers) until his family astrologer had drawn a chart of his prospective bride's planets and found them auspicious. Dwight went back to his hotel, his head spinning.

The following day he walked across the road to the Gateway of India at exactly the same time of day – in the fading glow of early evening – he had met Indru months ago. He retraced his steps, he passed the ice-cream seller, he bought a Thums-Up and lingered at the rail of the harbor, then took a seat, hoping that the ritual of these precise repetitions might conjure her up.

Without a word, she appeared and approached and sat beside him on the bench. That was another Indian surprise: Indians might spend hours or days waiting until you showed up – his driver, the courier, even J. J. Shah. When you wanted them they were there, standing at attention, or as in Indru's case, uncoiling in the half-dark and smiling.

'I waiting you so long.'

'I want to kiss you.'

She giggled. 'Not here. Follow me.'

To anyone who glanced his way he was a foreigner, a *ferringi*, perhaps an American – the baseball cap with the suit was a giveaway. He was alone, detached, strolling in the crowd of people, on Apollo Bunder, heading north, and now towards Chowpatty. But in fact he was watching a girl in a white dress, and guided by her he crossed busy streets, and negotiated side-walks that were dense with pedestrians.

At the point in a busy road where in the clouds beyond a gleam of summer lightning broke through, like the shivered splinters of a precious stone smashed by a hammer, the smithereens puddling in a watery afterglow on the slop of the sea at Chowpatty Beach, Indru glanced back at Dwight and her smile touched his soul. Then she walked down a narrow lane and through a gateway, where a woman was washing a baby in a tin basin in the strange light like a child in a slop of mercury. At a distance the houses were lovely; here at the base of this apartment house the smell of packed-down and heated dirt was so strong it built in his head like a loud noise.

Indru was on the stairs, three flights, he caught up with her on the last landing, as she was turning her key in the metal door.

'Please you come in.'

He summed it up quickly in the twilight, before she switched on the lamp – two rooms, a string bed, cush-ions on the floor, a chair.

'Please sit.'

He chose the chair; the long walk in the humid heat had worn him out.

'How did you find this?'

'Money you gave me was ample.'

'The ring?'

'I am sold,' she said, looking fearful.

Instead of saying anything, he kissed her to reassure her.

'But first, sir.'

She took his shoes off, plucked off his socks, slipped a mat under his bare feet. Then she got a bowl and filled it with water and knelt before him. And when she bent over and washed his feet, massaging his toes, he felt strengthened, and the distant rumble of thunder from Chowpatty echoed in his head as he thought, I am happy, I am home.

4

He asked the firm for another month. Thanking him for his willingness, they granted it immediately, emailing him a list of new clients, with specifications of product lines for outsourcing – sports clothes, leather goods, brass fittings, molded plastic tubes for patio furniture, gardening implements, lamp bases, glassware – and Kohut added, *Glad it's such a success*, because no one had ever asked for an extension. Most had wanted to come home early.

After the meetings, or the flights to Bangalore and Hyderabad – usually a day in each place and the late flight back to Bombay – he went to Indru's room rather than the Elephanta Suite. He lay in the half dark, listening to her stories, which she told in a monotone: how her father touched her – the shame of it; how her mother beat her, blaming her, and her father sent her away to her auntie's village; how her auntie locked her in a dark room, with the grain sacks and the rats; and how, when Indru went to the police, they didn't believe her; and the village boys threw bricks of cow shit at her, and when her uncle happened by to rescue her, he drove her on his motorbike to the river bank where he dragged her among the bamboos.

'He touch me here, he touch me down here on my privates, he bite me with his teeth and call me dirty dog.'

They were harrowing stories, the more terrifying for the factual way she told them, lying on her back on the string bed, her fingertips grazing her body to indicate where she had been violated. She seemed to understand how they seized Dwight's attention and silenced him. And some evenings when he seemed distracted, his gaze drifting to the window, sleepy and satisfied, she would prop herself on one elbow and drop her voice and show him a scar on her wrist, whitish on her dark skin.

'One uncle tie me with ropes. He say, "Is a game." I be so scare. He take my sari. He say, "I no hurt you."'

And what she told him next in that soft voice was more powerful to him than the racket at the window. He took a deep breath and gagged and thought, *Not a success at all. It's a failure.*

The smell of failure in India wasn't only Indian failure. It was a universal smell of human weakness, the stink of humanity, his own failure, too. His firm of lawyers was bringing so many people down.

He remembered telling Maureen that he was being sent to India – like a threat, a risk, a martyrdom. *I'm going to India. Take that!*

His marriage hadn't worked, but he thought, How can any marriage work? Everyone had their own problems – who was normal? If the two people remained themselves, with separate ambitions, there was strife. Submission was possible in the short term. But if one or the other surrendered to become absorbed in the other's life, then it was the annihilation of a human soul, something like slavery or an early death, and resentment was inevitable. Love was not enough, sexual desire didn't last, you had to make your own life.

He'd had hopes, the usual ones, of partnership and plans, and had tried. But early on he'd lain beside his wife of less than a year and thought, *It's over*. He suspected that she was thinking the same.

To calm himself while lying beside Maureen, he mentally moved out: his restless mind roamed through the whole apartment, room by room, selecting the things he wanted to take with him, rejecting the things that were hers. It was an inventory of the place but also a way of processing the marriage, making a pile of belongings he planned to leave behind.

He had loved her for more than a year, the passionate part of the whole business; and then he proposed and set a date. But the nearer they got to the date the less love he felt – panic set in – and his heart was almost empty as he went through the motions on his wedding day. The wedding itself, the expense, the decisions, their first arguments, seemed a ritual designed to break your spirit. After that it was just a struggle, as though marriage represented the end of a love affair, the beginning of mutual strife. She kept working, she wouldn't take on the name Huntsinger, she rejected the idea of having kids, she didn't cook – but then neither did he. He asked Sheely, who could be trusted with confidences, if these were signs, but Sheely in his lawyer's way just shrugged, gave a lawyer's equivocal answer: Maybe yes, maybe no.

Maureen was also a lawyer – tax law and trust funds, but a different firm – and she seemed too preoccupied to notice his mood, the question on his face, Why did we do it?

He was the first to mention splitting up. He did it in a cowardly way – 'Maybe just spend a little time apart.' But she could see he meant divorce, because the same thought was lurking in her own mind. She'd said, 'My mother will be so angry. She said I couldn't do it – that I was too selfish.'

Maureen began to cry, and for the first time, with acute pain, Dwight saw how vulnerable she was. He held her tenderly, he felt protective, he said, 'We'll figure something out,' and he despaired, because it was turning out to be so much harder than he had imagined. Showing her weakness for the first time, the fear that she had expected the marriage to fail, made the break-up a nightmare. Losing her as a wife was painful, but he guessed he'd get over it; losing her as a friend – someone he had pushed overboard when the storm broke over them – that seemed unbearable, and something she would never forgive.

Not much remained to divide. They sold the apartment and split the proceeds.

'Short marriages,' Sheely said. 'Pretty common. Like a chess move. I know three people, not counting you. Couple of months and they're gonzo. Better now than later. Probably a book on the subject.'

In the melancholy months afterwards they still saw each other. They didn't know anyone else and their feelings were so raw they didn't want to make new friends.

Maureen had been depressed by the men she'd met. She had no one else to tell, so she told Dwight. 'The first drink is fine. On the second drink I hear about their marriage. How it ended. What a bitch she was. How she took him to the cleaners.'

So, as friends, they dated each other for some months, even recognizing that it was a failure and that they were too timid to enter the wider world and contemplate romance again. Dwight was amazed that after that anyone would take the same risk twice, going through that shredder.

At last, they disengaged. He was surprised because at that point he had become comfortable, seeing her on weekends, and going to movies. She asked how he was doing. With his new frankness – the divorce had made him blunt – he told her, 'This is good. I'm happy.' Maureen said, 'It's not good. I can't stand this anymore. I don't want to see you. I'm starting to really dislike you.'

Was it because he was happy again? If so, she succeeded in making him miserable by saying this. That was his reason for saying, 'I'm going to India,' in the look-what-you're-making-me-do tone of voice.

At last, he saw his divorce as a triumph. No one else did, which was another reason he was happy to be in India. Perhaps failure was the severest kind of truth. His work was a punishment and a wrecking ball: he took manufacturing away from American companies and brought it to India. The American manufacturers hated him – and they failed; the Indian companies were cynical, knowing that if they could not produce goods cheaply enough they would be rejected. Every success meant someone's failure. He could not have any pride in that process: he was part of it.

The old woman pimping the children to passers-by: he recognized himself in her. And in Indru too. Her stories were painful, but the experiences had damaged her so badly her endearments were meaningless. Yet he belonged with her, not in the Elephanta Suite but in the oddly bare room, a stinky alley outside the window. In that human smell like the odor of sorrow he saw his connection to India.

He stopped blaming Maureen, and he could hardly blame Indru for anything. Human frailty implied human strength. Most of the world is poor and weak, beset by the rest of them.

A young man visited Indru's apartment; he was there one evening and seemed reluctant to leave. He was from the countryside, he said. *Willage*. Then he was there more often. But he looked more confident and better dressed than a villager, and he frowned at Indru in a proprietorial way. He was sometimes impatient to leave the place with Indru ('Let we go marketing'). He nagged her in their own language, which wasn't Hindi – Dwight had asked. Indru sometimes replied in English, sulking and saying, 'Not chivvy me' or 'I fed up!'

'My brother,' she said. She left Dwight in the apartment and went out. He looked out the window and saw them – not holding hands but walking close together, touching shoulders, a kind of intimacy. He was rueful but it was better to know, and he'd been so hurt by his shattered marriage he had kept from committing himself to her. Giving her money when she said 'Ring money gone' was his way of possessing her, since it had more value to her than to him. The Indian deals were making him wealthy.

Dwight was startled one evening when he went to the flat and before he could turn the key in the lock, the door was opened by a small, pretty girl in the sort of white dress Indru wore. Why?

'I am work at hair-and-nail salon.'

Another one, younger than Indru – sixteen? seventeen? Who could tell? – who said she was from Indru's village. Her name was Padmini. She did menial jobs in the two-room apartment in return for a place to sleep. Dwight believed the hair-and-nail salon story because her nails were lovely – polished and pointed – and she wore fresh make-up and always a hairstyle that interested him, because unlike most Indian girls her hair was cut short, boyishly. Dwight remarked on it.

'I bob it,' Padmini said, plumping her lips prettily.

Dwight said, 'Is that her brother?'

Padmini joined him at the window, standing close, as Indru and the young man with the unpronounceable name turned the corner towards Chowpatty.

'I am not know, sir.'

She was frightened. *Not know* meant she knew and that the answer was yes, or else she would have said no, because as a villager she too was a relative.

Dwight smiled; she was slow to smile back yet she did so. He gave her to understand that they were conspirators – both being manipulated by Indru. He thought of kissing her, as a test, but didn't – they seemed to resist that. Was it his breath? But she let him hold her loosely, she allowed him to grope. His touching Padmini quieted her; she stayed still with his hands on her, and seemed to purr, like a cat being scratched.

He knew that, had he wished, he could have gone

further – and Indru must have guessed at the situation she had created by inviting Padmini to stay; by leaving Dwight and the girl alone in the place. Indru was worldlier than she let on – they all were, they had to be to survive.

And he had become reckless. More than that, he was debauched – the word that had seemed like hyperbole before was appropriate now. He had never known such sexual freedom, had not realized that it was in him to behave like this. It was India, he told himself; he would not have lived like this back in the States. All he had to do was leave India and he would be returned to the person he'd been before – forty-something, oblique in business deals, cautious with women, cynical of their motives, not looking for a wife, still smarting from his divorce, even a bit shy, and, like many shy men, given at the wrong time to laughing too loudly and to sudden gauche remarks, of which 'You bet your sweet ass' was one.

His sexual experiences in India had opened his eyes and given him insights. The world looked different to him. That business about 'my brother' had not fooled him, nor had it discouraged him. It gave him another opportunity, for the next time the brother appeared and took Indru away on some obscure errand, Dwight beckoned to Padmini and drew her down to the charpoy.

'No,' she said, and when he began to tug at her clothes – the white dress she wore for work at the nail salon – she resisted, turned away and covered her face.

'Okay,' he said. He sat up and swung around, putting his feet on the floor.

No meant no. He would not use force on a woman – had never done so in his life. Any suggestion of intimidation killed his desire. But when he got up from the charpoy Padmini rolled over onto her back and smiled at him in confusion.

'You no like me,' she said.

'I like you too much,' he said.

But she just laughed, and yanked at the tops of her knee socks, and tossed her head, and when he gave her money that day she took it reluctantly, as though acknowledging that she didn't deserve it.

He continued to give Indru money. He suspected that she was giving it to the young boy she called her brother. Deceits and failures and betrayals: but it was part of the India he had come to understand. He belonged here. He had found his level.

Although India advertised itself as a land of sensuality, he had regarded it as hype. They were trying to sell tickets. And where were the sensualists? The businessmen were two-faced, and so shifty they turned the women into scolds. Most of the people he'd met had been too angry – pestering and puritanical – with red-rimmed and tormented eyes. If they'd been liberated they wouldn't have been such agitated nags. They scowled, they carped, they pushed, they honked their horns. Serenity seemed unattainable; the way the bosses screamed at their underlings, the shrill orders a manager gave a secretary, the bullshit, the buck-passing, the cruel teasing, the racism, hating each other much more than they hated foreigners – it all revealed to Dwight a culture of punishment and sexual frustration, for the two always went together.

Long ago, as a youth, as a law student, he had once behaved that way himself – on edge, because he'd been unsuccessful with women. His first trip to India had reminded him of that – everything wrong, the yelling crowds, the food, the bad air, and the women were either virginal with their eyes downcast, or married and plump and indifferent, in both cases impossible. The predatory divorcee or widow was just desperate, with no option except to be devious, and scheming turned him off. The society was packed too tight, jammed and impenetrable, and all a stranger could do was drift hopelessly around its dusty edges.

Or so he had thought. He was wrong about this – wrong about everything, wrong in all his assumptions. India was sensual. If India seemed puritanical it was because at the bottom of its puritanism was a repressed sensuality that was hungrier and nakeder and more voracious than anything he'd known. The strict rules kept most people in their place, yet there were exceptions everywhere, and where there were exceptions there was anarchy and desire. If India had a human face it was that of a hungry, skinny girl, starved for love, famished for money.

From his first encounter at the Gateway of India, when the canny woman had tricked him with that elaborate scam that involved the charade with the old man and the children, Dwight had seen India differently, accommodated himself to it, and begun to live a double life. He had sunk to the bottom and had entered a new level of the Indian experience – the lowlife of the truly desperate. When Shah said, 'I ring you at your hotel last night – you not there,' he explained that he had shut off his phone, and he was certain that Shah did not know that he was elsewhere, living his other life in the grubby flat in Chowpatty. And he was glad, because he was not able to explain what he was doing and who he had become. His relationship with Indru in the two tiny rooms was equally unexplainable.

When you could not explain your absences, when you were living your secrets and were happier living them than you'd ever been, you were leading a double life. He knew that. He also knew that living this way you had to accustom yourself to telling lies and remembering them and building on them, so that a whole world of obvious and gabbling falsehood was a front for the hidden and wordless reality. Something else he discovered about the double life – you began to lose track of your identity, at least he did. Someone said 'Huntsinger!' and his instinctive reaction was to think, *Who*?

How had it happened? Was it the sex, the young women, all the layers of living in India – the rooms, the religion, the castes, the crowds, the city of twenty million? His first visit to India had been a suspension of his life. Most Americans he knew came to India holding their noses, did what had to be done – found a contractor who would produce goods for one-fifth the US price – and returned home, resumed living, fearing to be called back. That had been him once.

But he had found a life in India, or rather two lives: Indru's little flat and the Elephanta Suite, the life of hidden and vitalizing sexuality which he was still learning and the boardroom existence he knew well – the world of contracts, competitive pricing, manufacturing and outsourcing, the easy task in India of finding people who could produce good quality samples (that is, copy the American sample at their own expense) and then signing them up, saying, 'We'll grow together.'

The most recent deal was with a maker of blue jeans in Poona – he looked so hopeful, so eager to please, with suitcases of swatches and samples. *Look at pocket formation, look at seams, quality, double stitching. We can supply unlimited units. It is a good pant.*

'What about a buck twenty-nine a pair, delivered,' Dwight said.

Shah conferred with the man, and then turned to Dwight. 'He can manage. Do you not agree, Mr Hund?'

'Deal.' And later he said, 'It's like shooting tuna fish in a can.'

Shah smiled in bewilderment – how did you explain? – and Dwight was reminded of the days when he had feared Indian food, how he'd come with a box of tuna fish in cans with pop-off lids that he'd eaten standing over the sink in his hotel bathroom.

Now he ate the food, most of it – not just the enamel dishes of it that Indru and Padmini prepared, that they ate sitting on the floor of her little apartment, but also the dishes that Shah habitually ate. Adhering to the Jain rule of not eating any living thing, keeping to leaves and grains and lentils, Dwight had not been sick once. The idea was to keep it simple – no fish, no meat, no roots. He liked the okra dishes that Shah called *bindi*, the chickpeas – channa and gram – the rice cakes, the chapattis, the pooris. He ate no cold food, nothing from the street, nothing that had sat uncovered, no salads, nothing that had to be washed, lettuce was fatal, so was water – water was a source of illness in India. Fruit that he had not peeled himself he didn't eat.

He and Shah usually presided over a ceremonial meal in a restaurant as a way of sealing a contract. The deal with the blue-jean manufacturer was one of these, the restaurant called the Imperial, a pleasant place near Church Gate. Dwight was asked to order first and he glanced at the menu. *Dine Like a Maharaja*, it said. *Chunks of mutton steeped in a savory broth* and *Slow roasted chicken in a clay tandoor oven* and *Thick fillet of pomfret Kerala style with coconut milk in a spicy sauce*. He clapped the menu shut and handed it to the waiter.

'Just a dish of dhal makni, some yogurt, and rice.'

'Will that be all, sir?'

'Unless you have bindi.'

The waiter wagged his head yes.

And someone at the table said, 'Mr Shah, you are a bad influence on our friend from America.'

'Oh, yes, exceedingly bad.'

Everyone except Dwight and Shah ordered from the menu. 'The *sali boti* is justifiably famous. Mutton and fried potatoes. Much talked about.'

Shah made a pained face.

'The prawns here are also very good I'm told.'

'I don't take prawns,' Shah said.

'I understand they raise their own chickens.'

'I don't take.'

'The fish is flown in fresh from Kochi.'

Shah smiled as the men were served enormous portions of meat and fish, while he and Dwight dabbed at their simple portions like a pair of monks.

Dwight was complimented on his choice of diet,

which was seen as a way of life, not as an affectation; it was a humble and healthy way of experiencing India. Almost without realizing it he'd become dependent on the food.

'No coffee for me,' he said at the end of the meal. 'Nor me,' Shah said. He frowned, as though preparing to deliver unwelcome news. 'Doxins.'

Dwight nodded in agreement, feeling at ease and slightly superior to the meat-eating Indians. He looked around the over-decorated restaurant – it was elegant but with a gamey aroma of roasted meat in the air, and incense, and the mildewed air conditioning. He looked closely at the other tables and noted with satisfaction that he was the only non-Indian in the place.

He tried to imagine what Maureen would say had she seen him looking so at home in the Imperial. 'I'm going to India' didn't sound suicidal anymore; it meant 'I don't need you.' Had Sheely or Kohut been in the restaurant with him they'd be wigging out – frightened, rigid with culture shock, dying to go back to the hotel, or on their cellphones reconfirming their flights home, so as not to have to stay a moment longer in India. Beyond the dumb arrogance of mere bigotry they would be terrified and angry, hating the place and the people. Dwight knew: he had once felt that way himself, like India's victim.

That memory shamed him. How could a prosperous American lawyer with a first-class plane ticket feel that way, surrounded by the poorest people in the world?

Yet his partners would never have done what he was doing – sitting here in the Imperial among the Indian businessmen, scooping dhal with the torn-off ear of a flaky poori, spooning yogurt, nibbling the slippery bindi. He did not know anyone in the office who would have sat so comfortably here. He was pleased with himself, he'd proven to be strong. India no longer scared him – rather the opposite, it aroused him, made him feel engaged with the world, most of all made him feel powerful.

In that confident mood after the dinner at the Imperial he shook hands with the businessmen. He could look them in the eye and tell them that he was enjoying himself in India and mean it.

'You are welcome, sir,' one of them said.

'I'm learning so much,' Dwight said. 'And I feel I have a lot to offer too.'

After the men thanked him and left, Shah said, 'Shall we walk?'

'I was going to get a taxi.'

'Taj Hotel is just that side.'

But Dwight had not planned to go to his hotel. He was headed to Chowpatty, to see Indru as usual. All through dinner he had imagined her waiting for him, lying in the charpoy, watching the little TV set he had bought for her, Padmini squatting nearby, their faces bluish from the light from the screen.

'Good idea,' Dwight said. 'Let's walk.'

The walk was a delay but he felt close to Shah – the man was his guide, his partner, his benefactor, his friend. Yet he could not imagine disclosing to Shah the facts of the other life he was leading. No one must know what he seldom thought of himself; it was better that his secret remain almost a secret to him, at least something unpacked and unexamined.

How did you go about examining it, anyway? Words weren't enough. That had been the trouble with his brief marriage, with life in general – no matter how much you told you, were only hinting at the truth. There was always too much to tell in the allotted time. He thought he'd known Maureen before they were married – what a doll, he'd thought. She'd been like a party guest who'd shown up in his life, anxious to please, eager to be a friend, grateful to find a kindred spirit, someone to talk to; and so she'd been quick to agree, appreciative of his attention, polite, undemanding, good company, Dwight relieved and thinking, We've got so much in common.

Eight months of courtship convinced him they were a perfect match. He was unhesitating in proposing to her. Then came the planning for the wedding, and a different Maureen appeared, a fretful and uncertain woman, prone to fits of anger, moody, argumentative. Or was it him? Perhaps it wasn't the details of the arrangements but the fact of the wedding looming in the months ahead.

'I don't suppose your parents could get involved?' he asked.

'We're too old for that!'

He was forty, she was thirty-eight; they felt conspicuous in their ages. Dwight said, 'It'll be fine.'

'No, no! You always say that!'

He thought, *You always* was a dangerous way to start a sentence.

'The lettering is all wrong. It has to be raised. The ribbon is a cheesy look. Don't you see?'

Early days – they were discussing the invitation. She

had revealed herself to be a perfectionist. But perfection is unattainable – the trait made you unhappy. Never mind the invitation. He worried about his own imperfections.

'We have to get it right' was her cry, 'It'll do' was his. Dwight was satisfied with passable, which infuriated her. The church service, the bridesmaids' dresses, the flowers, the reception, the music, the guest list – it all became so contentious that by the time it was over and they were married, and they knew each other's personalities so much better, they were convinced they'd made a mistake.

No, that wasn't true. He could not say at what point the marriage had begun to fail – it was only his cynical liking for ironic symmetry that made him think that it had started to falter as soon as they said, 'I do.' But whatever he might say about it was no more than a fragment. There was too much to tell; you didn't know someone until you were living under the same roof, sharing space in the same room, in the same bed, naked, for a long time. Then you knew, not from anything that was said, but by the way they smelled and breathed and murmured, by rubbing against the other person, and being rubbed.

That was how he had gotten to know Indru, and that first girl Sumitra, and now Padmini. He had not possessed them, he had helped them through a crisis – and a crisis was a daily event in India. Explain this to Shah? Impossible.

They were still walking. Shah had never suggested a walk before, never offered his companionship that way. And what made it even odder was that they were in a district of new nightclubs and bars, they were passing the awnings, the lurid lights at the windows – the music blaring through the curtains at a door, glimpses of people dancing, the smell of incense, the grubby red carpet at the entrance, unrolled like a welcome. Out front the bold young men who worked at these places, seeing two men in business suits, stepped forward.

'Mister – very nice club. Good premises.' And, lunging at Dwight because he was still walking, 'Sir, nice girls. As you wish. Pop music. Drinks. Eatables.'

Though Dwight had slightly slackened his gait, Shah kept walking at the same speed.

'For some people, that is reality,' Shah said.

Another awning, more young men, a pretty girl in a red sari standing just inside the door. Club Durga. An image of the blackish-faced goddess with her necklace of skulls he'd remembered from Sumitra's room, as she danced beneath it.

'Kali,' Shah said. 'Durga, the Inaccessible.'

Dwight said, 'I just remembered that I got an email today from my firm. They're talking about my flying back to chair a seminar on doing business in India.'

'How did you respond?'

'I said, "If I come to the meeting I'll have to stop doing business in India. I'll lose some deals."'

'I can keep the parties cooling their heels,' Shah said. And then, 'This was never here before.'

He meant the lane off the main road, which was brightly lit, thick with clubs, loud music, taxis dropping off well-dressed men. Dwight knew: bar girls, rotten whiskey, pimps. He passed this way often; it was one of his short cuts.

'You know what is the meaning of "phenomenal distinction"?' Shah asked.

'Something like differentiating between the look of things.'

'Not just look. Also sound, odor, flavor, touch,' Shah said. He waved his hand in the direction of the night-clubs. 'Better to leave behind all phenomenal distinctions. Like those.'

Did Shah suspect something? Dwight said, 'But that's the way things are.'

'You mean reality?'

'More or less.'

'No, that is only appearance.'

And Dwight thought: In the idlest conversation in India, wading through platitudes, deep water was never far off. He said, 'You are making the usual big distinction between appearance and reality.'

Shah wagged his head but it didn't mean yes. He started to speak but had to pause, because the music was deafening. When they had passed that noisy doorway, he resumed, saying, 'Both appearance and reality are merely names.'

'That's a quibble,' Dwight said. 'Of course they're names.'

'But reality is many-sided,' Shah said.

Dwight slowed his pace again, and made a face, and said, 'Never heard that one before.'

'Is Jain, also Buddhist concept.' He looked for a reaction on Dwight's face before adding, 'I am eclectic in spiritual matters. My Mahavira was a contemporary of Buddha. Both preached about karma. You know karma.'

'Karma is a kind of luck, eh?'

'Not luck. Karma is deeds. Karma is particles that can build up, by wrong action. Especially passion.'

The mention of passion would have made Dwight suspicious, even defensive, except that Indians were always mentioning it. Meat was a cause of it, and so was alcohol and loose women.

'You're saying karma is matter?'

'Indeed so. It is almost visible. Better not to allow the mind to dwell on worldly thoughts. The world gives false messages – distracts with sounds, odors, flavors. Touching, too, can be harmful, a way of acquiring karmas.'

What was he driving at, and why now? Dwight put it down to this sleazy neighborhood of clubs and bars and obvious lowlife. He said, 'Just – do what then?'

'Develop a clear pure mind by not accepting appearances of things. And observe the three jewels.' He used his fingers, flipping one upright and then the others. 'Right belief. Right knowledge. Right conduct.'

'That's deep,' Dwight said. 'I should tell the partners.'

'It would do them much good.'

'I mean we could include it in that seminar they want to give about doing business in India.'

Shah nodded, but his nod seemed to mean 'maybe'. He said, 'Seminar is a practical matter. I have myself created a packet of materials for helping to understand business practices here.'

'A business manual?'

'Let us say guidelines.'

They were still walking. The Taj was ahead, its distinctive entrance, the palms, the perimeter walls that were meant to keep panhandlers away, the big bearded Sikh in his top-heavy turban, his gold braid and frock coat, saluting a departing guest.

'Ever been to the States?'

'Not yet.'

'You know what I think?' Dwight said. 'You should go to the States, not me. You can run the seminar. They're holding it at a great hotel in Boston. Wonderful food and hospitality. The weather's perfect at this time of year. They'll look after you. And it's money. The people who attend are all potential clients.'

'I cannot,' Shah said, but what made it unconvincing was his smile, the activity behind his eyes: he was reflecting with pleasure on going to the States. Dwight had seen that look on the faces of other Indians: a glow of anticipation at the very mention of America.

'You're perfect. You've got all the papers lined up.'

'Packet of materials,' Shah said.

'The guidelines! This is a big deal for the firm. They see it as a way of attracting clients – easing them into thinking about outsourcing. We're not giving away any secrets, just intending to convince them that we know what we're talking about.'

'The attendees?'

'Yeah. Show them our track record. Sign them up.'

Though he did not say anything just then, Shah had become animated, his face twitching with interest as he'd listened. Dwight could tell when Shah was thinking: his thought process was observable as a subtle throbbing of veins beneath his features.

'How will you manage here?'

'I'll be fine. You've been a great teacher. You've given

me lots of wisdom. "Don't accept the appearances of things." That's great.'

'It is from Diamond Sutra,' Shah said.

The word diamond caught his attention, and he squinted at Shah.

'The idea of fundamental reality is merely name only. Material world is not material. Money is not money. World is not world.'

'Right,' Dwight said uncertainly.

'Words cannot express truth,' Shah said. 'That which words express is not truth.'

'You just lost me.' But he thought, Yes, words were not enough.

Now they were at the driveway of the hotel, well lighted, the tall sturdy Sikh doorman opening the door of an expensive car to allow a little man in a dark suit to step out.

'Come to dinner at my home,' Shah said. 'It will be a humble meal but your presence will do us a great honor.'

5

Instead of going up to the Elephanta Suite, Dwight lingered in the lobby of his hotel, and when he was certain that Shah was on his way home, he signaled for the Sikh to hail him a taxi and he went to Chowpatty – not the lane, but nearby. He didn't want anyone to know the address, not even a taxi driver.

Inside, the stairwell reeked of urine and garbage. A rat on the stairs was not startled by his stamping but only crouched and became compact, twitching its whiskers in a way that reminded Dwight of Shah's active thinking. It was a familiar rat – you got to recognize them, Dwight thought; the stinks, too. Or was it all false? Appearances were meaningless, phenomenal distinctions were misleading, and this great smelly cloud of shit was just an illusion.

Indru's outer door was made of rusted iron grating like the slammer on a prison cell, for security and for the air, though the air was sour even here on the third-floor landing.

She had heard him. She approached the door holding a circular brass tray with a flame burning in a dish of oil. And while Padmini unlocked the steel door and swung it open and made a *namaste* with her clasped hands, Indru passed the flame under Dwight's chin and applied a dot of paste to his forehead.

'You are welcome,' she said.

He kicked off his shoes and followed her to the second room. It was open to the alley, the TV sets of the neighbors, the smell of spices and boiled vegetables, the whine of traffic, horns beeping, distant music that always seemed to evoke for Dwight an atmosphere of strangulation.

'Don't put the light on,' he said. 'Just keep that candle.'

'Oil lamp,' Indru said, 'is how we make pure the air. Shall I wash feet?'

'That would be very nice.'

Somehow Padmini had heard. She brought a basin of warm water and a cloth, and set it down before him. Still watching, she backed away as Indru began gently to massage his bare feet in the water.

'Have you eat?'

But he didn't hear. He was watching her head, her hair, her swinging braid that slipped against his legs like a long tassel as she knelt before him. She was so intent on her task, canted forward, narrow shoulders working, that he could look down to the small of her back, her white dress tightened against her buttocks.

'That's fine.'

'Not quite finish.'

'Stop,' he said. His throat constricted, his face went hot. 'Close the door, please.'

The way she got to her feet in pretty little stages, first lifting her head to face him, tossing her braid aside, then raising herself by digging her fingers into his knees for balance, almost undid him. Then she was peeling off his shirt as he approached the charpoy. He watched her shimmy out of her dress, using her shoulders; when her dress simply dropped to her ankles she stepped out of it, kicking the door closed with one foot.

'I know what you want,' she said as he took her head, cupping her ears, and moving it like a melon on his lap.

He lay there in the half dark, the string of the oil lamp flickering in its dish on the floor by the wash-basin; and he thought of how different his life was now. And what about Indru? She seemed happy. He had come home to her, she had been waiting for him. She was grateful, he could sense it from the warmth of her mouth, her eager lips.

He had done her more than a good turn; he had rescued her – rescued Padmini too, and if that young man did not happen to be her brother but another lover he was helping that fellow as well. But who in the other world would understand? It was impossible to explain. *That which words express is not truth* – right! He would be seen as a sensualist, an exploiter, another opportunist in India. No, he was a benefactor.

In his rapture, with Indru's palms flattened against his thighs, his sighing with pleasure, he was sentimental and told himself that there was no other place he wished to be.

Warmed by this thought, luxuriating in where he lay, he raised his eyes and saw past Indru's head and her braid coiled on the dampness of her bare back to the door of the room, the shadow of Padmini in profile against the vertical bar of light where the door was ajar. One bright eye shone in the light of the oil lamp. He said nothing – could she see his face? – and it was a long time before the door silently shut, squeezing the light, and by then Indru was too frenzied to notice.

Afterwards, he drew her into his arms and thought, Yes, their benefactor.

'That is my father,' Shah was saying, holding a framed photograph.

The old man in the silver frame was bearded, very thin, gripping a walking stick, carrying a cloth bundle.

'All his worldly possessions.'

The ascetic and rather starved face contrasted sharply with the elegant frame, the polished side table on which it rested with other silver-framed pictures, more of the old man, and the cut-glass lamp, the linen tablecloth, the candlesticks.

And Dwight sat at a table that had been set with delicate porcelain plates thin as eggshells, linen napkins, gold-trimmed salvers, crystal goblets. But there were yellow lentils in the plates, beans in the salvers and water in the goblets.

'Please take some more dhal,' Mrs Shah said. 'It's a family recipe. Dhal tarka – very creamy, you see.'

She was a lovely woman, younger than her husband, with a smooth serious face and a slightly strained manner, a kind of concern, that Dwight understood as the effort of being hospitable to a big American stranger who had a reputation for bluntness. Shah must have warned her, but Shah was much more confident these days.

'And this,' she said, serving him with silver pincers what looked like a flattened muffin, 'this is my mother's uttapam.'

'Delicious,' Dwight said. 'I'm not eating meat ever again.'

'Thank you,' Mrs Shah said. She rang a bell and a young woman entered with a bowl of rice. As the woman stood next to Dwight, serving him, he had one thought in his mind. These days when he met a woman in India, he thought, Would I? To this one, he nodded and smiled, thinking, Yes, I would.

'My father was a businessman,' Shah said, glancing at the framed photograph as he spoke. 'He started as an accountant, then created a firm and eventually had a huge business – bought his building, branched out into real estate and investment. He did very well. My brother and I had a privileged upbringing. But as he got older he prepared himself, and at last he embarked on his journey.'

'Where did he go?'

'Not where, but how, is the question. He walked, he slept on the ground. He begged for alms, holding bowl. He wished to become a saint. It was his aim.'

'Renounced everything?'

'Completely,' Shah said. 'Not so, my dear?'

Mrs Shah tipped her head in regret.

'Obeying the mahavratas,' Shah said. 'The big vows. No injury. No lying. No stealing. Chastity. Lacking all possessions. Meditation and praying only. And walking to the shrines, day and night, begging for food.'

Now Dwight looked at the picture of the wealthy investor, who out of piety had reinvented himself as a beggar. Dwight said, 'It's quite a trajectory.'

'Jain trajectory – Buddhist, too,' Shah said. 'My brother and I looked after my mother. And my turn will come.' He suddenly became self-conscious, and smiled at his wife. 'Then my son will look after my wife. It is our way.'

'In this other picture he's wearing a mask,' Dwight said.

'So as not to breathe in microbes and fleas.'

'So as not to get sick?'

'So as not to kill them. *Ahimsa*. Not killing a life, even flea's life.'

'I get you.'

'I will share with you some literature about our beliefs,' Shah said. 'We are not extreme – not like the Digambara, who are sky-clad.'

'Sky-clad, meaning . . . ?'

'Nakedness. They go about mortifying themselves in the nakedness state. No one on earth could live more simply. But we are Svetambara. We follow the tenets of our faith. It is ancient, I tell you – older than your Christianity, from long before.'

'Maybe you can tell me about it sometime.'

'We have sweetened curd for dessert,' Mrs Shah said, ringing the servant bell again.

'I anticipate being a saddhu myself – giving up the world. Just wandering, as my father wandered. He was so contented.'

'I guess that's an Indian solution to life.'

'No. It was penance. He was not pure previously. I am not pure.' He smiled at Dwight, who read in Shah's smile, *And you?*

Dwight saw himself with a wooden staff and a loincloth and a turban, striding down a dusty road in the sunlight in sandals, eating an apple – did they eat apples? Birds sang, a fragrant breeze cooled his face, he carried a bowl full of flower petals. He smiled, mocking himself with this image, knowing that he would be visiting Indru later.

Shah's apartment was luxurious, with gilt-framed mirrors and brocade cushions on a white sofa that could have held five people, a thick carpet – he'd left his shoes at the door – windows like walls with panes of glass that went from floor to ceiling, and a balcony that gave onto Bombay, from this height a magical-looking city of twinkling lights and toy cars.

The food could not have been simpler, yet it had been served in the thinnest porcelain; even the bell that Mrs Shah rang to summon the serving girl looked precious. The colored portraits on the walls could have been deities, objects of veneration, as well as a valuable collection of paintings.

All this time, Shah was talking about Jainism, atonement, penance, poverty. '*Nirjara* – process of atonement,' he said. '*Ahimsa* – respect for all living things, great and small, all *jiva*, all life and soul.'

The mention of living things, great and small, made Dwight think of his partners in Boston. He said, 'Have you given any thought to my proposal? I've cleared it with the firm. They're pretty excited.'

'I have reflected deeply on it,' Shah said. He kept a studied tone of reluctance in his voice that Dwight recognized as an eagerness he didn't want to show. 'I will accept. I will do my level best.'

To match Shah's tone, Dwight was subdued and quietly thanked him; but inside he was rejoicing. He wouldn't have to make the long trip back to Boston – Shah was perfect for the business seminar.

Leaving Shah's apartment, plunging back into the city, he was reminded how it had been the second time he'd been inside the house of a wealthy Indian. Like the big soft apartment of Winky Vellore, it was a refuge. All of India had been shut out, more than from the fastness of the Elephanta Suite. At Shah's, India almost did not exist, except in the paintings and the photographs of Shah's father, the wandering holy man, and the talk of atonement. The apartment had shone with polished silver and white porcelain, and crisp linen on the gleaming table.

Now Dwight recalled that music had been playing softly, the sounds of string instruments, the soft chanting, the odd and irregular harmonies. And the big glass doors had been shut, so that Bombay was its lights and shadows, and it had sparkled, silent and odorless, far below. What floor had they been on? It seemed that they'd hovered at a great height in the splendor of a glass tower. And he knew he would always remember the experience for its comfort, the softness of Mrs Shah, the beauty of the serving girl, the glint of the silver in the candlelight. Bombay had looked like a city of crystal.

Now he was at Indru's, in the stew of stinks and harsh voices from the lane, in the cement stairwell – his secret, his hiding place. Approaching the building he'd heard a groan and looked aside and saw a cow, visible because of its pale hide, sounding human and helpless in its distress.

He kicked the stairs as he climbed, to scatter the rats, and when he got to Indru's landing he tapped a coin on the iron bars of the outer door.

Padmini scuffed forward, unlocked the door, held the round brass tray with the oil lamp flickering in its dish. On tiptoes the small thin girl stretched to apply the mark with her thumb.

'Never mind that.'

She stared, her eyes shining in the firelight. On the days she worked at the salon her hair was lovely, her make-up like a mask, her nails thickly varnished.

'Where's Indru?'

Padmini hesitated, then said, 'Brother come.'

Dwight shut the door. He lifted the tray from Padmini's hands. In the sounds of the traffic, the yakking voices of television sets, car doors slamming, the loud blatting of motorbikes, he heard the moaning of the cow suffering in the alley.

He waved his hand at the dark insects and white moths strafing the naked bulb above his head, he shot the bolt in the door, and when he turned Padmini was gone.

'Where are you?'

From deep in the far room, 'Here, sir.'

She was squatting cross-legged in the back room on the mattress that was spread on the floor, where she slept – not even a string bed, but what did that matter? The only light was the light from the street filtered through a high dirty window.

Padmini was indistinct. He tried to read her expression, to see her posture. He thought, Reality is many-sided.

'Is bolt in door?'

'Yes.'

A quality of air, no more than a ripple, told him she

had relaxed, hearing that. But when he held her she was stiffened, like someone about to take a leap. She wouldn't let him kiss her, though she allowed him to touch her. She seemed to grow limp as he did so, murmuring in her throat, and still the cow moaned in the alley.

6

In Shah's absence, Dwight kept himself scarce. He spent less time in the boardroom, and when he was there he avoided looking down the long table for a view of the Gateway of India. Huge though it was, even when he did accidentally glance in that direction, he hardly saw it. The three-portalled archway did not loom for him anymore. Too much had happened to him for the thing to seem important in his life. It was just another monument in a country that was cluttered with monuments.

Unwelcome visitors were another reason for him keeping away. Incredibly, he was regarded as the expert on India now.

'I'd like to pick your brain,' people said in phone calls. That meant his dispensing free advice over a hotel lunch to another nervous American on his first visit to India.

And the odd thing was when Dwight spoke to these newcomers he said unexpected things, surprising himself in his opinions.

A man named Todd Pinsker visited. He was a Hollywood lawyer – he'd done a contract with Ralph Picard from the Boston office; he was passing through Bombay on his way to Rajasthan for a luxury vacation. As a favor to Ralph, Dwight saw him for a drink at the Taj.

'And this is my son, Zack,' Pinsker said. 'He's making a movie.'

The boy's smug expression matched his clumsiness. He wore a baseball cap on backwards, he sat with his legs sticking out, he demanded that the waiter remove the ice from his drink.

'Ice can make you sick,' he said. 'I mean, you can get a bad ice cube.'

'He's got this dynamite idea,' the boy's father said. 'Sort of meld the Bollywood idea with an American movie. I mean, get some major talent from the States and shoot it here.'

'I have no contacts at all in the movie industry,' Dwight said. 'I'm contracting for US companies who want to outsource here.'

'That's Zack's project,' the man said. 'I want to set up a concept restaurant in Manhattan. I've got some backing in LA. I'm looking for ideas here, for a theme. Maybe head-hunt a chef.'

'Wish I could help you. I don't even eat in restaurants anymore,' Dwight said. He wondered, Is this true? And he surprised himself again by saying, 'I mean, I'm a committed vegetarian.'

'That's cool,' the man said, but his squint gave away his caution.

'Following kind of a Jain thing,' Dwight said.

That got Zack's attention, 'A Jain thing? Those people that don't kill bugs?'

'*Ahimsa*,' Dwight said, in almost a whisper, because the boy's voice was so loud. 'It's part of the philosophy – non-killing.'

'Vegetarian options would play a big part in this

restaurant,' the man said. 'I've just got to meet some people. Have you been to Rajvilas?'

'No. I've hardly been out of Bombay.'

'Clinton stayed there,' the boy said, and sucked on his glass of Coke.

Dwight became impatient; this father and son were annoying him with their presumption. They were both trying to get rich here, do some business, use the Indians, as everyone else did.

'You won't have a problem finding what you want here,' he said. 'Whatever it is. Everyone gets what they want. But at the same time you're going to find something you didn't bargain for.'

'Is that some kind of warning?'

'I suppose it is,' Dwight said. He thought: Where is this coming from? Why am I saying this? But without any effort, and hardly knowing what was coming next, he said, 'But it's a fact. India's cheap, so it attracts amateurs and second-raters and opportunists. Backpackers, little-leaguers. Because India's desperate, Indians do most of the work for you.'

'Isn't that a good thing?'

'Depends,' Dwight said. 'Indians never lose. No matter how well you think you're doing, they're doing better. You're glad because you can get a pair of blue jeans for a buck twenty-nine. But eighty cents of that is profit for them.'

'I'm trying to put a restaurant together. Zack's doing a movie.'

'You'll get it done. And you'll get something else you never expected. The Indian extra. The Indian surprise.'

He knew he was being enigmatic, he was not even

sure what he was saying. Certainly he was warning them, but he didn't like them enough to explain the warning in detail. What alarmed him was, having given no thought to these opinions before, they seemed to be bubbling up from his unconscious. *Maybe I am warning myself?*

After an hour, he said he had an appointment. They swapped business cards – even the punk kid Zack had one. And then Dwight took a taxi to Indru's. Probably that was what he meant when he mentioned the Indian surprise.

It was true that Indians did most of the work. And there were plenty of manufacturers eager to service clients – too many of them, perhaps, and they were ruthless with each other. They were persistent with him and tended to call his cellphone at all hours, offering to cut deals. It was no good his saying, 'You can't do an end run on the tendering process' – they didn't understand the metaphor and anyway backstabbing was a standard business practice, even part of the culture, with real backs and real knives.

But Dwight had always found someone suitable to make the product – not movies or concept restaurants, time-wasting negotiations that brought together those natural allies, the dreamer and the bull-shitter. He preferred deals for making plastic buckets, rubber gaskets, leisurewear, nylon plumbing fixtures, sports shoes, electronic components. The insulated wire that was a crucial part of a spark plug for a car engine – no one wanted to make it in the States anymore, but Shah had found a man in Hyderabad, a former rope-maker, who had retooled his shop to make these wires for a few dollars a spool. That kind of thing. The hard part was the contract, the final wording, the up-front payments, the penalty clauses – and for that he needed Shah's scrupulous shit-detecting Jain eye.

Still following up some contacts here, Shah emailed, and it sounded like procrastination.

Fine. Dwight handed the competing Indians to his secretary, Miss Chakravarti. Indians understood delegating. 'I can do it, sir,' they'd say, and give the job to someone else, a menial; and that menial would delegate it to someone lower. And Dwight had more time, because he found that an email or a letter, if left unanswered, became stale and less important as time passed; and then diminished to something so thin and tentative it was easy for him to delete it. Filing it or keeping it fresh made it into an artificial demand.

Time was the test of any demand. He had never in his life felt the passage of time so palpably as he had in India. And he had concluded that, really, nothing was urgent – nothing at all. Maybe nothing mattered.

Now and then he forwarded a message to Shah, still in Boston. *You have given me a wonderful opportunity*, Shah emailed; and he stayed on.

On most days, but especially on the weekends, Indians walked along Chowpatty Beach, a great expanse of tainted shoreline – dirty sand, sodden litter, scummy water, beached plastic – where it was always low tide. These days, with more time on his hands, Dwight walked along the beach with Indru, and sometimes Padmini. He saw no other foreigners doing this, and thought: Maybe I'm not a foreigner anymore.

They walked, he bought them ice cream, they sat on the benches, they used the promenade, they gazed at the Malabar Hill beyond the bay, the mansions, the villas. They looked at the sea, which seemed idyllic, but Dwight knew – and so did the unbuoyant, non-swimming Indians – that it was polluted and that if you looked closely you'd see that the seawater had the yellow-gray color and deadly fizz of battery acid.

Strolling made Indru talkative. 'My mother treat me so harsh,' she said. 'My father touch me. Shame for him.'

She was provoked to tell her stories whenever there was a lull in the conversation. Usually she spoke without emotion, lapping an ice cream, as she was doing now.

'My granny lock me in the dark room.'

'So you said.'

'After he make me naked, father say, "Go away, you bad girl."'

'I remember. You went to the police. They didn't believe you.'

'Police not believe me at all. "You are talking blue lies." They take me to the *sarpanch*. He touch my privates. Oh, my god.'

She spoke without anger, rotating the ice cream on its cone, licking her fingers when it dripped.

'And the boys in the village were cruel,' Dwight said.

'They throw things at me. They throw *kanda*. The cow-dung women make for the fires, they throw at me.'

The same stories, in their way tragic perhaps, but hearing them so often irritated him. He had been moved the first time. Then he learned them by heart. He could recite them verbatim, and what was more annoying than that? They became parodies. Apart from the stories of cruelty and abuse, which he only half-believed (she told them a new way each time and sometimes improved on them, with variations and discrepancies and gaps), Indru had no other conversation.

Obviously, she had remembered how, the first time, he had listened; how she had captured his attention, silenced him, with her stories, a Scheherazade of sadism.

They were an important justification for him – for seeing her, being kind to her, sleeping with her – the poor kid, how she'd suffered. He needed the stories. They gave him the right to sleep with her and to be her benefactor.

She needed them, too, for without the stories she was just a wayward girl in Bombay, filling in at a hair-and-nail salon and lazily looking for someone to pay her way.

'My uncle, so cruel. He touch me and threaten me.'

'He had a motorcycle. He gave you a ride. He took you to a riverbank and raped you.'

'His friend also did things to me.'

That was a new twist. Dwight said, 'Give it a rest, Indru.'

The trouble was that, bored by the stories – he had been outraged before – his own behavior seemed crass. She was not a victim he was helping but rather an opportunist overdramatizing her past.

He doubted the stories, not just because she told

them without feeling; she seemed to repeat them because of his reaction to them. She believed they were the key to his sympathy, and they had been, but not on the twentieth retelling.

'What about you, Padmini? Any family problems?'

'No problem. I happy.'

'They beat Padmini at nail salon,' Indru said with indignation, as though looking to create drama.

'I spill nail varnish on customer sari,' Padmini said. And she began to laugh. 'She so angry!'

'Did they really beat you?' Dwight asked.

'Oh, yes, but customer refuse to pay. She get out of chair and say "Goodbye" and hurry out to street and rickshaw-wallah hit her – whoof! – and she plop down. Ha!'

The memory of the angry customer being struck by a rickshaw was stronger than the memory of being beaten.

Padmini didn't look for sympathy, which was probably why he liked her, and why, when Indru's brother showed up and took her out, Dwight didn't mind: he had Padmini, who was younger and prettier and in her way shrewder. Because she didn't ask for anything, he gave her money and presents; he was less inclined to give Indru presents, since she asked for them constantly these days.

Indru believed that her horror stories helped, but all they did was diminish her, turn her into a figure of melodrama, make her impossible to love and hard to like. Yes, he could pity her but there were a billion others worthy of pity.

Both were living off him. Indru had stopped

working. And Padmini worked less often. And when Indru asked Dwight for money or a present, he suspected that she was asking on behalf of her brother. Even Padmini admitted that she sent some of Dwight's money home to her parents in the village.

That made him think. Behind Indru and Padmini, radiating outward from the two-roomed apartment, were more people living off them, each girl with a family, each family a village, each village a hierarchy, like the *sarpanch* whom Indru had mentioned, a great assortment of hungry people with their hands out. He was supporting them all, yet he could not call himself a benefactor.

Indian money was peculiarly filthy, the frayed little ten-rupee notes, the tattered hundreds, a stack of bills looked like a pile of dirty rags. The money smelled of all the people who had fingered it and used it. The thought of this killed his desire, and he began to see Indru and Padmini as two lazy girls, older and shrewder than they looked. He saw himself as even lazier, or worse – credulous and weak. As he saw their cynicism he liked himself less. He feared that one day he would come to despise them.

Meanwhile, so he said, Shah was at Disneyworld in Orlando. He was visiting New York City, where he had a cousin. He'd found clients all over New England. He'd been invited to Harvard Business School, to speak informally to a seminar. Kohut had given a dinner party for him in Sudbury. *Autumn leaves*, Shah had reported, *magnificent colors*. And, *I trust all is well, Mumbai side*.

Was it? These walks along Chowpatty Beach, because they were interludes, because they required conversation, were revealing, and proved to Dwight that he was kidding himself. He was a man who had discovered sex in India and thought it was magic; but it was an illusion, the consequence of his having power and money in a land of desperation. Sex was a good thing, because sex had an end, and when his desire died he saw he'd been a fool. But now, with more power and less conviction, his passion diminished to casual playing, he took more risks.

Seeing a boy with a CD player and headphones, Indru said, 'Buy me one of those.'

'What will you do with it?'

'Listen music.'

'Maybe,' he said, to tease her, and saw she was agitated with greed. He said to Padmini, 'Do you want one, too?'

Her whisper was so soft, he could scarcely hear it, yet he knew her vibrant lips were saying yes.

'But what will you give me?'

He was ashamed, he had no right to feel powerful when he said this, making the request like a greedy king addressing his subjects, asking, *How do you intend to please me?*

They were at the beach, another of their Sunday strolls, watched by groups of chattering boys who were attracted by the pretty girls, curious about the tall white man in the Indian shirt and kadi vest of home-spun, which Dwight had begun to wear since Shah's departure for the States.

Padmini glanced at Indru, who was smirking and looking coy, as though challenging Padmini to give the right answer.

'Sir, we will be good to you,' Padmini said.

Indru laughed and skipped ahead. Her laugh got the attention of an old woman who was walking in the opposite direction. Dwight looked up at Indru and saw the woman. He wouldn't have noticed her at all, except that she hesitated and stared at him.

She had not changed – she was fat and slow, wearing a billowing sari banded with gold embroidery, gold bangles on her wrists, browny-gray hair, with a shawl thrown over it.

For a moment Dwight wondered how she'd singled him out – but of course, he was the only white man on the beach. He was glad that Indru and Padmini had gone ahead. The old woman's unfriendly smile was like mockery.

'Hello,' he said.

Instead of replying, the woman called out sharply. Among the crowd of strollers on the beach, three figures hurried over – the children, the little girl, the young boy, the tall skinny dancer in her gypsy dress. He only recognized them because the old woman was there. The boy was taller but thinner, with a resentful face; the little girl wore a new dress but seemed sickly, hollow-eyed, with lipstick and eyeshadow, a parody of a whore. Sumitra, the dancer, looked at him with hatred. She was bony and her hair full and frizzed, with dry patches on her strangely hairy arms and lines in her face, as though she'd become old. In the way they stared they seemed brutalized and rude.

The old woman gabbled in Hindi. Dwight knew she must have been saying, 'It is the man. You remember him from the Gateway of India.'

Were they speculating on whether they could con him again – somehow entice him?

'Nice to see you,' Dwight said.

But as he made a move to go they crowded him and blocked his way.

With a yelp, a passing boy called out to his friends – and Dwight thought how suddenly stupid the boy became in his eagerness. The other boys hurried over, attracted by the odd public scene: the yakking old woman, the scruffy gypsy-looking children, the white man – the towering, isolated white man. In just seconds, there were more spectators, all boys, laughing, perhaps suspecting trouble – that slack-jawed look of anticipation was also moronic. Dwight had seen this before in India, how subtle and crafty Indians could be individually, how ignorant and obvious in a large crowd.

At that moment, in what seemed to him a standoff, Dwight heard a screech.

'Yaaagh!' Another animal noise – Indru's shriek, and followed by Padmini she broke through the cluster of people.

Indru snatched at Dwight's hand, and a jeering cry went up from the boys. But Indru screamed at them, something that had to be worse than 'go away', because they howled back at her.

Glancing around to make his escape, Dwight saw the old woman smile. It was a sour smile of contempt. Even she recognized what he was now, and she began to mutter defiantly. What was she saying? Something wicked about him to these foolish boys.

Dwight stepped back, while Indru continued to yell

at the boys. She wasn't like a girl anymore, she was a howling woman with big reddish teeth in her wide-open mouth.

Now the old woman, who seemed fearless and slightly superior, was saying something sly to Indru – vile words, they had to be, because Indru spat at her, a gob of reddish saliva that darkened in a streak on the old woman's sari. The boys laughed, and punched the air in delight.

'Come on,' Dwight said, and pulled Indru away, as the old woman craned her neck and screamed.

Indru said, 'That auntie say she know you. You give her money. You bad man.'

When they had crossed the expanse of Chowpatty sand and were back on the sidewalk, Dwight said, 'I am a bad man!'

He was disgusted with himself. He deserved this humiliating scene at the public beach on a busy Sunday, with the horrible boys watching, the cow shit, the yellow froth at the sea's edge, the poisonous water, the spectacle of a predatory American confronted by the victims he had paid off.

I am a bad man had shocked Indru into silence. She merely followed him to the apartment block, and when they got there, Dwight shook his head. He saw that Padmini was just catching up with them, still looking flustered from the business at the beach.

'No,' he said.

'Yes,' Padmini said. She took his big hand in her small one.

That gave him some strength. He climbed the stairs slowly, feeling weak.

In the room, while Indru watched, Padmini said, 'We be good to you.'

The words made him sad, but she had turned away and dropped her sari, and now her little brown made-up face made him sad, her skinny neck, the fuzz of hair on her lower back, the tight globes of her buttocks.

Indru had taken most of her clothes off. She lay on the charpoy, wearing a sarong, her heavy breasts hanging, one to the left, one to the right. There was something lewd in the asymmetry, and the way she lolled, half propped up, watching Padmini bend to pick up her sari and fold it.

Dwight tried to laugh, but he was numb all over. The thought that saved him was: I created this. I brought these people here. I gave them my wedding ring, to rent the place – it's all mine. And so I can do whatever I want.

They were staring at him. He said, 'What's my name?'

Padmini began to giggle. Indru said, 'I am know.'

'Tell me.'

'Mister,' she said, but she could not go any further, she was murmuring, *ferringi*.

'I'm Dwight Huntsinger.'

Hearing this, they both laughed, for the name was impossible to say. They champed at a few syllables, and laughed some more.

Padmini stood naked before him and said, 'What you want?'

Just as he was thinking the same thing, a clumsy matching moment that helped him see clearly.

He said, 'I want to go.'

They were still calling to him as he descended the

stairs. A door opened on a landing below, and a chubby-faced woman looked out and seemed to pair the girls' appeals to his fleeing – more humiliation.

On his way back to the hotel he almost succeeded in losing himself in the crowd, yet he felt that his face was vivid with shame, a pink and sweaty, guilty-looking *ferringi* face, debauched; different from everyone else.

His shame was strongest on that walk when a woman approached him to beg from him, as though testing his willpower. India was weird that way, a culture of confrontation. Here he was, a few minutes' walk from one humiliation, and a woman was stopping him to challenge him with another. *Give me money.* He was so fearful he could not bring himself to give her a rupee. She hissed at him and his agony was complete.

That night he went to the hotel's business center, as he did most nights, to check his email. Usually he forwarded the messages to Miss Chakravarti. Rarely was there a message on a business matter from Shah, though everyone in the firm praised him. *He's developed some contacts at Harvard Business School* and *He found some great people in Boston who want to create a hi-tech facility in Mysore* and *The partners like him. He might be the key to setting up a branch office in Bombay.*

But tonight, the message from Kohut was, *Shah is talking about bringing his wife to the States.*

Dwight began typing, *Urgent. Please . . .*

Before he finished the message, he looked at the clock. It was morning in Boston. He deleted the message and found Kohut's number on the speed dial of his BlackBerry.

'Huntsinger!'

'Ernie, listen to me. I need Shah back here.'

'Why are you pleading? You're our guy in India. Anyway, Shah was planning a trip there. He's got some great business lined up.' Perhaps aware of the huge distance, Kohut was shouting in the phone. 'So, hey, Dwight, how's it hanging?'

7

In the days before Shah returned, Dwight stayed at his hotel, either using the business center or else sitting on the veranda of the Elephanta Suite, which was enclosed, a high wall protecting him from the road. He was slowed by a kind of fear. He could not bring himself to go out. The risks were too great – strangers would approach him, obstructing him, as they always did in India, and they would challenge him, ask for money or food, or ask that he give them a job. A young boy had tapped Dwight's Rolex watch and demanded to know why it should not be given to him.

Once, he regarded dealing with people like this at close quarters as his strength, staring them down, like a chief or a king, or acceding to the request, with the power to change a person's life. Not just Indru and the others. Those experiences had made him bold – he was known on the street as a soft touch. Now he had come to see himself as a victim, but a corrupt one.

He called Maureen – dialed the number impulsively, not quite sure why, until she answered in a small, beaten voice. 'Yes?'

'I'm so sorry,' he said, feeling tearful.

'Who is this?'

'Dwight,' he said. 'It was all my fault, the break-up. I could have tried harder. We could have worked out our issues. But my damned pride prevented me. Can you ever forgive me?'

She came awake, she said, 'It's two o'clock in the morning, for God's sake!'

'I'm sorry.'

'Dwight, don't talk to me about issues. We have no issues. Your coupons have run out.'

'Honey?'

'Don't ever do this again.'

He was left holding a buzzing phone. He deserved it, for having been so reckless in India. From where he sat on the veranda, he could see other Americans doing the same – lawyers, lobbyists, facilitators, dealers, wholesalers, all of them being wooed by Indians. They were traveling down the same road, under the promising billboard, *You Can Make Anything in India*. It was the crux of the whole effort, the test of a person's character. You had to be strong to survive it. But most of the people he saw had failed.

The middle-aged American with the pretty and pliant Indian girlfriend, the American woman with her saluting driver, the American lawyer with his submissive hacks, the young American traveler being helped by the groveling concierge, the Pinskers – the father starting a gourmet Indian restaurant in New York, the son trying to set up a movie, hustling in Bombay and vacationing in Jaipur – everyone had a scheme to hook up the Indians and make money and behave badly.

With rising anger, Dwight saw an American brat – nine or ten years old, long hair, hat on backwards – in the hotel dining room. The boy sulked as he was being asked by a waiter in a turban and a frock coat and a crimson sash, 'What do you desire for your meal, sir?'

The white-gloved waiter bent low and abased himself to the child, while the parents studied their menus.

'May I suggest the soup?'

'I hate soup.' The child made himself ugly and turned away.

'Perhaps tasty grilled cheese sandwich?'

'I don't like that either.'

'Maybe young sir would prefer breaded cutlet?'

'What's that supposed to be?'

'Meat, sir.'

'I want spaghetti, but no red stuff on it, and no cheese.'

'I will request kitchen to make, sir,' the waiter said, bowing, clicking his pen, while the brat's father and mother still frowned at their menus.

Dwight wanted to slap the snarly child, then slap the parents; then tell the waiter to stop groveling; and then he wanted to slap himself. But it was too late. They were all lost. No hope for them, not much for him.

How had he been corrupted so quickly? It wasn't as though the Indians were sensualists. They were forthright, they asked for what they wanted. He'd had the best of intentions, but he had been weak. The girls had not been beautiful, either, only young and hungry. Hunger was a terrible thing, that turned you into both predator and prey. Winky Vellore was no beauty; she was greedy. Padmini had connived with Indru. It was all like the sort of deal he had been negotiating for months with Shah and the wholesalers. *Sir, we will be good to you.*

It wasn't food they wanted. They craved dresses and shoes and electronics, an iPod, a better TV set. They were not starving; they were greedy for gold. He couldn't blame them. He blamed himself. He needed Shah to return, to protect him, somehow rescue him. The man was saintly, he didn't swat flies, he didn't eat eggs, he wouldn't drink water at night for fear of guzzling an insect that might be floating on the surface.

At last, Dwight got the email from Shah with his arrival time. Dwight did not go to the airport to meet him – Mrs Shah would do that – but he checked that the plane was on time and he waited the next morning for Shah to call. Without quite knowing how, Dwight trusted Shah to release him from his misery.

He was convinced of it the morning after Shah's arrival, when he met him for breakfast. It wasn't his manner – in fact he seemed somewhat changed: he was more urbane in a self-conscious way, wearing what looked like a Brooks Brothers suit and a Harvard tie and a matching hanky stuffed into his breast pocket. But he was a reassuring presence, and his choice of food was proof of his unchanged goodness, the simplest items on the menu – dhal, some rice cakes, a plate of warm flaky pooris, some Indian cheese.

'This is paneer. Please don't make a face, but cow dung is used in preparation.'

'Gives it a distinctive taste,' Dwight said.

'Exactly.'

'I'm so glad to see you back here.'

'Thank you, my friend.'

'Fruit, sir?' the waiter asked. He was holding a basket of oranges and bananas and apples.

Shah said, 'An apple only, but you must assure me

that it was not picked. That it fell from tree and was garnered.'

'Apple fell to earth, sir.'

'I will take, then,' Shah said. 'Please, Mr Hund. Take yourself.'

Dwight selected an apple. He said, 'It wasn't picked. It fell. I like that.'

Though he was scrupulous in what he ate, Shah's method of eating was noisy. He chawed the apple, biting hard and loudly; he chewed with his mouth open, flecks of fruit on his lips, a smear of juice on his cheek. He talked with his mouth full, heedlessly spraying masticated apple flesh, and doing this while boasting made it all seem ruder.

'In America they could not believe what I was saying. They offered me apples and whatnot. I said, "Only if they have fallen. Not if they have been picked by human hand." They were so surprised! And then I had to tell them, "I do not take water at night. Insects may be adhering to surface." The blighters were shocked, I tell you.'

This detail, which Dwight had admired in Shah, seemed pointless now that he was booming about it. He was changed – not the certain yet modest Shah but an overconfident man who took pleasure in these triumphant stories, like Indru's tales of rape. In America he'd had a fatal revelation: he had been persuaded that he was interesting.

'I told them, "No potatoes. One might inadvertently eat the living things, such as fungi and microbial substances." They thought I was joking. I said to them, "Not at all, my friends!"'

He was a bit too happy about this, and the other giveaway was his repeating himself. He must have told the stories fifty times, not remembering that he'd already told them to Dwight.

Dwight remarked on the new pinstriped suit.

'Brooks Brothers,' Shah said. 'Flagship store. It's a good cut, I think. I like the drape.'

'Probably made in India,' Dwight said.

'Oh, no,' Shah said, protesting as he tugged on his lapel, reacting a bit too sharply to what Dwight had intended as a joke. 'Italian made. Very good weave.'

When he took out his new cellphone he said that he'd bought it on a trip to New York, that it took photographs and could store five hundred of them in its memory. He located one and displayed it for Dwight: Shah smiling beside a tweedy man with beetling brows and horn-rimmed glasses.

'John Chapman Thaw. Harvard man. He presented me with this tie, as a matter of fact.' He held the phone in his hand to admire it. 'A very humble man.'

'New watch?'

'Oh, yes. From duty-free in London. So many functions.' He pinched the face of it. 'I have two time zones here. It's seven at the office. Mr Kohut will be calling Mrs Kohut and saying, "I'll be late, my dear." What a delightful chap. Very faithful to his missus.'

Dwight smiled at him. The old Shah had been – not Americanized, but enlarged, made self-aware. He had been appreciated, someone had listened to him, he'd been praised. He seemed a new man. He wasn't sinuous and oblique anymore, and unexpectedly Dwight found this new assurance irritating. Dwight reminded himself that Shah had been in the States for almost two months.

'I hear you went on a course at Harvard Business School,' Dwight said.

'Your fellow Elfman fixed it for me. Very decent chap,' Shah said. 'I met so many Indians in Cambridge. It was like a little India. I invited the prof. He will be visiting.'

'Indian?'

Shah opened his camera phone again. He said, 'No, Chappie. John Chapman Thaw. Harvard man. You must know him?'

'I went to BU.'

'Very famous. Very accomplished. Very moral chap. Truthful in all things.' Gazing again at the man's picture, Shah hadn't registered Dwight's remark. 'Family money. Excellent set of contacts.'

That was another thing – the new friends. In Bombay, Shah had seemed to circulate in a small circle of businessmen, most of whom Dwight knew. But while enlarging his personality, his experience in America, where modesty was usually a fault and never a virtue, had widened his network of friends. He was impressed by the people he had met. He wasn't cynical, yet he always made a point of saying how impressed they'd been to meet him, an insect-preserving Jain, an abstemious man who lived by strict rules. But Elfman? God, he'd finally found someone to share his fatuous passion for Harvard.

'They said to me, "Shah, you don't deviate." And I said' – he sat back on the banquette of the hotel restaurant – '"I am ruthlessly consistent."'

Dwight smiled at the way Shah had praised the

Americans he'd met: *very moral, very decent, very faithful, very humble, truthful in all things.* Did he know something? But he was glad Shah was back. And when, later that day, they got down to business, working through the list of new appointments that Miss Chakravarty had prepared, Dwight placed his hand on Shah's forearm and gripped it in gratitude, feeling the energy: he was the man to emulate – his work ethic, his sense of appreciation, his moral code.

Over the next few days, they kept the appointments; Dwight resumed his normal office hours in Jeejeebhoy Towers, and when he was in the boardroom he didn't look down at the Gateway of India. He watched the efficient way that Shah dealt with the clients, he commented on the deals, and he reflected on the Diamond Sutra, what Shah had told him that evening – how the world gave false messages, with sounds, odors, flavors – and the Three Jewels of Jainism: right belief, right knowledge, right conduct.

Never mind Shah's self-interested stories, Dwight was consoled by his being near and giving him strength. He often thought of his last visit to Indru's, when he had asked them what his name was and they hadn't known it, or remembered it; when Padmini had asked him what he wanted; when he had said, 'I want to go.' Had it not been for him holding to right conduct, he would have gone back.

'Bangalore next week,' Dwight said at the end of one meeting about information technology.

'I'll have to stay in Bombay. Chappie is coming.'

'I can look after him,' Dwight said.

Shah did not reply, yet he reacted, something involuntary, a twitch visiting his head and shoulders, almost recoiling, as though to the drift of a questionable smell.

'I need you to do something important,' Shah said.

That was fine – what Dwight needed was to be kept busy. Shah himself had returned so much more confident than before – a good sign – and with a list of contacts and accounts to pursue. Dwight had imagined they'd be working together, yet Shah's confidence and his full schedule kept him distant and somewhat aloof.

This is his city, Dwight told himself. But the master–servant relationship of before, in which Shah had been a punctilious helper, a junior partner, seemed to be over, and at times Dwight suspected that the roles had been reversed – Shah the active partner, Dwight the assistant, who required direction.

'I need your help in releasing a consignment of rice from a certain warehouse,' Shah said. 'A ton or so.'

Shah was giving *him* something to do? Dwight said, 'Maybe we could do it together.'

'I will be extremely busy,' Shah said. 'I need a few days. I'll give you details of the shipment, bill of lading, whatever. It will be coming by lorry from Chennai to the bonded warehouse. You'll have to see to the paperwork.'

'Paperwork' was an ominous word in India. So were 'bill of lading' and 'bonded warehouse'. Dwight saw in advance the clipboards, the carbon paper, the inventory numbers, the perforated certificates, the forms to be filled out, the seals to be broken, the forms in triplicate, the coarse smelly paper, 'You must apply for permit,' and at the end of it, baksheesh.

'Payment will be made by wire transfer from a bank in Baltimore, Maryland.'

What? But he did do it. The chore took five days, back and forth to the warehouse in Bhiwandi, an hour by taxi from the Taj Hotel.

'Why Bhiwandi?' he had asked.

'Because it is adjacent to Grand Trunk Road.'

All this time, negotiating for the release of the shipment of rice, and moving it from Bhiwandi to a secure facility nearer the railway junction at Kalyan – following Shah's specific instructions – Dwight had the feeling he was working for Shah. And what he was doing any office manager could have done – Manoj Verma, Dinesh Patel, Sarojini Dasgupta, Miss Chakravarty, any of them. The other, better question was: what did a consignment of rice have to do with client business? Agricultural products had never been a priority. Five days of this bafflement went by without his setting eyes on Shah. Maybe he was at home, in his lovely apartment, dining off his porcelain?

The phone rang at midnight.

'Hund?'

What happened to 'Mr Hund'?

'It's kinda late.'

'I am just now proceeding from the airport, speaking on mobile. Sorry to wake you. I wasn't sure you'd be in your room.'

'Where else would I be at this hour?'

Shah didn't answer. He said, 'Just to thank you for your assistance with consignment of food grains. It is not entirely billable, but I will compensate you.'

'You'll pay me for moving that ton of rice?'

He intended to sound sarcastic. Literal-minded, Shah said, 'Indeed, for facilitating in business just concluded.'

'The rice?'

'The visit of Chappie.'

'I don't get it.'

'John Chapman Thaw. Harvard prof. He's putting some of his people into Bangalore to study IT and related areas. It will benefit us with tech transfer. He is amply funded, but a humble and humane individual.'

'I'd like to meet him,' Dwight said.

'Chappie and tech team have just departed. I saw them off. Lufthansa flight to Frankfurt.'

Dwight tried to draw a breath, but his concentration was too intense, the air too thin, his punctured lungs would not inflate, for he had begun to understand.

'Gone?'

'I would have introduced you, but his schedule was jam-packed.'

He still said *wisit* and *shed-jewel*, yet he was a different man, and this was the proof of it. While I've been dealing with a ton of rice in forty-pound sacks, Shah has been wining and dining this Harvard professor and his team. An American contact, an important lead, has come and gone; and I haven't seen him. How had this happened? Dwight was not angry; he was sad – he felt the bewilderment of a younger brother, a rejected suitor, an excluded bystander, a bypassed partner. And the silly name Chappie rankled.

'I must fly home,' Shah said. 'We meet tomorrow.'

It was not like Shah to exclude him from a negotiation. And it was absurd that Shah had taken the initiative to give Dwight five days' unpaid work while he shepherded the Harvard team around Bombay. And Dwight was his boss! Yet Dwight was grateful. For those five days he had worked at this menial task. He had not gone to a club. He had not called Indru or Padmini. He had hardly thought of them. He had felt – not virtuous, he was not virtuous; but serious, and he understood the fatigue that creates a passivity that empties the mind and gives access to spirituality, the trance-state induced by routine that helps in the practice of meditation.

'Many thanks,' Shah said the next day at Jeejeebhoy Towers, before the usual meetings – a parade of eager manufacturers with ring-binders of products, a lining-up of contracts.

Shah was his old submissive self, deferring to Dwight and calling him Mr Hund.

The last deal today was a process for applying rubberized coating to metal roof-racks – not just the pieces that were fixed to the car, but kayak cradles, bike-holders, attachments for skis and ski-poles. This created an enormous inventory, since many of the racks and clamps were unique to a specific model of car.

Shah itemized the list of attachments and fittings, wetting his thumb and moving through the clipboard of papers. Two companies would be involved, a steel fabricator and the rubber coater. Shah knew about carbon quotients, potential bruising, the matrix of the rubber solution, even the windage – the resistance of the carrier on the car roof.

Dwight looked on in admiration, forgiving Shah for putting him to all that trouble with the rice shipment, which was obviously a dodge – he didn't want him to meet the Harvard team, for whatever reason. Never mind. He was grateful to him for the days of pious mindless toil. He had almost forgotten his debauchery.

At the end of the day, Shah saw the businessmen to the door. Then he turned to Dwight and said, 'Now we will go on our spiritual journey.'

8

'What's that?' Dwight asked when the driver opened the trunk of the car. It was early morning, just after dawn, a sourness of damp streets, women scraping twig brooms in gutters. Out of the corner of his eye Dwight saw two girls with enormous backpacks walking up the driveway. They had stringy hair and sandals, one very pretty, the other one heavy with a beautiful smile, saying, 'This is unreal.' American girls: he envied them their innocence and wondered what their Indian surprise might be.

'Sack of rice,' Shah said. 'Symbol of gift. Remainder will go by train.'

'Will go where?'

'Mahuli,' Shah said. 'Adjacent to Mahabaleshwar.'

'Is that where we're going?'

'Indeed so. We take luncheon at Poona, and proceed to Mahabaleshwar, for Mahuli. You have checked out of hotel?'

'I'm going to miss that suite.'

Then they were on the road, sitting side by side in the back seat of the small car. The driver fought the other cars, jockeyed for position in the traffic, and once they were clear of Bombay – it took over an hour – struggled to pass the big filthy trucks that hogged the road, staring at *Horn Please*. Living in Bombay could be horrible, but nothing was worse than a journey like this.

On the first clear stretch of road, Dwight's own head cleared. He was able to recall the obvious thought that had occurred to him in the confusion of the previous day.

'You didn't introduce me to those Harvard people.'

'Chappie?'

The silly name sounded even sillier the solemn way that Shah uttered it. Dwight said, 'And his team.'

'They will prove to be excellent partners. Don't think of Harvard as a mere college. It is a billion dollar business, a tremendous source of contracts and expertise. Pay-dirt. And skill sets, my God!'

Something he has just found out and is preaching is something I've known since I got into this business, Dwight thought. Yet he was glad for Shah's enthusiasm, because that always implied willingness, and 'pay-dirt' made him smile.

'But you didn't introduce me.'

'They were so busy – tied up most of the time. And they went sightseeing. Chor Bazaar. Crawford Market. Towers of Silence. Elephanta Caves. Side trip to Agra. They much enjoyed themselves.'

All the things that he had never seen, while his own interest had been elsewhere. He said, 'You thought I'd corrupt them.'

'Not at all,' Shah said without conviction. He said nothing more, and because Dwight was looking closely at him, he saw Shah's nostrils widen – a breath instead of another denial, but it was the more telling for being a deliberate breath.

Now Dwight was surer of himself. He said, 'You were afraid I'd lead them astray.'

Without blinking, Shah took another breath, flaring his nostrils again. He was a spiritual soul, his pieties were obvious in the office, yet he had the manner of an accountant – discreet, over-cautious, revealing nothing and yet giving off a distinct hum of repressed fuss. Something of the Indian businessman informed the spiritual one, with his credit and debit columns in the ledger of karma.

'You heard something,' Dwight said.

Anyone new to India would not have detected the slight head-wobble, or would have assumed it to be an involuntary twitch, a sideways nod on a bad stretch of road. But Dwight knew it was not a pothole. It was Shah's acknowledgement: that tilt of the head was an emphatic yes.

'What did you hear?'

Shah did something with his lips, his mouth, compressed his lips in another subtlety, as though he'd tasted something and found it unpleasant, while at the same time, out of politeness, refraining from showing his disgust.

He said, 'Are you knowing Cape Cod in Massachusetts?'

'Very well. I grew up not far from there. We spent our summers in Chatham.'

'Exactly. When I visited Harvard to pursue that research angle of business, they took me by road to Cape Cod. We visited lovely towns. Saw Kennedy compound from road. Went for a fine walk on expanse of beach. An impressive place with many vivid sights.'

Get to the point, please, Dwight thought, staring hard to speed him up. Shah had the Indian businessman's way of speaking (and it had also been Winky's way) that seemed designed to force you to submit, to cry 'Uncle!' But this manner was his strength in the firm.

He raised a skinny finger. He said, 'One sight was more vivid than any other that day. Can you guess?'

'Maybe one of those big sailboats in Hyannis harbor?'

'Not at all,' Shah said.

'Kennedy compound?'

'Not.'

'I can't guess.'

'It was me,' Shah said.

'You were the sight?'

'I was the sight. That day, in that place, I was indeed the most unusual feature. There were no other Indians anywhere we went – none in the restaurant, none in the museum. At the botanical gardens in the town of Sandwich. With this face and these hands' – now he looked at Dwight; until then he had been looking away – 'I was the most visible.'

Wisible too was how Dwight had felt in his shame.

'I get it,' he said.

But Shah went on, saying, 'Had I drunk beer in a bar, or gone about with a woman, or given money . . .'

'I said I get it.'

'In India, we see everything. We hear everything. And if you are visible . . .'

'Please stop,' Dwight said. He put his head in his hands: he saw himself, a big white goon, at the Gateway of India, at the charity ball with Winky Vellore, talking to Indru, whispering to Padmini, sneaking to their flat, kicking the sand at Chowpatty Beach. *Wisible*.

His shame silenced him, the emotion fatigued him

– or was it the early start, back-seat nausea, the rutted road? He slept and was awakened by Shah saying, 'Poona city. We will take luncheon.'

Shah said he knew of a Jain restaurant. He gave directions to the driver. The place was just a shop with trestle tables and creaky chairs. No menu. The usual humble meal, which Shah kept calling luncheon, served by an old man and a boy.

'He is a good man,' Shah said of the restaurant owner, as he was clearing the plates. 'Very strict. And a teacher, too.'

The man smiled. He seemed to know that he was being spoken about.

'We Jains call such people "passage makers". He shows the way.'

'You do that, too,' Dwight said.

'It is kind of you to say that. But . . .' His voice trailed off and he shrugged, ambiguous again, neither yes nor no, but probably yes.

Walking towards the car, Shah said, 'That lovely gateway was once entrance to a great palace, Shanwar Wada. And over there . . .'

He gestured, he walked ten steps to a narrow street overlooked by old stone and stucco houses.

'Very nice,' Dwight said.

'Was a place of execution,' Shah said.

Dwight stepped backwards, looked harder, but saw only a bumpy, weedy street contained by the leaning buildings.

'Men who transgressed were brought here. They were bound hand and foot. They were summarily executed.'

Gazing at the tussocky street, the potholes, a grazing cow, a skinny boy in a white shirt marching with a school backpack, the sun slanting into dust motes, Dwight said, 'How?'

'Elephants were released that side. The men were trampled to death.' Shah winced, as though he had gotten a glimpse of it. 'For their indiscretions. Under the elephants' mighty feet.'

He said no more. He led Dwight to the car. In the car he tapped on the back of the driver's headrest and said, 'Mahabaleshwar, for Mahuli.'

The Poona meal had made Dwight drowsy. He hugged himself and crouched in a corner of the back seat, and sank into sleep. The country was dry and hilly and looked crumbled and cracked: Dwight carried the landscape into his dreams. The road, the honking of the car, the sunlight in the window – it all became part of his vision of punishment, and the rumble of the wheels was like the pounding in his heart. When he awoke, strangely refreshed, yawning with vigor, relieved to see the day, he looked out of the car window and saw a rural land of great simplicity, a landscape he had never visited before and hardly imagined – men squatting in the shade of low huts, children carrying water in squarish tin containers, women slapping muddy chunks into Frisbee-sized dung pats for fuel.

Those serene people thrived in a dusty setting that Dwight saw as the counterpart of the tortured landscape of his heart. Lucky people, he thought. They've learned how to live here – how to flourish in a quiet way.

'I can see you are suffering,' Shah said.

'Suffering?'

'You were crying out in your sleep.'

'What did I say?'

'You were pleading for relief,' Shah said. 'Don't be embarrassed. Was it my mention of the execution ground?'

He didn't know. He remembered the sight of the big sun-baked land, the dusty, stunted bushes, the dead trees, the yoked buffalos turning over dry curls of soil. But seeing Shah's serious face he recalled, *trampled . . . indiscretion . . . mighty feet.*

So he said yes, and, 'That would be an awful way to go.'

With the take-charge energy that Dwight noticed in Shah after his return from the States, Shah said brightly, 'What I heard in America was people saying, "I know I have a problem. But I don't know what to do."'

'I understand that,' Dwight said. He had been fearful of speaking the words, but they had run through his mind.

'Or, "There are no answers",' Shah said in a stilted quoting voice.

'Tell me about it,' Dwight said.

'Yes,' Shah said. 'It is a Western confusion, a kind of spiritual ignorance. "I don't know which way to turn." We in India never say such things. Why, do you think?'

The little car had tipped forward and they were descending into a steep-sided valley on a road that was like the bewildering track Dwight saw when he thought of his own life. *Going nowhere*, people said, when it was obvious that they were traveling hard on an awful road like this to somewhere, even if the place was unknown.

'I don't know,' Dwight said, not replying to a question but summing up every doubt in his head.

'In India we have answers. Real answers. That is Indian strength. It is our spiritual heritage. Never "I don't know." Always "I can know."'

'I wish I did.'

'It was my late father's lesson to me, dear man, when he set off on his journey to be holy. A lack of holiness impedes enlightenment.'

It was the voice Shah used in the boardroom when he was speaking to the wholesalers – the plastic fabricators, the rubber people, the textile men. He was the wordiest man Dwight had ever met, but he could also be blunt, with his lawyer's love of precision. He was that way now. He was saying, 'Excess of karmic particles.'

'I'm listening,' Dwight said.

'Process we call *nirjara*. I have mentioned this to you in connection with my late father. Cessation of passionate action.'

'I think I know what that means.'

'Also fasting.' Shah splayed his fingers and enumerated. 'Eating properly. Solitude. Mortification. Meditation. Study. Atonement.' He tugged at his thumb. 'Renunciation of ego.'

The list could have seemed intimidating and demanding, but – because it was different from anything he'd known, and a new thought – Dwight found it restful to contemplate.

'You will see,' Shah said, pointing ahead.

The land was hillier, emptier, with mountains showing in the distance like low clouds. What farms they saw, hacked into the hillsides, were even smaller than the ones they'd passed earlier. The corrugations of newly plowed gardens lay against the slopes. Farther on, a scene of almost Biblical simplicity – women drawing water at a well, one with a clay pot on her shoulder, in an orange sari, another woman heading up a dusty path in thin sandals, a flock of goats bleating at her.

'You see? We are leaving the world behind,' Shah said. 'Soon we will be in Mahabaleshwar.'

It was twilight when they got to the edge of the town. Dwight could make out more hills beyond these, and in the car's headlights people walking in the road, boys in white shirts, men in dhotis. He expected the car to stop now that they were in the town, but the driver kept going, past the lighted shops and into the darkness of the winding road, towards the solitude of the over-hanging forest.

'Pratapgarh,' Shah said, tapping the car window. And after a few minutes, 'Mahuli.'

He spoke in Hindi to the driver, who began to brake, and then turned into a long driveway that rocked the car.

'We have arrived.'

No lights, no sign of a building, just a dark place on an even darker road. And when they got out of the car the air was cool and damp. All that Dwight saw was the sky thickening with night, pierced by scattered pinholes of stars.

'I can't see anything.' Yet the shadows were perfumed with an aroma of incense.

'Tomorrow you will see everything.'

Preceded by a flame, a woman appeared, holding a platter on which an oil lamp flickered. She rotated the flame under Dwight's chin, as Indru and Padmini had once done, and marked his forehead with paste.

'Welcome,' she said.

Without thinking, merely reacting to her, Dwight fell to his knees and touched her feet in a single fluid movement, and while he knelt with his head bowed tears of gratitude and relief blurred his vision.

Shah made no sound, and yet – how was this? – Dwight could tell that the man approved, that he was delighted and proud of him.

'What did you just say?' Dwight asked as he got to his feet, hearing Shah speak to a man in a white robe who seemed to materialize behind the woman with the flaming platter.

'I told him, "Swamiji, this man has brought you a gift."'

Dwight brushed his eyes with the back of his hand. 'What are you talking about?'

Now the light from the trunk of the car was illuminating a tall gateway he had not seen before, yet had passed through. The driver was directing a young man to lift it – the Indian chain of command: a driver was not a carrier.

'The rice. A full ton of it.'

'I didn't do that,' Dwight said.

'Collecting the money in America was the easy part. Buying it was simple. The hard business was shifting it. The paperwork, the supervision, the permits and signatures. So it is your gift.'

Dwight had resented his unpaid work in dealing

with the rice shipment; he had even suspected Shah of fobbing off this chore onto him to keep him away from the visiting Harvard team. He now saw the design in the whole effort. He could take credit: it hadn't been easy.

'Swamiji is thanking you,' Shah said.

'Who is he?'

'He too is a passage maker,' Shah said. The old man was still speaking. 'He is inviting us to eat. But before we go in to take some food he must ask you to give him your mobile phone.'

'Glad to get rid of it.' He rummaged in his pockets.

'All electronic devices,' Shah said.

Dwight handed over his cellphone, then his BlackBerry.

'He is asking if you have a computer.'

'Laptop's in my briefcase.'

'Shall I put it in my safekeeping?' Shah said.

'Go ahead.'

'As you saw, I too am a passage maker.'

Dwight felt lighter, out of touch, relaxed. Nothing would ring or buzz; nothing would interrupt him. He followed the two men to the dining area, feeling happy.

They ate from clay bowls, by candlelight, in a cool clean room, seated on mats.

'Swami says again he is grateful for the rice,' Shah said. 'He is asking if you are Christian.'

'I spent a lot of time in church when I was a boy,' Dwight said.

The old man and Shah spoke awhile in Hindi, and then Shah said, 'He is complimenting you. He knows Jesus Christ. Jesus, who said, "If you want to be perfect, go and sell everything you have and give it to the poor, and you will have treasure in Heaven."'

'That's nice,' Dwight said, feeling that he was hearing it for the first time.

'My late father did so,' Shah said.

Now the old man was speaking – a shock to hear him speaking English.

'There was something that Jesus did not say.'

'What did Jesus leave out?'

'He did not describe world of ego – fleeting world.'

'I thought he did.'

'Not at all,' the old man said.

Shah was beaming, the flames lighting his face. Dwight waited for more.

'What is the world?' The old man gestured towards the door – towards Bombay, Dwight guessed, where his memories were so painful. 'It is almost nothing, do you not agree?'

Dwight said, 'It was something to me.'

'But do you sincerely want to leave it behind?'

'Very much.'

'That will not be hard if your heart is right.'

'What is it, then?' Dwight asked, and realized hearing the reverence in his tone that he had become a student, an initiate; he had surrendered his will, and was happy.

'It is a falling star,' the old man said. 'It is a bubble in a stream. A flame in the wind. Frost in the sun. A flash of lightning in a summer cloud.'

Dwight was too moved to speak. He blinked – tears maybe, or maybe he was overcome by the perfume in the incense that thickened the air.

'A phantom in a dream,' the old man said. 'Why are you rising, sir?'

Dwight did not answer. He knelt and bowed his head and touched the old man's feet, feeling a surge of energy in his fingers that jolted his wrists and stiffened his arms.

'Do you want to be free?' the old man asked softly.

'Yes, yes.'

'It is possible. To be free, you must see things as they are.'

'That's all?'

'That is a lot,' the old man said, and got to his feet. 'Now sleep.'

He led Dwight through the courtyard. 'Stars,' Dwight said. 'You don't see these in Bombay.'

As though obeying a subtle cue, the old man walked a few steps away, towards a gateway carved with images of animals and gods.

In an urgent whisper, Shah said, 'You are so lucky. No one knows you here. It is as though you don't exist. You can be peaceful. You can think about your life. Meditate, my friend. Open your heart. What is the world? A flame in the wind. A flash of lightning in a summer cloud. So beautiful.'

Dwight said, 'How can I thank you?'

'Trust me with your valuables,' Shah said, clutching the briefcase.

'They're nothing. A bubble in a stream.'

The old man was watching, the light from the candles giving him the bright eyes of a nocturnal animal.

'I'll leave first thing,' Shah said. 'And then I'll be away.'

'Whatever.'

Shah said, 'I'll stay in the States for a while.'

Dwight said, 'I think I'll stay here for a while.'

In the darkness of his cubicle, Dwight slept as though drugged. He lay on his back, lightly covered by a clean sheet, breathing the residue of the night's incense.

At first light he was aware of Shah leaving, gathering his bags, scuffing his sandals on the path outside. Dwight simply held his breath and waited for silence to descend. The car doors slammed, and the engine raced, and then like a fly-buzz fading, the sound of the car was overlaid by silence again. And with that silence and Shah's departure a sweet fragrance filled his room.

Dwight imagined Shah in the car, heading back to Bombay, rubbing his hands, probably making a gleeful call on his cellphone, hooting into it, something like, 'It is done!' Shah thought he'd pulled a fast one, secured the Harvard account, ingratiated himself with Sheely and Kohut and Elfman – all the while keeping Dwight in the dark. He had maneuvered him to this ashram, divested him of his laptop and was going off to get rich. He believed that he had fooled Dwight.

No, it had been a favor, a gift.

Once, at Shah's house, at that dinner, hearing Shah describe his mendicant father, Dwight had had a vision of himself as a holy man on a dusty road, swinging a stick, eating an apple. He had laughed then, because it had seemed so improbable, and it had been a way of jeering at himself. Now lying on a narrow cot in the tidy room freshened by the fizz of leaves and the morning air at his open window, he saw himself again, a skinny sunburned geek in a turban and loincloth, carrying a wooden staff and strolling down a country road, craving nothing except more life – happy, seeing things as they were.

The Elephant God

I

Walking towards the railway station, its dome like a huge head, its scrollwork and buttresses suggesting big ears, Alice smiled at the way the old building glittered like a great gray creature of granite, but closer it was just fakery, India mimicking England, a hodgepodge of disappointed Gothic. Alice hesitated at the archway, then stepped through the entrance. Inside it was a nuthouse, and it stank. The smells of India still terrified her. From a distance, India was splendor; up close, misery.

A man with stumps for hands, just rounded wrists, approached her with pleading eyes and lips. She gave him a ten-rupee note but could not bear to see him manipulate it. She had to brave the waiting room because her friend Stella was late – as usual. Pretty girls were never punctual – was it another way of being noticed? Pretty girls were always forgiven. Pretty girls could be peculiarly reckless and were seldom harmed or blamed, because they were pretty. And the weird thing was that pretty girls never believed they were pretty enough.

Alice was never late, and she knew what that implied about her, but she told herself she didn't care. They had been friends at Brown but not close. She had been the pretty girl's plain friend, a protector, to be patronized. Now, as this was not Providence but the world, over the weeks of their traveling together Alice had begun to see Stella in a new way. She pitied her for her egotism, her passivity, her abrupt changes of mind. Pretty girls had a free pass, they could do anything, especially get away with a child-like sort of helplessness. Alice wanted to say, 'Some day it will be your undoing.'

Having to search for Stella in the crowded station made Alice conspicuous and meant her having to stare at the people pushing, or ones quarrelling or sleeping in heaps on rectangles of cloth by the wall. Beaky old women sat abjectly in front of dishes of coins, exhibiting their misery. A mother with a limp baby made 'give me food' gestures – her fingers fluttering to her mouth, presenting the baby as the object of suffering. Was the baby dead?

The Indian novels she'd read in the States had not prepared her for what she saw here. Where were the big fruitful families from these novels, where were the jokes, the love affairs, the lavish marriage ceremonies, the solemn pieties, the virtuous peasants, the environmentalists, the musicians, the magic, the plausible young men? They seemed concocted to her now, and besieged in up-close India all she thought of was Hieronymus Bosch, turtle-faced crones, stumpy men, deformed children.

'Yes?' It was someone else from Bosch, a dark brown man with dyed orange hair and red eyes. He pressed close to her and stroked her hair with a lizard-like hand. He held a tattered canvas bag in his other hand.

'Please leave me alone,' Alice said.

The man looked gleeful. He said, 'There are more

than one billion people in India. You will never be alone.'

A furious-faced mustached man, in a khaki woolen uniform, with a truncheon under his arm, demanded to see Alice's ticket. Roosterish and aggressive, he was not in any of the novels. The first man backed away, still smiling.

'What do you want?' She had been told that some of these people wanted bribes.

'Security. Where going?'

'Going Bangalore.'

'Flatporm pyve.'

'Me waiting friend,' Alice said, and smiled, hearing herself.

'Prend coming?'

'Friend coming just now.'

The man left her, and there she waited, as though abandoned, feeling scrutinized, assaulted by people's stares, but what could she do? They had agreed to meet at the front of the station platform for the trip. Alice had not gotten used to Stella's lateness, and she thought, Why should I? But the late person always seemed to think that after many instances of being late they were understood and pardoned and the waiter was habituated to it. But the opposite was the case – the blame grew.

When, finally, Alice saw Stella approaching through the throng she knew her friend had something on her mind. Mental conflict showed in the way she walked. They'd been traveling for three weeks and in that time Alice saw how obvious Stella was, how easily she could be read. She touched her right eye when she was being untruthful, she jogged her left leg when she was impatient, she quickly agreed to anything Alice might say when she wanted to talk. And then she talked and talked, as a way to prevent Alice from asking any questions; talked in order to dominate and conceal. She had talked a lot lately, and ever since arriving in Bombay Stella's pretty-girl presumptions had been obnoxious. She was used to being treated as someone special, she was passive; she only needed to smile to attract notice.

The most obvious thing about Stella today Alice did not see until they were next to each other. She had no bag. She wasn't coming.

They had set off from Delhi with much-too-big rucksacks. Stella's had a teddy bear dangling from it – another of her affectations. ('Teddy doesn't want to see the temple.') Without the rucksack she looked smaller and straighter and a little devious.

'Where's your pack?'

'Long story. I left it at the hotel.' Stella's hand flew up and she touched her right eye.

Before she said anything more, Alice knew that Stella was trying to find the right words to say that she wasn't coming to Bangalore – would not be traveling with Alice, after they had spent every day together since leaving the States on the graduation trip that they'd planned since last January. Alice knew that from Stella's wan smile and her now contorted posture, digging her toe into the platform where someone had spat. She was staying behind – but why?

'I've been thinking really hard about us traveling together,' Stella said. 'How really fun it's been.'

Alice said, 'So you're bailing.'

'Don't say it like that.' Stella was shocked – she disliked Alice's bluntness. 'You make it sound like I don't care.'

'The plan was to take the train to Bangalore. To visit Sai Baba. He's there at the moment. There's a darshan this week. We have beds reserved at the ashram. And the trip to Madras to see the temple. That was the plan, right?'

'I know, but – oh, gosh, I'm so confused, I don't know what to do.'

'That was the plan,' Alice insisted. 'And this is the train. It's leaving in twenty minutes.'

'I'm really sorry, Allie.'

'So you really are bailing?'

'You make it sound like I'm betraying you.'

It was not at all what Alice meant but now she realized that it was what Stella was doing. She had guiltily uttered the exact word that she was denying, another of her traits, just as 'It's the truth, Allie' was always a lie.

'Bombay's a zoo. That's what you said. So why are you staying here?'

'I don't know. It's a long story.'

But her expression, and especially her unreliable eyes, indicated that she knew. Well, of course she did. She was an only child. She always did what she wanted, and if there was a better deal she took it, even if it meant breaking her word.

Alice had given up any hope of Stella coming along, but she hated being lied to and she was genuinely curious as to why a weak, spoiled girl like Stella had changed her mind and was staying in a city she said she disliked for its noise and its crowds and its smelly sidewalks.

'This is like a scene in one of those great movies when the characters have this painful farewell on a railway platform.'

'No, it's not,' Alice said. 'In the movies it's always lovers. We weren't even room-mates.'

'It's like a farewell though.'

'It's not painful.'

'It's painful for me,' Stella said.

She's going to cry, Alice thought, seeing Stella's pretty mouth crumple, so she said, 'You're the one who's bailing. So why is it painful for you?'

Stella started to cry, but managed to say, 'You're being really harsh.'

'If you cared so much you'd be coming along. And what I don't get at all is why you're deciding to stay in Bombay alone.'

As soon as she said the word 'alone' Alice knew why. Stella would never travel alone, never stay alone; she had met someone else – she was with that person. The fact that Alice had only just realized this made her feel foolish – obtuse, anyway. But who was it? Where had they met?

'You're staying with that hippy chick from Bennington we met at the bazaar.'

'God, no. She was so gross, like she flossed her teeth in that restaurant,' Stella said, in such an outburst Alice was sure she was telling the truth.

But she knew that Stella had teamed up with someone else. She said, 'Don't be enigmatic, Stell. We're supposed to be friends. Who's the guy?'

It was a shot in the dark, but from the way Stella reacted, grimacing – the tears were gone – Alice knew she'd guessed right.

'Nobody special.' She touched her right eye again. 'But that kid, Zack, um . . .'

When she uttered the name Alice knew everything. Zack with his baseball cap on backwards, Zack from the ticket line at the Regal Cinema and the Bollywood movie, who had gone to NYU Film School and wanted to make a Bollywood movie himself, with big-named American actors, Zack in the T-shirt that said *Choose Death*, whose father was (so he said) a connected Hollywood lawyer, who was staying at the Taj Mahal Hotel. Zack with his cellphone that worked in India for US calls – Stella had called her mother on it. Zack's father knew Bill Clinton.

'You said he was a brat.'

'That was a first impression. He's got a spiritual side, plus he's really funny.'

'He just wants to nail you.'

Stella looked appalled and on the verge of crying again.

'He already has!' Alice said. 'You're screwing him. That's what you were doing the other night when we were at that club and you said you had a headache and went back to that fancy suite his father got for us.'

Hearing the raised voices, and especially 'You're screwing him', some Indian men paused and drew closer to listen to the two women, whose faces were flushed.

When one pressed close to her, Alice turned on him and said, 'Do you mind?' and the man stepped away but remained within earshot.

'I told you, it's a long story.'

'It's not! It's a short story. You met a guy. He said his father was in India to go to that luxury spa near Jaipur.'

She saw it all. Zack had gotten his father to pay for them to spend one night at the Elephanta Suite, and afterwards Zack had invited Stella to travel with him and his father to the spa in Jaipur, where Bill Clinton had stayed. Stella was as interested in the father as she was in Zack – perhaps more so, since spoiled children were always looking for protectors, who would let them have their own way. Now she was glad that Stella – shallow, selfish Stella – was not coming. She began to laugh.

Hearing her laughter the Indian men stepped closer, as though to inquire what was so funny.

Alice said, 'I think you're right. This is like one of those partings on a railway platform in a movie.'

And Stella looked happier.

Right at the beginning of the trip they had agreed – no boys, or if there had to be boys, no relationships. Also, no expensive hotels, no patronage, no accepting drinks from strangers. We'll pay our own way, even if it hurts.

And of all people Zack. Now Alice remembered with scorn how Zack had remarked on an image of Ganesh, the elephant deity, fat and cheerful and beneficent, bringing luck to any new enterprise, seated on his big bottom, with jewels on his domed head and his floppy trunk and his thick legs.

'He looks like a penis,' Zack had said.

'I guess you haven't seen too many penises,' Alice said.

Stella had looked alarmed and glanced with concern at Zack, who said, 'More dicks than you have, girl.'

That meant, You're plain. When she was heavy at Brown she heard fat jokes, and now that she had lost weight she heard ugly jokes. And the amazing thing was that people actually said them to your face, as though there was some subtlety in them, rather than: You're fat, you're plain, you can't get a date. And they also said them because if you were plain or heavy you were supposed to be strong and have a sense of humor.

Now she remembered Zack saying, 'Want to text-message your folks?' and she smiled angrily at Stella and said, 'Aren't you the clever one.' Meaning, You're not clever at all, but Stella with the pretty girl's deafness to irony took it as a compliment.

'Maybe we can hook up somewhere,' Stella said.

'You're on your own now, girlfriend,' Alice said.

She had to summon all her strength to say it, because she knew that Stella was taken care of. As soon as she spoke she was breathless.

Seeing that the foreign women had become more conversational, with lowered voices, the Indian men lost interest and wandered away down the platform, where people were pushing to board the train. Suitcases were being hoisted through the windows of the coaches, families hurrying to board, red-shirted porters with boxes on wheelbarrows.

Now a man approached with a clipboard and sized them up. He said, 'Boarding time.'

Alice showed her ticket and said, 'She's not coming. She found another friend.'

Stella began again to cry. She hugged Alice and said, 'I love you, Allie. I have to do this. I can't explain.'

'This is a bad movie,' Alice said, and broke away.

After she boarded and found her seat she saw Stella outside, gaping, looking cow-like. Stella leaned and waved. Stella remained watching until the train pulled away. She was still tearful, but she was meeting Zack and staying at Zack's fancy hotel; it was Alice who was on her own.

But no sooner had the train pulled out of the station and was rumbling past the tenements and traffic of the Bombay outskirts than an unexpected feeling came over Alice, glowing on her whole body: she was alone and liked it. Free of Stella, she felt stronger and more decisive. She could do whatever she wanted, without consulting her fickle friend. Just fifteen minutes into the twenty-four-hour trip, she realized that Stella had been a much bigger burden than she'd imagined. Now Stella was at risk and it was she who was happy in the swaying train, like being in the body of a bulgy creature that protected her while plodding forward in the heat.

With the whole day ahead of her, she sat by the window and watched India slip by in a stream of simple images – women threshing grain on mats, men plowing with placid oxen, children jumping into muddy streams, clusters of houses baking in the sun, here and there a level crossing where a blue bus or a man on a bike was stopped by the passing train. These human sights became rarer, for after Poona there were only fields, or stunted trees, or great dusty plains to the horizon, an India Alice had not seen or read about before, and because she was not sharing it with Stella it was all hers, a secret disclosed to her, a discovery too that India was also a land of empty corners.

And so all that hot day in the hinterland of Maharashtra Alice marveled at this revelation of big yawning India. It was the antithesis of crowded, damp and noisy Bombay, the words 'critical mass' as a visible image. She liked what she saw now for being unfinished and unpeopled. Stella knew nothing about it – might never know, for Zack harped on about being a city person and was talking importantly about setting up a movie and you could only do that in a big stinking city.

'You can have him,' Alice said clearly, still at the hot window.

She was startled when a voice said, 'Pardon?'

The seat where an elderly Indian woman had been sleeping wrapped in a thin sheet just a moment ago – or so it seemed – was now occupied by a young Indian man. He was fat-faced and bulky, with big brown eyes, a lovely smile, and wore a clean neatly pressed shirt. He was sitting cross-legged, barefoot, where the old woman had been, and both his posture and his face conveyed the assurance that he was harmless, even if a bit innocent and fearful. He sat with his chubby fingers locked together, in a patient posture of restraint.

'I was just thinking out loud,' Alice said.

'Talking out loud,' the young man said.

'Not exactly,' Alice said. 'The thought was in my head but it somehow got turned into some words.'

'Something worse?'

'No. Some words. The thought became a statement.'

'Thought in head becoming utterance.'

Now 'utterance' was one of those words like 'miscreants', 'audacious' and 'thrice' and 'ample' and 'jocundity' that some Indians used in casual conversation and Indian writers used in sentences, in the same way that out the window the Indian farmers were using antique sharp-nosed hand-plows pulled by yoked oxen and women carried water jars on their heads. India was a country of usable antiques.

Alice kept a list of these Indian English words in her notebook. Comparative linguistics was a subject she had thought of pursuing in grad school (what else could an English major do?) but first she wanted to take this year off after graduation, the trip with Stella – who had slipped into thin air, just bailed, selfish bitch. But Alice smiled to think that here she was, enjoying herself in this adventure to Bangalore, while Stella and Zack were sneering at Bombay and discovering how shallow each other was. It gives me no pleasure to think that you're unhappy, Alice thought, and smiled, because it did.

'You are ruminative,' the young man said.

'Ruminative,' Alice said, thinking: Write that down. 'That's me.'

'Cudgeling your mind.'

'The expression is "cudgeling your brains", only I'm not.'

'You are indeed thinking out loud.'

'You learn fast,' Alice said. 'Where are you going?'

'Bangalore,' he said.

He was going the whole way in this sleeping compartment?

'Job interview,' he said. 'Eye Tee. Bee Pee Oh.'

'A call center?'

'Can be call center or tech support center. Voice-based or computer-driven. Wish me luck.'

Alice was touched by the fat young man saying that. She said, 'I really do wish you luck. I hope you get the job. Maybe I'll call the tech support line someday and you can help me fix my computer.'

'It would be my pleasure. You are smiling.'

'Because we're in this train. India out there, rolling along. It's so Merchant–Ivory.'

When Alice glanced out the window she saw that dusk had fallen and they were pulling into a station. It was Gurgaon. Many people got onto the train, and just as the train started again a woman entered the compartment with two suitcases. She did not offer a greeting but instead concentrated on chaining her luggage to a stanchion by the door. Then, muttering, she claimed the lower berth and sent the young man to the upper berth and out of sight. It was as though a chaperone had intervened, for he was at once both obedient and less familiar. While he appeared to read – Alice heard the rattling of magazine pages – the woman made her bed and lay down to sleep. Alice was reassured by the woman, whom she saw not as an intrusion at all but a typically bossy Indian woman who would keep order.

A man came by with a tray of food – dhal, rice, two puris, a pot of yogurt, the sort of meal that Stella had begun to call 'the slimy special', but Alice found delicious. And after she ate it and the tray was collected, she lay down and read a Sai Baba pamphlet, 'The

Meaning of Love', in preparation for the ashram, but had hardly turned a page when she fell asleep, rocked by the train.

In the morning a coffee seller came by. She bought a paper cup of coffee and some bananas from a woman with bunches of them in a basket, and she sat in the sunshine, feeling on this lovely morning that a new phase in her life was beginning.

'Can you please inform me, what is your good name, madam?'

She looked up and saw the tubby young man smiling at her, sitting in a lotus posture. She had forgotten him.

'Sure thing. Alice – Alice Durand.'

He was now leaning over, his arm extended. 'My card. May I obtain yours?'

'I don't actually have a business card,' Alice said. 'But I'm sure I'll see you around. We're both getting off at Bangalore.'

'No. You must be getting off at Cantonment, for Whitefield.'

'How do you know that?'

'Sai Baba Center. You have been perusing pamphlet.'

Anyone's watchfulness slightly unnerved her, but she also admired this man's. He was a fast learner. He would get the job.

'We are sitting on eight o'clock. Cantonment is coming up.'

'And what is your good name?'

'Amitabh. On the card. Also mobile number and hotmail account. Also pager. You will find me accessible.'

He was still sitting, wide in his solid posture, when

Alice hoisted her top-heavy rucksack and struggled off the train to face the squawking, reaching auto-rickshaw drivers, who seemed to know exactly where she was going.

2

The passage of time was not easily calculable in the ashram. You didn't count hours or days, but rather months, maybe years. A month had gone by, though time meant nothing here, even with the routine, up at four to queue for a place at the hall for the darshan and a chance to hear Swami at six-thirty; then bhajans until eight, and breakfast; then chores and food prep and more queuing until more of Swami at two and more bhajans, of which Alice's favorite began:

> *Jaya Jaya Jaya Hey Gajaanana*
> *Gajaanana Hey Gajavadana . . .*

> *Victory to Gajaanana,*
> *The elephant-faced God . . .*

'Work is worship,' Swami said, and 'Hands that help are better than lips that pray' and 'Start the day with love, spend the day with love, fill the day with love, end the day with love. That is the way to God.'

Alice's days spilled one into the other, full and fluid, guided by the Swami. And the passage of time was a consoling liquefaction of weeks in which she was gently turned, as though tumbled downstream, without any effort, feeling the buoyancy of happiness chanted into her ears.

Swami was smaller, slighter, older than his photographs suggested, the hair a less symmetrical frizz-ball, his smile more fatigued than impish. But he was eighty. His direct confrontation, his practical advice, his refusal to preach – the essential Swami appealed to her. He seemed to single her out at the daily darshan and to hold her gaze and, while seeming to preach, said, 'I am not here to preach. Only to listen. Only to make suggestions. I tell you' – and here Alice felt the warmth of his attention – 'if you are Christian, be the best Christian you can be.'

'He will leave his body at ninety-six,' Alice's roommate Priyanka said. 'And after some eight years, the third and last incarnation will be born. Prema Sai. I wish to observe this.'

Priyanka and her friend Prithi had gotten robes for Alice and allowed her to share their room, claiming they were spiritual sisters, since single women were discouraged from applying for rooms. The room was spartan and clean – well, she cleaned it, after bhajan. She was glad that Stella was not here to distract her. Stella would have hated the food, made a fuss about the flies or the heat, or else said (as she had at the temple at Muttra), 'I don't see why I should take off my shoes here, since the floor is a heck of a lot dirtier than my feet.'

Alice loved the simplicity of the place, the strict routine, the plain food, the safety of the perimeter wall, the knowledge that Swami was right next door, beyond the gate in his funky yellow house. It was like a nunnery, and yet there were no vows. She could leave any time she wanted. But the routine suited her, and the city – what she had seen of it – seemed pleasant enough. Too much traffic, though; too many people; honks, shouts, the crackle of music, new stinks.

Against Priyanka's advice – 'Swami doesn't like us dibble-dabbling in the town' – Alice took a bus to Lalbagh Gardens and lost herself among the giant trees, the first real trees she'd seen in India, big old ones that spoke of space and order, that provided damp shade and coolness. Indian families wandered in the gardens, lapping at ice creams, and Alice regarded these people wandering among the great trees as worshippers of the most devout sort, without dogma, lovers of the natural world, as Swami was.

Some of the Bangalore streets were lined with flowering trees, like any good street in Providence, and the same sort of solid, smug-fronted houses and bungalows. Stella would have shopped – there were silks and pashminas and bangles – but Alice only looked. The Christian churches, a large somehow unexplainable number of them, helped calm her, because all those Christians were a link with a world she knew and the faith itself had Swami's approval.

But the dust-laden and echoey churches were not enough. She was drawn to another place of worship – the Ganesh temple in the heart of the city, the elephant image smiling at her from the inner sanctum. That was how it seemed: another big soft gaze in her life. The other deities sat glowering – with horror-teeth, like Kali's, or else solemnly dancing, like Shiva; with half-closed eyes, like Saraswati playing the sitar, or goofy-faced, with pouchy cheeks, like Hanuman. But only the elephant god smiled, always the kindly eyes directed straight at her, and the full satisfied mouth chomping on the tusks like a tycoon with two cigars. The way the fat thing sat on the rounded cushion of his bottom, his center of gravity in his broad bum, was also a pleasure to see, but most of all his eyes reassured her with the *What can I do for you?* look, and the guarantee, *I can help you*.

The afterlife was not intimated in any of the elephant god's intercessions. He was worldly and efficient, not granting grace or forgiving sins, but promising to bring his heavy foot down to flatten a problem.

Alice's problems were small but they were problems nonetheless. One was the memory of Stella's dropping out. She wanted to forgive her but she could not rid her mind of the betrayal, and she remembered Zack trying to impress Stella, saying how his favorite line in *How to Marry a Millionaire* was Marilyn Monroe talking about maharajas: 'Those jewels – and all those crazy elephants.' Stella had laughed and now she had what he wanted.

One afternoon, having ducked out of the ashram to be soothed by a visit to the Ganesh shrine, she decided to walk back to Whitefield. A taxi always meant bantering with the driver and having to answer too many questions. In an area of narrow lanes she passed the courtyard of an old house and saw what looked like a stable. The air was rich with sweet decay here. What she sniffed as a relief from the sourness of traffic fumes she realized was manure that had the density of compost, the powerful suggestion of a healthy animal and also of the fertile earth. She took a few steps into the passageway and saw a large dusty elephant.

The tubby smiling creature with the swaying trunk seemed linked to the deity she'd just prayed to, as though it was his living embodiment. She could not separate the two, but, having prayed, saw this animal as the privileged answer to those prayers. Its big staring eyes held her and seemed to fix her as an image, as though photographing her – certainly remembering her. As it stared, it danced from side to side, swinging its rubbery trunk. It reached towards her with the big hose-like thing and then lowered it, wrapped it round a broken stalk of sugar cane and clenched the pink edges of its nose holes, then delicately plucked the fragment and with one upward bend of its trunk popped it into its mouth and crunched it. It had teeth too.

The elephant still swayed, holding Alice's attention like a promise fulfilled. And for the first time in India she did not feel lonely.

She saw with sadness the collar of metal around the lower part of its left rear leg, and the heavy chain fastened with an iron spike. The elephant was male yet he appeared to Alice like an enormous plain woman, chained to a post, overwhelmingly frustrated, murmuring to herself to get attention.

'Ha!' A man stepped forward, wearing a dhoti like a diaper and a badly tied turban, and sprayed the elephant with a hose.

She decided to try the word that was in her mind. She pointed at the man and said, 'Mahout?'

He smiled – 'Mahout, mahout' – and went on spraying, and the elephant too seemed to smile.

Alice lingered a little, watching the elephant being

drenched, its gray dusty skin blackened by the water, thick and wrinkled, looking like cold lava. Then she clasped her hands, said '*Namaste*' and was delighted when the mahout returned her greeting and somehow encouraged the elephant to nod its great solid head at her.

'You were missed,' Priyanka said, when Alice got back to the ashram.

Priyanka had a haughty, well-brought-up way of speaking that annoyed Alice, not for its Indian attitude but its English pretension.

The other young woman, Prithi, said nothing, but Alice knew what she was thinking.

They were her friends but not so close that she could tell them that she'd just made a new friend. They were just a little older than she was, Prithi a runaway fiancée, Priyanka a runaway bride. Told that a husband had been selected for her in an arranged marriage, Prithi had been rescued by Priyanka and had found peace here under the benign presence of Sathya Sai Baba.

Priyanka had her own story, another arranged marriage, to an abusive husband in a house with a nagging, possibly insane mother-in-law. She had suffered it for two years and then done the un-thinkable – slipped away, disgraced her parents, infu-riated her in-laws and hidden here. The ashram was her refuge. Although she was damaged, scandalous, unmarriageable, she was safe. And she had money.

Prithi also had money. She said to Alice, 'Until I was seventeen, I had no idea there were poor people in India. I thought everyone lived like us, in a big house, with servants and a driver, and a cook and all the rest of it, surrounded by flowers. I thought our servants had lots of money. Their uniforms were beautiful.'

'Your father probably bought them their uniforms,' Alice said.

'May I finish?' Prithi smiled in annoyance. 'I wanted to walk home from school one day. The other girls weren't met by a chauffeur, as I had been all my life. The driver begged me to get in. He called me on my mobile, but I refused to answer, and I walked home while the car followed me.' She folded her hands primly. 'So there.'

'I don't get it.'

'I saw how people lived. Not like us. It was quite a shocker.'

But Prithi said that she still had never been on an Indian bus or train. She had flown to Bangalore from Bombay and had not left the ashram for eight months.

So it seemed more and more to Alice like a nunnery, yet with none of the fear, no talk of salvation, nothing of sin, no rejection of the outside world; simply the pleasure of being in a safe and loving place, among happy people, where everyone was accepted. Not like an organized religion at all but perhaps like the first followers of Christ, the people who had been so moved by the Sermon on the Mount they had left their houses and families to follow the Master and to witness miracles.

Swami performed miracles, always reluctantly, which made them more startling, and always with a smile. He had a magic ring; cookies materialized in his hand for children, and sometimes money. The devotees applauded, as though at a party trick, and Alice realized they were like the earliest Christians, whose heads were turned by Christ's words and his marvels, not seeing him as a figure foretold by scripture or a human sacrifice, the Lamb of God, but a handsome man with a new voice, a beautiful spirit, a reformer, a liberator, someone who was able, in the most memorable words, to make sense of the world.

'I love Swami,' Alice told them.

'We were worried – isn't that so, Prithi?' Priyanka said. 'You have such a good education. You are so independent and strong. Such people seldom tarry here, you know.'

'I feel that we are here at the beginning,' Alice said, still thinking of the listeners to the Sermon on the Mount. 'Seeing Swami in the flesh. Hearing him at the darshan. I love watching him nod and smile as we chant the bhajans.'

'Yes, we're lucky,' Priyanka said. 'I see that life has a meaning. Even my divorce has a meaning. It allowed me to come here.'

More time passed, some weeks perhaps, and one day both women approached Alice while she was sweeping the room.

'We have something for you,' Prithi said.

She took her hands from behind her back and presented Alice with a large cloth pouch, decorated with small round mirrors sewn to it, a piece from Rajasthan, red and orange. It glittered on Alice's lap.

'It's great,' Alice said.

'Open it.'

Alice untwisted a woven cord that held it shut and saw that it contained a soft brick of rupees, held together with rubber bands. Because they were worn and dirty they seemed somehow tested and proven to be especially valuable.

'I can't take them.'

'Yes,' Priyanka said. 'You must.'

'But you don't have to keep them,' Prithi said. 'You can give them to Swami.'

'Swami doesn't want money – he says so, all the time. "Where money is asked for and offered, I have no place." I love him for that.'

'It is one of his most spiritual qualities,' Prithi said. 'But still ghee butter costs money. Pulses cost money. That broom.'

Alice was holding the broom in one hand and the chunk of money in the other. She said, 'Yes, he can buy some more brooms!'

A day or two later Alice realized what the women had done. They were helping her pay her way, giving her the money as an oblique present so as not to embarrass her. One of the devotees was always passing the hat – actually, it was a brass bowl – and the residents put money in. Alice usually slipped in a one hundred-rupee note – about two dollars. This had been noticed.

She had believed that sweeping and washing and tending to the pots of flowers and weaving garlands for Swami was enough. But no – it seemed you had to pay.

This face-saving gesture, done so sweetly, saddened her. She had come to India in a spirit of renunciation, looking to Swami – with the help of Ganesh – as an example. Stella had hindered her in her quest – she saw that after Stella had gone off with Zack. But this need for money was a surprise, because she wanted to go on living at the ashram and clearly she could only do that by getting a job, somewhere in Bangalore. Well, wasn't that why most people came to Bangalore?

'I'm looking for a phone,' Alice said to Priyanka, slightly distracted by the way Priyanka ate – using her fingertips on the chapattis but one-handed, eating with the fastidious concentration of a watch mender.

Priyanka let her fingers hover and dangle, while she looked at Alice with amazement, as though she'd asked for a forbidden thing.

'Whatever do you require a phone for?'

'The usual thing,' Alice said.

'Idle phoning is discouraged by Swami.'

'Who said it was idle?'

'Phones are frivolous, Swami says. Ashram is complete and self-sufficient. He is the only link we need.'

'Maybe I want to phone Swami,' Alice said, and she could tell that she was becoming angry in her sarcasm.

'He won't pick up.'

'I thought you had a cellphone. You mentioned it once.'

Priyanka smiled while she chewed her mouthful, then she dabbed her lips. 'I left my mobile with Daddyji. He was flabbergasted.'

'My Daddyji doesn't even know where I am,' Alice said.

'Phoning parents is discouraged by Swami.'

Alice said, 'Why am I a little sorry we had this conversation?'

And it occurred to her that had Priyanka known who and why she was planning to call, she would have been even more scolding and unhelpful.

She put on her walking shoes and sunglasses and went to the main gate – the gate-keeper saluted – and she walked along the busy road, on the broken sidewalk, stepping past the fruit vendors who were crouched on low stools, selling oranges and mangoes. She had not gone thirty yards when she saw three or four storefronts advertising telephone services – *International Calls, Best Rates, Fax and Internet Connectivity* – with lists of countries and prices per minute.

After the solitude and order of the ashram, the street – and this was right outside, just over the wall – was startling in its dirt and disorder, the hawkers crowded against the wall of the ashram, fruit sellers, people seated at small tables selling picture frames and pens and cheap watches and hair ornaments. It was a relief to see someone selling fresh flowers, a pile of marigold blossoms, but the rest of it was a bazaar of cheap merchandise. The shops that lined the road sold rubber tires and shoes and clocks and sacks of beans and rice and spices. At one storefront a man was mending shoes, at another a boy was on his knees, his forearms streaked with grease, laboring to fix a bike. The large number of pedestrians made it hard for Alice to walk, and when she dodged them to buy a bag of roasted chickpeas, cars honked at her. She thought of turning back, yet she had to make the call.

'What country, madam?' the clerk said, showing her an assortment of phone cards.

'India.' Alice handed over the business card. 'Right here. Bangalore.'

'Is mobile number, madam. Better you purchase card.'

She bought a 300-rupee card, feeling that she was being cheated – the man claimed he had nothing smaller. Could that be true?

Feeling helpless – Indians fussing around her created that illusion – she waited while the clerk dialed the number.

'Ringing, madam.' He handed Alice the phone. Once, long ago, a phone like this had sat on a small table in Alice's house: black, solid, heavy – but always a small voice issuing from it.

'This is Shan.'

That's what it sounded like, an Asiatic name but with the twanging palate of a forced American accent.

Alice was so surprised by the voice she could not respond.

'How can I help you? Is there anyone there? Hullo?'

The voice was extraordinary – nasal, the mouth wide open, the suggestion of a smile in the tone, and though it had an American sound, something unnatural subverted it, so that it was hardly human, a cartoon voice. Alice was reminded of a parrot – a mimicky voice, as if the speaker had no idea what he was saying, just uttering words in a tortured way, swallowing and gargling.

'I think I have the wrong number.'

'Who are you wishing to speak to at this time?'

The sing-song was odd, too – the whole effect so weirdly comic Alice did not put the phone down.

'I'm calling Amitabh.'

'This is Amitabh' – still, in an American accent, the name was approximate.

'I thought you were Shan.'

'I'm at work. I'm Shan at work. Who am I speaking to, please?'

'This is Alice – from the train. I wanted to talk to you about something.'

'I'm on late shift till three a.m. Can we maybe meet tomorrow?'

The voice was still bizarre. Was it really him? 'I guess so. Can you come to Whitefield?'

'Sure thing. Whitefield! Now I remember – you're the Sai Baba woman from the first AC compartment.'

'That's me,' but she thought, *Sure thing*? She saw a sign, *Vishnu Hotel and Lunch House*, and read Amitabh the address. He took it down expertly, then read it back to her.

After she hung up she kept walking, away from the ashram. It was too late to line up for the darshan – she'd be at the end of the line, at the back of the hall, Swami barely visible. She had a better idea. She felt a need to make a superstitious gesture, and so she waved down an auto-rickshaw and gave the driver the address of the elephant's stable.

She liked the side street, the quiet gloom from over-hanging trees, the archway to the courtyard stable, the sight of the elephant's hindquarters. He was snatching at hay with his trunk and stuffing it into his mouth, but when Alice approached the elephant lurched, his chain clanking, and he swung around and nodded at her.

Now she saw the mahout with a hayfork, piling the fodder near the elephant.

'*Namaste*,' Alice said, clasping her hands.

The mahout held the hayfork with his knees and returned the greeting. He then beckoned her closer.

Alice said, 'I know you have no idea what I'm saying, but thank you. I need a job, I need some money. I am here because I love this elephant.'

The mahout smiled, the elephant smiled, the odor of manure was sweetish, the stable was shadowy, cool with the aromas of drying hay.

Alice held out some roasted chickpeas for the mahout, and he took some; but instead of eating them he poked his hand towards the elephant's trunk and allowed them to be seized from his hand. The elephant swung its trunk backwards and blew the chickpeas into its mouth, and then reached for more – not to the mahout but, in a show of cleverness, lifting its trunk towards Alice and seeming to gesture with its twitching nose holes, wrinkling the pink flesh around them. A faint stink reached her from the holes at the tip of its trunk, a gust of sour breath.

'Here you go, darling.' She held the chickpeas in the flat of her hand and let the elephant scoop them up.

The mahout nodded, and went back to forking hay, the elephant to eating it; but she could see that the elephant was looking directly at her with its great round eye.

'Thank you, thank you. *Namaste.*'

The mahout waved the hayfork and Alice thought, he looks like Gandhi. She returned to the ashram refreshed, at peace, as though she'd visited a holy place.

And the next day she slipped out to meet Amitabh. He was waiting at the Vishnu Hotel and Lunch House, seated at a table, holding a cup of tea and studying his cellphone, perhaps reading a number and wondering if he should answer. There was no doubt that it was

Amitabh – smiling, fat-bellied, fleshy arms and big brown cheeks and beautiful eyes.

'Hi,' he said. 'Take a chair. This is real positive, seeing you.'

The tone of voice belonged to someone else – the words too. Yet he was smiling as he spoke – this was a novelty. His mouth was set in a grin and he was open-mouthed as he twanged at her.

'How long has it been? Like six weeks or more?' He was sipping tea, sucking it through his open mouth.

'I don't even know how long,' Alice said. 'I wanted to ask you a few things. Looks like you got the job.'

'The job, yeah' – he said *jahb*. 'I was working when you called. That's why I gave you my work name.'

'Which is?'

'Shan.'

She said, 'Would that be anything like Shawn?' – seeing it as Sean.

'You got it. Shan Harris.'

'You have two names?'

'Don't you? You sure do! It's kind of strange. My mother calls me Bapu. It means Dad!'

She said, 'Amitabh, why are you talking like this?'

'American accent? That's my job just now, at the call center. I'm a consultant – working towards being an associate.'

'For a company?'

'We service Home Depot.'

Alice had heard of such jobs, but this was the first time she was seeing an employee at close quarters. She said, 'Good news – that's great.'

Because she was thinking: His accent is grotesque,

I can do much better than that – and she smiled at the thought of operating a phone at a call center in Bangalore, fielding calls from Rye and Westchester, maybe people she knew, though she didn't know anyone who shopped at Home Depot.

Amitabh said, 'How can I offer you excellent service?'

She almost laughed, but thought better of it. She said, 'I need a job.'

'Have a cup of tea,' Amitabh said. 'Then tell me what you want to do.'

Over tea, Alice explained that she was short of money. She said that she had been an English major but was computer-savvy.

'I'm open to doing anything,' she said.

Amitabh's face gleamed at this. He savored it, working his mouth, then said, 'You got a good attitude. Plus it's my day off. Let's get a taxi.'

Waiting for the taxi, Amitabh made a call on his cellphone. When he used his thumb to end the call, he said, 'Plus you're real lucky. Miss Ghosh is interviewing today. They have a major manpower need.'

She was glad that there was no delay, that she would not have to report to the ashram and hear 'Swami doesn't approve.' As this thought turned in her mind, Amitabh asked about Swami.

'Sai Baba – is he as great as everyone says?'

'Greater,' Alice said. 'He'd be glad I was doing this. Work is worship. Are we going into Bangalore?'

'No. Electronics City. Phase Two.'

He would not shake the accent. *Electrahnics Siddy*.

It was not far, though it took more than half an hour in traffic on a dusty road of two-wheelers and auto-rickshaws, limping cows and mobs of tramping people. They turned off the main road onto a new empty road of the industrial area where there were tall glass buildings and many more roughed out in concrete, and although these looked like bombed ruins she saw that they were rising.

'This is Info-Tech,' Amitabh said. He showed his pass at the front desk and walked down a side corridor. 'I can introduce you to the head of personnel.'

He knocked at an open door and became obsequious, bowing, losing something of the accent, laughing softly, as he greeted the woman at the desk.

'Please sit down,' the woman said to Alice. 'Amitabh tells me you're looking for a position.'

'That's right.'

'Perhaps you could fill up this form and we'll see if we have anything.' She handed Alice a set of forms. 'Please take them outside.'

Alice sat in the corridor and answered the questions, filling in the blanks and elaborating on her education and previous jobs. When she had finished and handed the form to the woman, she sat and watched the woman examine the form. The woman had a solemn, unimpressed way of reading, pinching the form with her thumb and forefinger, holding it away from her face.

'I can't offer you anything permanent, but we could extend something informal. No benefits, no contract. Just a week-to-week arrangement.'

'That would suit me. Is this at the call center?'

The woman smiled. 'Not exactly. With your skill sets you could be useful in the classroom. We have lessons most days.'

'To teach . . . ?' She left the question hanging, for a space to be filled in.

'American accent and intonation.'

'I can do that.'

So she had a job, and a secret, and smiling an elephant smile, she discovered that Bangalore was not one place but two.

3

Alice knew herself to be single-minded, and successful because of it – how else to explain her *magna cum laude* at Brown, all the loans she had floated to pay tuition and, most recently, her ability to overcome Stella's defection? The face she showed the world was dominant and determined; she was reconciled to living with the personality her body suggested, the one people expected – she was heavy, with her father's features – always the pretty girl's plain friend. She had to be decisive, because she also knew that people like her got no help from anyone. She had had to learn to be the helper, the humorist, to be self-sufficient and ironic, too. She coped with that role yet she was someone else – sensitive to slights, appreciative of attention, spiritual, even submissive, more sensual than anyone imagined, yet no man had ever touched her.

With the job, her life changed; the inner Alice was released, and she was able to be two different people in the two different parts of Bangalore. That was how it seemed. But really she was the same person, using the two sides of her personality, just as perhaps Bangalore was one place with two aspects – indeed, as the elephant god, whom she esteemed rather than worshipped, had two aspects, the spiritual enabler and the fat jolly workaday elephant, spiritual and practical, as she believed herself to be.

She had made the traveler's most important discovery. You went away from home and moved among strangers. No one knew your history, or who you were: you started afresh, a kind of rebirth. Being whoever you wished to be, whoever you claimed to be, was a liberation. She wrote the thought in her diary and ended, *So now I know why people go away*.

And in between the ashram and Electronics City was the stable where the elephant was chained and the mahout lived. The elephant was more eloquent than the mahout: smiled more, was more responsive, hungrier, and hunger said so much. She visited at least once a week, usually on her way home from Electronics City. She paid the taxi driver and then lingered to feed the elephant, or just watch, and afterwards she walked back to the ashram in a better mood.

This elephant had two personalities, too. Usually the mahout welcomed Alice – in his way, a downward flap of his hand meaning, 'Come closer,' or cupping his hand to indicate 'Feed him.' But one day he made an unmistakable 'Keep off' gesture, pressing his palms at her, pushing them towards her face.

And he said an Indian word that Alice recognized, because it existed in English too. Pointing at his eye, he said, '*Musth*.'

She peered at the elephant's eye and saw that it was leaking brownish fluid, staining its coarse skin, like rusty water dripped from an old pipe. The elephant's eye was glowing, his chain clanked, he looked trapped and agitated.

'*Musth, musth*,' Alice said. Of course, the elephant was half-demented with frustrated desire, chained against venting it, lust and anger mingling in its big body and leaking out of its eye. For the first time she heard that fury in the elephant's trumpeting, and the sound of it made her step back.

The mahout was relieved. He too gave the elephant room and he forked the grass and branches very carefully into a pile that was at the limit of the elephant's reach. That the mahout with all his knowledge, and what she guessed to be his history with this animal, was so cautious, and even perhaps fearful, impressed her greatly.

That very evening she knelt and prayed to Ganesh, and chanted, *Jaya Jaya Jaya Hey Gajaanana*, reminding herself of what she had seen at the stable, the explosive elephant chained to a post.

In the morning, as always, she was an attendee at the Swami's daily darshan; and later a cleaner, a menial, a mopper, an acolyte, an arranger of flowers, a collector of rupees, her hands clasped before her.

She sat with Priyanka and helped weave garlands of marigolds to drape before the big statue of Saraswati at the edge of the pavilion.

'My personal favorite,' Priyanka said, smiling at Saraswati holding the sitar. 'Making beautiful music.'

Was it because Alice smiled that Priyanka asked her to whom she prayed?

She did not say the elephant god, Ganesh. She needed her secret. She said, 'They're all related, the Indian gods – fathers and daughters, sons and mothers, avatars and incarnations. It's a family, isn't it? I pray to the family.'

Priyanka had a way of twisting her head, contorting

herself in a way that said 'I don't believe you', and she assumed this posture of disbelief today. Looking sideways, perhaps because the answer had come so neatly. But Alice's was an Indian reply – indisputable and yet untruthful, too well-rehearsed, a little too elaborate, a little too general not to be hiding the truth. She had been hearing such replies since arriving in India.

She was well aware that Priyanka was suspicious of her. But that was all right. Alice was now used to the Indian habit of inventing the person they supposed you to be, assigning you particular traits. Alice was American, middle-class, good school, funny about food, careful with money, always with her nose in a book, a bit too quick to point out that some Indians were poor, not quick enough to venerate Swami, with a deplorable tendency to treat him as a fallible human, because Americans made a point – didn't they? – of being hard to please.

And for Alice, a lot of these devotees at the ashram were little more than cultists, even though Swami rejected any idea of its being a cult. But they had come from rigid, structured backgrounds – good families, like Priyanka's and Prithi's; they were well brought-up and had lived sheltered lives, and could say with wide-open eyes to an American, 'I had no idea there were poor people in India!'

Alice had read the books. In their adulthood, such people needed an authority figure; they needed to be with like-minded companions, they needed moral certainties, they needed a path – no, they needed *the* path. Sai Baba was a power figure, the ashram was the center of their world, they would have sat all day knitting shawls for him and been perfectly happy.

If not a cult, pretty close to one.

'As for me, I'm just curious,' Alice told herself, and she was glad she was not much like them, nor much like Stella – worldly, selfish Stella.

And she had another life, at the far side of Bangalore, Electronics City. From this vantage point she was able to keep her life at the ashram in perspective.

She had taken the job because she needed money, but she saw it was more than about money – the job kept her clear-sighted. Her notion of the devotees at the ashram as resembling cultists – that insight came to her one night at InfoTech as she saw the employees, her students, making their way from the company cafeteria. They were laughing and talking, comparing notes, whispering among themselves, one or two making calls on their cellphones, all dressed differently, all of them young, all free. They were doing what they wanted, they were independent, being paid, and hoping to get to the next level. They had supervisors but none of these bosses was an authority figure in any solemn sense. They followed company rules and protocol but they had no path except their own, they had not forsaken anything – far from it, they were embracing the world and pressing their smiling faces against it, hoping it would smile back.

Alice's sari worked in both places. It was the perfect disguise. She liked slipping out of the ashram and becoming anonymous on the busy sidewalk, then hailing a taxi. She liked moving from the comfortable decrepitude of Whitefield to the unfinished modernity of Electronics City, which sometimes seemed to her a city already glittering in decay, so many buildings under construction the place looked like an elaborate ruin. So often in India you could not tell whether a building was going up or falling down, and the construction sites were a mess, but with tall buildings here and there, the fragments of a crystal city.

And then to InfoTech, which was a compound behind a high wall, the glass tower with tall palm trees in the lobby, and the annex behind it where her classroom was located, and the ugly power plant.

'Good evening, madam. How was your day?'

Yesterday's lesson had included that catchphrase, as well as the word 'catchphrase'.

Some of the others repeated it. They were confident. The quality of poise that Alice had seen in Amitabh when they'd met on the train was a trait that all of them shared. Speaking Hindi they bowed their heads, they were deferential, they sounded elaborate and oblique and evasive. In Basic English they were direct, even blunt, certainly unsubtle. Basic English was a good telephone language: its edges had been knocked off, it was informal yet helpfully intrusive, demanding a reply.

Amitabh had proven to be the best student, the quickest learner. Any word or phrase he heard became part of his permanent vocabulary.

'It takes very little brains to learn a language,' Alice had told the students. They seemed to resent her saying this, but she insisted on it. 'Anyone can do it. Children do it. You just have to make the right noises. But what you say – that's a different story. So you can be fluent and have nothing to say. I can't teach you to be good sales people but I can give you the tools.'

All of them were altered by speaking American

English, they were given new personalities, but Amitabh was changed the most. On the train he had been a strange figure, with his obsolete words. India clung to the past, and so for all the new buildings and new money, nothing changed very much. These were the words the East India Company had brought from England hundreds of years ago, and still they were spoken and written, however dusty they seemed. Perhaps Indians used these archaic words to give themselves dignity, power, or presence, but the effect was comic.

Yet saying 'We can ramp up a solution', Amitabh underwent a personality change. 'Or we could go another rowt,' he might add, 'depending on whether you have the in-surance. Pick up a pin and make a note of this, or with one click of your mouse we could have a done deal.'

Alice smiled to think that it was all her doing. She herself said 'root', not 'rowt', for route. 'Ramp up' made her laugh. 'In-surance' and 'pin' for pen were southern but spreading. Why not hand them all over, to give these callers credibility? They often dealt with mechanical objects – nuts and bolts, metal sleeves, tubes and rods – *toobs* and *rahds*.

'I'd so appreciate it if you'd share the serial number of your appliance with me. You'll find it on the underside – that is the bottom of the appliance, stamped on a metal plate. Thank you so very much.'

And after they'd rehearsed this, in a classroom chorus, Alice said, 'The bahdum of the appliance.'

'The bahdum of the appliance!'

'Thank you so very much,' she said.

'Thank you so very much!'

The expression made her laugh, but it was American.

These students, who were known in the company as sales and technical associates, worked for a company that retailed home appliances and power tools. Manning the phones, they needed information from the person on the other end, in American, so that they could find solutions in the user's manual. Once they found the specific model and the serial number, they would try to solve the problem. They needed polite but exact ways to ask for information.

'And plus, I'd be very grateful for your attention at this point in time. Kindly turn the appliance so that the power cord is facing away from you. You will be looking at the head of the appliance, which is green in color.'

'And plus, I'd be very grateful for your attention at this point in time!' they repeated, twanging the words.

Alice surprised herself in finding pleasure teaching informal American English – not essay phrases but telephonic American. 'What I'm hearing is that your product might be defective' and 'Let's focus in on the digital messages you see on the screen' and 'Have you remembered to activate the On switch?'

Speaking in this way, with Alice's urging, the students were, even after just a few weeks, slightly different people – more confident, like Amitabh, but also friendlier and funnier, more casual, more direct. Alice smiled to think that in teaching American English she was giving them magic formulas to utter: they were getting results on the phone, helping customers, effective in troubleshooting.

And Miss Ghosh was complimentary, adding more hours to Alice's schedule and reporting that the employees at the call center were more effective in their jobs.

'We can perhaps revise your contract to reflect a month-to-month contingency,' Miss Ghosh said. 'We're chalking that in.'

Alice agreed. The money helped. Now she was paying her way at the ashram, though they asked for very little. How odd to pass from InfoTech to Sai Baba, from Electronics City to Whitefield; yet had it not been for the elephant in between, she would have been lost.

'*Musth*?' she inquired of the mahout a week after that visit when she had seen the agitated elephant beating its chained leg against the post, its eye leaking.

The mahout smiled and shook his head, and he gave her to understand – waving his open hand in the air – that he had been wrong, that it had not been *musth*. Another gesture, pointing ahead – the *musth* would come later. He welcomed her into the courtyard. The elephant nodded, seeing her, and when she gave it a handful of peanuts which it crushed and shelled with its trunk, blowing the nuts into his mouth and expelling the husks, she knew he associated her with food, and she brought more and more. She found he liked cashews. They had no shells. She brought bags of them, and fed the grateful animal and felt she had a friend.

The elephant calmed her, kept her centered – another expression she delighted in teaching the employees, who called themselves InfoTechies.

'Aapka naam ke hai?' she asked the mahout one day, having found the sentence in a Hindi phrase book.

'Gopi,' the mahout said.

Alice pointed to the elephant and said, 'Aapka naam?'

With a smile, perhaps at the absurdity of the question, the mahout said, 'Hathi.' Alice knew that this was the word 'elephant', for Hathi Pol was the Elephant Gate at the Red Fort in Delhi.

But she was glad that the animal had no name, that it was Elephant, a designation that made it seem a superior example, as though it represented all elephants.

At the ashram, wobbling her head in a knowing way, Priyanka said, 'You're proving to be a dark one.'

Alice stared at her until Priyanka smiled. All she meant, apparently, was that Alice had a secret.

'I'm working,' Alice said. 'I don't want to be a parasite here. And as Swami says, work is worship.'

'There is work, and there is work,' Prithi said, at Priyanka's side.

She was trying to be mysterious but Alice knew she disapproved of her leaving the ashram to go to an unnamed job.

'Have you ever had a job?' Alice said, and when they smiled at the thought of such an absurdity – their families were wealthy: why would they ever need to work? – Alice said, 'I've had plenty.'

Alice did not say where she worked, but when she hinted that it was in education this suggestion of uplift and intellect reassured the two women and they left her alone.

She did not reveal that she passed from the world of speculation and the spirit, and the Swami's talk of dignity and destiny, to the other world of Bangalore, of tech-support and 'skill sets', and her new students who dealt with cold calling, hot leads, and diagnostic parameters.

'How can I resolve your issues today?' was a sentence she drilled at InfoTech, but not one that Swami would ever have spoken.

'Hey, guess what?' Amitabh said to her, as she was going into the class, and did not wait for her to reply. 'I've been made Team Leader. They bumped up my pay! Thank you so very much.'

He was so different she hardly recognized him. She was well aware that in having taught Amitabh a new language she had altered his personality. At first she thought 'in many ways', and then she came to see that the alteration was profound. He was someone else speaking American. He bore no resemblance to the awkward, slightly comic, rather oblique and old-fashioned job-seeker she'd met on the train. He was radically changed from the mimic she'd met at the Vishnu Hotel and Lunch House who'd said, 'This is real positive, seeing you.' He was a new man.

Saying, 'Hey, can you spare a minute?' he was no longer the fogey. He was a big importuning brute, hovering over her and demanding an answer.

The rest of the class, thirty-seven of them, women and men, had undergone a similar transformation, and she marveled at the changes.

''Scuse me' was not the same as 'I'm sorry', and 'Huh?' or 'What?' were not the same as 'Pardon?'

It seemed to Alice that Indians were much ruder speaking American. They sounded more impatient.

Naturally confrontational, these Indians now had a language to bolster it and no longer had to rely on the subtleties of Hindi. The obliqueness of Indian English, its goofy charm that created distance, was a thing of the past. The students were, without any doubt, more familiar, even obnoxious in American. 'Can you please inform me, what is your good name, madam?' had become, 'So who am I talking to?'

And she was the teacher, the cause of it all!

She had succeeded because they needed to be direct, with a certain obnoxious control of language, as techies in the call center. They were only effective on the phone if they were listened to.

'If you'd just let me finish' was another rasping way of dominating a conversation that Alice had given them.

But Alice was regretful, for in acquiring the new language a weird adaptation had taken place: they had become the sort of Americans that Alice thought she'd left behind back in the States, and Amitabh, the quickest learner, was the best of them, which was to say the worst – her personal creation, a big blorting babu with a salesman's patter. He was full of gestures – the chopping hand, the wagging finger, even backslapping. In a country where people made a virtue of never touching each other in public, he was all hands – that also was part of speaking American.

'I gotta talk to you,' Amitabh said to Alice one day after the classroom drills. She winced at the way he said it and she cringed when he tapped her on the shoulder.

The lesson that day was concerned with useful

Americanisms for 'I don't understand.' She had drilled them with 'Sorry, I don't follow you' and 'You've lost me' and 'Mind repeating that?' And 'I'm still in the dark.'

Amitabh she knew to be a fundamentally patient and polite young man, but in his American accent, using colloquialisms, he sounded blunt and impatient. Speaking Indian English he allowed an evasion, but his American always sounded like a non-negotiable demand. It worked on the phone – well, that was the point, but in person it was just boorish.

Now Amitabh was saying, 'How about it?'

Alice smiled at his effrontery, the liberty he was taking with her, his teacher; and yet she inwardly groaned, knowing that she was the one who had given him this language – this new personality.

She said, 'It just occurred to me that I don't think I've spent enough time on please and thank you.'

'Hey, whatever,' Amitabh said, flinging his cupped hands in the air.

'No, really, Amitabh, I'm pretty busy.'

She had hoped to stop and feed the elephant – she was sure the elephant was expecting her; and yet she was overdue at the ashram. She didn't want anyone to notice her lateness. The devotees, with all the time in the world, were very punctual – often pointlessly early, making the twiddling of their thumbs into a virtue, almost a yoga position, as though to abase themselves to Swami, to please him with the obedient surrender of their will.

'There's one or two things I want to go over,' Amitabh said.

'And you want to do it now?'

'That's about the size of it,' Amitabh said.

'Maybe someone else can help you.'

'Nope. I'm focusing on yourself.'

'Not "yourself". "I'm focusing on *you*."'

'I'm focusing on you.'

'Better. But I wish you wouldn't.'

It seemed that whenever she was in a hurry or had a deadline in India, she encountered an obstruction: a traffic jam, or the sidewalk was mobbed and slowed her, or someone wanted money, or the office was closed. Or, like today, she wanted to feed the elephant and rush back to the ashram and here was Amitabh, in her face, with a question. But she had given him the convincing accent and with it, an attitude.

'The thing is,' Amitabh said, with the heavy-lidded gaze and the torpid smile he affected at his most American, 'you said you were kind of interested in seeing the gods at Mahabalipuram.'

He said *kinda* and *gahds*.

'Did I say that?'

'You mentioned the elephants on the Penance of Arjuna and the Ganesh temple.'

'I think I said Ganesh seemed the most dependable – maybe the most lovable. And the carvings of elephants there . . .'

Interrupting her, Amitabh said, 'I'll take that as a yes.'

Alice began to laugh. Had she taught him that? No – but as with other phrases he knew she might have used it in conversation. He remembered everything.

Using her laughter as a chance to interrupt again, Amitabh said, 'I know somebody, who knows somebody, who got me a couple of tickets on the so-called Super Express to Madras. You haven't been there, am I right?'

'Not yet.'

'I figured as much,' he said. 'So this is your chance to see the whole thing.'

How did he know that? Perhaps she had mentioned the elephant carvings at Mahabalipuram during one of her classes. She and Stella had spoken about visiting the shrine. One of the attractions of the ashram in Bangalore was that it was half a day by train to Madras and the famous bas-relief called the Penance of Arjuna, the temples called the Raths, one dedicated to Ganesh, all at the edge of the great hot Indian Ocean. 'That's on the list,' they said. This was before Zack had entered the picture.

'How about a trip there some weekend?'

Alice smiled at his presumption and squirmed away from his reaching hand.

'Sorry.'

'What's the problem?'

'The problem is that I'm a teacher and you're a student, and it's against the rules.'

Wagging his finger and opening his mouth wide to speak, he said, 'We're both employees of InfoTech. I'm Team Leader, full-time, and you're an associate instructor, part-time. Hey, you owe me – I got them to kick some work your way.'

'Listen, I got this job on my own merits and don't you forget it.'

'It's not about that,' he said, and shrugged. 'It's about the tickets.'

'If I wanted to go to Madras I'd pay my own way.'

She did want to go – he was reminding her of what she had planned to do; but she objected to big smiling Amitabh insisting that she go with him.

She said, 'Find someone else, please. I'm pretty busy.'

When she got to the stable and indicated to the mahout that she had brought some cashews for the elephant she could tell that he was preoccupied: he had already fed the elephant, he was just humoring her by allowing her to give the animal some nuts. But the elephant at least was grateful – forgiving, glad to see her, still smiling.

She was so late arriving at the ashram that she replayed the whole delaying conversation with Amitabh and began to hate him for his insolence. 'How about a trip there some weekend?' and 'Got them to kick some work your way' infuriated her. He now seemed to her a monster of presumption, without any grace. That night she sat in her room, ignored by Priyanka and Prithi, hating herself.

Two days later, at InfoTech, she went to Miss Ghosh to tell her how she felt. Not just her misgivings about the emphasis on the American accent, but her suspicion that with these fast learners, taking on this much language and accent, they were losing something important – some subtlety, an Indian obliqueness and charm, a fundamental courtesy.

She said that and then, feeling that she was rambling, she said, 'I'm starting to wonder whether I'm any good at this.'

Miss Ghosh said, 'I can sincerely offer assurance that you have been a resounding success.'

'I can see I've made a difference.'

'It is chalk and cheese, for which I am duly grateful.'

Miss Ghosh's Indian English and her dated anglicisms reminded Alice of how the students had once sounded. The archaic and plodding language made Miss Ghosh seem trustworthy and sensible.

'Block Four, I am thinking of,' Alice said. And she was seeing in her mind a roomful of rather shy but intelligent young people who had become a crowd of noisy Americans.

'You have worked wonders with them. They have developed a high success rate. We have taken them off Home Depot and have put them on call lists to obtain service agreements for contractors to sign up with mortgage companies in southern California. The percentage of sign-ups has been phenomenal.'

'I've been finding them familiar.'

'That worries you?'

'The rudeness does. Over-familiar, I mean.'

Miss Ghosh's head wagged back and forth. 'Rudeness will not be tolerated in any manner.'

'Some of them – the men especially – seem presumptuous.'

'How so?'

'The way they talk to me.'

'Not Mr Amitabh. He has come on very well as your protégé.'

'He's one of them.'

'He is scheduled for promotion. You would enjoin me to initiate action?'

Alice was turning *shed-jeweled* over in her mind. 'Not really. I can take care of myself.'

Miss Ghosh said, 'I think you are being modest about

your achievements. I want to show you the results of your efforts.'

No one was allowed to enter the inner part of InfoTech without a pass – a plastic card that was swiped on a magnetic strip beside the doors. Miss Ghosh got a pass for Alice and took her, swiping her way through the succession of doors, to the call center where her class worked, all thirty-seven of them, in cubicles, sitting before computer screens, most of them on the phone.

Alice had never seen the callers at work. The sight was not surprising: most business offices looked like this – people on the phone, tapping on keyboards, watching monitors. These all wore headphones and hands-free mikes that made them insectile in appearance – bulgy heads, antennae, a proboscis. But that was a passing thought.

What astonished her, overwhelmed her and even physically assaulted her, were the voices – the jangle of American accents, inquiring, pleading, importuning, apologizing.

'This is Jahn. Jahn Marris. May I speak to the home-owner?'

'Let me repeat that information . . .'

'I'm gonna need the serial number . . .'

'The mahdel number. I said, the mahdel number.'

'Are you sure this is our prahduct?'

They sounded like a flock of contending birds; even the room had a cage-like quality, the employees roosting in their narrow cubicles, like squawkers in a henhouse. Their sounds were strangely similar in harshness, as though they were all the same species of

287

bird, not hens at all, but a room full of macaws, the teeth and smiles of American voices but hardly human.

Miss Ghosh said, 'Why are you smiling?'

'I'm thinking of that line about a dog walking on its hind legs. You don't care that it's done well – you're amazed that it's done at all.'

'I'm not sure what you mean,' Miss Ghosh said, pursing her lips – she was offended. 'But this is your accomplishment.'

Miss Ghosh seemed to mean it as praise but Alice construed it as sarcasm.

4

The ashram was a retreat from the ambition and world-
liness of Electronics City. Electronics City was a refuge
from the selfish spiritualism and escapism of the
ashram. In his stable on the side street, the elephant
was balanced between them, sometimes swaying like
a prisoner, now and then the whole of its head and
trunk painted in colored chalk, designs of whorls and
flowers. One day the elephant wore a brass bell on a
heavy cord; when the mahout encouraged Alice to ring
it the elephant nodded and lifted its great head and
stamped its foot, its leg as thick as a tree. He knows
me, Alice told herself.

And in her traveling from one to the other, the
journey in a taxi or an auto-rickshaw was a weird
reminder of another India, of crowds and traffic and
skinny cows vying with cars, and people – thousands
of them – walking in the road carrying bundles. The
whole of it lay in a dust cloud during the day and was
eerily lighted at night, the dust-glow like the soft edges
of an incomplete dream, lovely to look at but at times
it gagged her.

Hers was a divided life, but shuttling among these
places she thought of the original idea of keeping the
ashram as a base, and traveling from there to the nearer
cities of Mysore and Madras, just to see the sights. That
had been the plan she'd made with Stella. Without

Stella, Alice felt that a trip to the coast to see Mahabalipuram would be a pleasure, especially now that she'd found a friend in the elephant. Her only hesitation was that Amitabh had reminded her of it. It annoyed her that he knew of her desire to see the temple by the sea – she was cross with herself for having mentioned it. Probably she had casually said something to someone in the class – 'You're from Madras? I've always wanted to go to Mahabalipuram.' But that was unlike her, because she made a point of never telling anyone the things she yearned for, since those were the very things that must never be revealed; speaking about them was the surest way of destroying them.

This irritated memory convinced her that she must go. She asked Priyanka and Prithi if they wanted to take the trip.

'I've never been on an Indian train and I don't intend to start now,' Priyanka said.

In the same reprimanding tone, Prithi said, 'We feel our place is here with Swami.'

That was another disturbing aspect of the ashram, the notion that the female devotees were like old-fashioned wives of Swami.

'I see this trip as a kind of pilgrimage,' Alice said, appealing to their venerating side.

'Isn't this enough for you?' Prithi said.

'This is your home,' Priyanka said.

Alice said, 'I'll find my own way of going.'

That casual remark was one she went on regretting, because its brashness she feared would attract bad luck or misinterpretation, as over-confidence often seemed to. And why? Because such confident certainty helped people remember your words and want to hold them against you.

For reassurance, she paid the elephant a visit, and in the course of fifteen or twenty minutes she emptied a big bag of cashews into the pink nostrils of its trunk, contracting and inquiring and vacuuming the nuts from her hand. It was a marvel, and it gave her strength. No wonder the first Central Asians worshipped great gilded bulls, and the earliest Hindus the smiling elephant Ganesh. A powerful animal was a glory of the natural world and such a suggestion of strength and innocence, so god-like, it seemed to link heaven and earth.

Instead of going to Bangalore Cantonment Station, which was near the ashram, Alice took a taxi to Bangalore City, so as to keep her plans secret. When she showed her passport as an ID at the Booking Hall, the clerk asked her if she was paying in American dollars.

'I could.'

'Upstairs. International booking for foreigners.'

'What's the advantage?'

'Quota is there.'

A better seat, in other words. Alice went upstairs, where she found a young bearded man bent over a low table, filling out a form. His backpack was propped against a pillar.

'Do I have to fill out one of those?'

'A docket, yeah.'

Australian – or perhaps a Kiwi, she could not tell them apart, though they could identify each other in an instant. She found a form, filled it in with as much information as she could muster, then brought it to the ticket window.

'Me go Madras, in a week or so. One person only.'

'We have four trains daily. Super Express is fastest day train. Which day had you in mind?'

The man's fluent reply was a reproach to her clumsy and patronizing attempt at broken English.

'Say the twenty-ninth.'

The man tapped his computer and peered at the screen.

'Down-train, departure is seven-thirty in the morning, arrival Chennai Central at two p.m., give or take. What currency are you proffering?'

Alice paid in dollars, a little more than five, which she counted into the man's hand, and received her change in rupees, with a freshly printed ticket.

'Have a nice day,' the man said.

She smiled at him, grateful for his efficiency, his effort to please, the accent even, which seemed like a favor to her, the man being himself.

But it wasn't a pleasure trip to the coast, as it had probably seemed to the clerk. She had told Priyanka and Prithi that the journey was more in the nature of a pilgrimage, and so it was, to Mahabalipuram. The elephant carvings on the wall and the great rocks at the Penance of Arjuna awaited her. It was not a comfortable summer-camp-like place, protecting her, as the ashram was, Swami in charge, the devotees like cultists and counselors, but rather a quest. She was not looking for shelter and ease; she sought revelation and inner peace. Stella had found an easy option with Zack. The devotees at the ashram were complacent in their piety, as the workers at InfoTech were boringly ambitious, and as for their mimicry – putting their education and achievement to use by making phone calls to the United States, something American housewives and college students had done as part-time workers in the past – these Infotechies were making a career.

It is not my career, Alice vowed. She was sad that the employees were satisfied by so little, but of course if they asked for more, if they demanded to be fairly paid, they would not have jobs.

She told Miss Ghosh that she would be taking a week off.

Miss Ghosh made an astonished face, her lovely dark eyebrows shooting up. 'You have applied for leave?'

'I guess you could say that's what I'm doing now.'

'This is rather sudden. We must have ample notification.'

Alice smiled at her, gladdened that Miss Ghosh was confounded.

'I am a casual worker, as you said. I can be dropped from the roster at any time, without prior notice. I have no medical benefits. I'm not even paid very well.' She smiled again, to allow what she said to sink in. 'And you tell me that I am obliged to give you ample notification?'

'We take a dim view of irregular shed-jeweling practices.'

'It's called a vacation. I haven't had one.'

The woman had spoken to her in the tones of a headmistress, and it was odd how quickly the tone had changed from the other day. Just when you thought you had a friend in India you looked up and saw a rival.

'The normal procedure is that one builds up leave over time.'

'But I'm casual labor, and on the lowest pay scale.'

The woman, Miss Ghosh, merely stared at her.

'So I guess I owe you everything and you owe me nothing.'

'May I remind you that this is a company and not a charitable institution. What if everyone did what you are proposing to do?'

'I don't believe this. Does this mean you're refusing me permission to take a week off?'

'What it means,' Miss Ghosh said, picking up a pencil and tapping its point on her green blotter, ' is that because of the precipitate nature of your request for departure I cannot guarantee that your job-slot will still be vacant on your return.'

This was the same grateful woman who had said, 'You have worked wonders' and 'I think you are being modest about your achievements.'

'What is your purpose in this holiday?'

'Excuse me?'

'Where are you going, may I ask, and who with?'

Alice said with a hoot of triumph, 'With all respect, I don't understand how that is any of your business.'

And she knew in saying that, in seeing Miss Ghosh's face darken – the prune-like skin around her sunken eyes, the way Indians revealed their age; the eyes themselves going cold – that she had burned a bridge.

Things went no better at the ashram. She did not need to seek permission to leave – after all, she was a paying guest. Yet when she broke the news to Priyanka who, because she spoke Hindi, held a senior position as a go-between and interpreter with the ashram staff, Priyanka became haughty and said in the affected way she used for scolding, 'I am afraid that Swami will not be best pleased.'

'It's only a week.'

'Swami is not happy to see people using his ashram as a hostel, merely coming and going, willy-nilly.'

'One week,' Alice said, and thought, I have never heard an American utter the phrase willy-nilly.

'But you are requesting check-out.'

'I'm not requesting check-out, as you put it. I just don't see any point in my paying for my room and my food if I'm not here.'

Priyanka turned sideways in her chair and faced the window. She said, 'If you like, I will submit your request. You will have to apply in writing, in triplicate. I will see that your request is followed up. But I'm not hopeful of a positive result.'

'Well, what's the worst that can happen? I'll leave my backpack in the storeroom and get it when I come back. And I'll hope there's a room available.'

'Ashram can't assume responsibility for your personal property, as though we are left-luggage at a station. This is a spiritual community.'

Alice said, 'Swami has personal property. People give him money. He has a house. He has a big car. He has another house in Puttaporthy. Are you kidding me?'

Priyanka pursed her lips and said in a stern and reprimanding way, 'Swami is our father and teacher. It is not for us to question him. He is the embodiment of love, he is a vessel of mercy.'

'Then obviously such a paragon of virtue won't have

the slightest problem with anything I say or do. He'll forgive me and give me his blessing.'

As soon as she said it she realized it sounded too much like a satire of Swami. Priyanka fell silent. Alice knew she'd gone too far.

Another bridge in flames. She went to see her last friend in Bangalore. The elephant looked miserable. Its leg dragged at the chain, and then she saw the stain running beneath his eye, gleaming on his rough hide. The mahout Gopi clasped his hands and with pitying eyes urged Alice to back away.

She boarded the Super Express to Madras in a mood of triumphant farewell. Although Priyanka had said it was impossible for her to leave her bag behind, Alice found one of the devotees willing to lock it in the store-room. She knew Priyanka was being destructive. Perhaps she saw that she was being left behind. Whose fault was that? She was the one who refused to travel on Indian railways. Alice was leaving Bangalore, the ashram, and the job at Electronics City, but she was well aware of her slender resources. Eventually, she might have to return and negotiate and be humble, but she hoped not.

The uncooperative people of the past few days only strengthened her, as Stella had done. I'll show them, she thought. I don't need them.

Though these Indians were difficult, India was not hostile, it was indifferent, a great hot uncaring mob of trampling feet in an enormous and blind landscape, damaged people scrambling on ruins. But why should anyone care about me? The country was so huge and crowded that if anyone seemed to care – to try to sell her something, as the hawkers were doing now in the train – it was because she was a foreigner and probably had money.

'*Nahi chai hai*,' she had learned to say. Leave me alone.

She had come to understand what the solitary long-distance traveler eventually knows after months on the road – that, in the course of time, a trip stops being an interlude of distractions and detours, pursuing sights, looking for pleasures, and becomes a series of disconnections, giving up comfort, abandoning or being abandoned by friends, passing the time in obscure places, inured to the concept of delay, since the trip itself is a succession of delays.

Solving problems, finding meals, buying new clothes and giving away old ones, getting laundry done, buying tickets, scavenging for cheap hotels, studying maps, being alone but not lonely. It was not about happiness but safety, finding serenity, making discoveries in all this locomotion and an equal serenity when she had a place to roost, like a bird of passage migrating slowly in a sequence of flights. The famous swallows that summered in Siberia, then wintered in the Zambesi Valley – they weren't taking trips, travel was an aspect of their extraordinary survival; they never lingered anywhere for long and yet the itinerant nature of their lives, their quest for food, had made them strong. The distances they flew were legendary but their lives were made up of short economical flights to breed and then move on. She wanted to become that bird.

She smiled, seeing that what had happened by accident to her was a gift, a further ripening of her personality. The jaunts in Europe hadn't done it, the experience of India had. By degrees she had been moved farther and farther from the life she'd known into a new mode of existence, as though soaring upward and finally, after some buffeting, moving with certainty onward, alone, no longer disturbed, in an orbit of her own, freed from her past, her unreliable friend, even her family, and liking the idea that the future would be like this – stimulated by the random lyricism of chance events, of good days and bad days.

Not a journey then anymore, not an outing or an interlude, but seeing the world; not taking a trip, not travel with a start and a finish, but living her life. Life was movement.

How had it happened? She guessed that it had come about by being alone, the circumstance Stella had forced upon her. She did not depend on anyone, certainly not a man. By earning the money she'd needed and, oddly, by being exploited, like most working people on earth; by being disappointed, abandoned, taken for granted, she had become strong. The elephant was an example, chained because he was powerful; becoming more powerful because he was chained. Released from that chain he would flap his ears and fly.

Her illnesses had given her heart. Needing a tooth pulled on her way through Turkey she'd found a woman dentist, and after a period of recovery the problem was solved. She did not tell her family until afterwards. The flu she'd picked up in Tblisi, the twisted ankle in Baku, and the bumpy flight to Tashkent, the plane's germ-laden air, the clammy days in Bukhara, and at last the flight to India – even Stella's illnesses, which she'd ministered to – all these had given her confidence, because she'd overcome them. You fell sick, you got well, then healthier afterwards. You didn't go home or call Mom because you'd caught a cold. You paused and cured yourself and continued on your way, stronger than before.

This is my life, Alice thought on the train to Madras – a good life, of my own making, all the decisions are mine. And here is my journey – a five-dollar seat, a ten-dollar hotel, a one-dollar meal – at this rate I can live for a month without working again.

The man with the narrow pushcart sold her lunch: rice, a chapatti, some dhal and green beans in a plastic dish, a pot of yogurt, some curried potato – perfect. Thirty rupees, which was seventy-five cents. And eating it, studying her thrift, she smiled and thought, I can go on and on.

She had enough money; the country was poor, the cost of living low. I'll be fine. She made a mental note to write a postcard home – not a letter, but just a few sentences, to say hello and to give no information, to show she did not need them.

This was what travel meant, another way of living your life and being free.

She began to read another Indian novel, much praised, by an Indian woman who lived in the States. Was this merely sentimentality? The book did not speak to her; the problem with it and the others she'd read was that they did not describe the India she had encountered, or the people she met. Where were these families? The novels described a tidier India, full of ambitions, not the India of pleading beggars or weirdly comic salesmen, or people so pompous they were like parodies.

As she was reading, the man in the adjoining seat started a conversation, interrupting her, but he was friendly, a Jain, he said, who would not eat a potato because they were crawling with living creatures.

'Full of germs and organisms,' he said.

'Not good to eat,' she said, trying to be helpful.

'No – good. But I must not take lives.'

Didn't want to kill the germs! Where was the book in which he appeared?

'So what do you eat?'

'Pulses. Beans. Curd. Also greens.'

'I get it,' she said.

'And later, when I am a bit older, I shall renounce the world and go hither and thither, barefoot, as my father did, in his dotage. Just wandering with no possessions, eschewing the material world.'

'I think I'm doing that now,' Alice said.

The man was corpselike, almost skeletal, a faster and an abstainer, even now mortifying his flesh. He smiled with too many teeth, a skull's smile. He didn't believe her, but that didn't matter. Another aspect of her freedom was that she didn't feel a need to explain her life or justify what she'd done.

'My father became a saint,' the man said.

He showed her a snapshot of a gaunt, bearded man, with a shawl over his narrow shoulders, carrying a walking stick.

'I will do likewise,' he said. 'My children will look after my wife.'

Poor woman, Alice thought – why can't she be a

saint? But she smiled and returned to her book, and found that she was unable to hold her head up. The book was a soporific. She was soon asleep in the overheated compartment, the sun pressing through the window burning one side of her face. She dreamed of sleeping by a fire, the noisy train creating in her dream a rumbling night.

When she woke up the Jain man was gone and in his place was Amitabh, as strange as if he had been shifted from her dream, and just as shocking and insubstantial.

She made a sound, an involuntary gasp – she couldn't help it. Amitabh waggled his head, as though pleased by her discomfort, a smile of satisfaction. He sat facing her, looking smug and ludicrous in a white long-sleeved shirt and dangling gray necktie.

'How did you get here?'

'Take a guess.' She hated his drawling accent, all the syllables in his nose, and what a nose. 'I have friends in lowly places.'

5

He was staring at her with the dumb frankness of a big hungry animal contemplating something tiny and edible. His gaze tugged at her face, she felt it on her cheek, and his leer lurking first on the upper part of her body and then her legs, lingering at her feet, flashing upward again at her hair, as though she didn't know. She kept her attention at the window to count the passing stations. She felt with disgust that he was regarding her with his mouth, his wet parted lips, his prominent teeth, the wet tip of his tongue just showing in a witless way.

At their first meeting on the other train months ago she'd found his bulky body a big hopeless thing, like a sack he stuffed food into; but now she found it absurdly over-large, even monstrous, refusing to obey her, obstinate and persistent like those eyes, that mouth.

At last, very softly but with unmistakable firmness, she said, 'I want you to go away and leave me alone.'

'I am holding a ticket. This is my assigned seat.'

She caught a glimpse of his mouth again, his tongue bulging against his teeth. He was fatter than when she'd last seen him. His size made him seem smug and immovable.

Alice sighed and prayed for a station and was reproached by what she'd thought earlier about being free – mocked, but glad she hadn't written it in her journal.

'The Sai Baba people don't like you at all,' he said.

'That's not true.'

'It is a fact. They believe you're selfish.'

It stung her, for though she denied it again she knew there was some truth in what he said.

'You look at India and see people everywhere and it seems like a mob,' he said. 'But it's not – it's like a family. We know each other. There are no secrets in India. Hey, this isn't China! Everything is known here. And where a *ferringi* is concerned it's all public knowledge.' He was smiling at her; he opened his mouth to laugh, and she got a whiff of the hot stink of his breath. 'It's funny how people come here from overseas – Americans, like you – and don't realize how we are in constant touch with each other. We're always talking, you have no idea what we're saying. Because we speak English so proficiently you have no need to learn Hindi. We know what's going on!'

Alice had vowed not to listen to him nor to follow his argument and yet she was intimidated by what he said – understood it in spite of herself.

'Please leave me alone,' she said.

'Give me a chance.'

She was so disgusted by his saying *gimme* she did not reply.

'I can help you.'

She prayed for a station so that she could see how far it was to Madras.

He read her mind, and that frightened her. He said, 'This is Tiruvallur. Twenty more minutes to Madras. Not far.'

She slid her train ticket she'd used as a bookmark

and palmed it. The arrival time was printed on it, 14.45.

'See? I'm right.' He was smiling again. 'And I'm going back with you. You can ignore me, but we'll be sitting right here, day after tomorrow.'

She was suddenly angry. She said, 'It's against the law for private information to be given out. Your friend at the ticket counter is going to be in big trouble.'

'Alice, want to know something? Huh?'

She went hot again with anger. She hated him; she feared she might cry, not from sadness but with frustration at his spoiling something she'd looked forward to, and paid for. He had no right to force himself on her.

He was still smiling and said, 'A lot of people in India think it should be against the law for women to be walking around alone. Wearing shorts! They think it's immoral.'

'Then they have a problem,' she said, and became self-conscious, because she was wearing shorts.

'Alice' – she hated his using her name – 'listen, most things that people do in India are against the law. That's how we survive. We're too poor to obey the law. You can bribe anyone, you can do anything if you have money. That's why we hate foreigners. We know they always bend the rules, too, just like us except they always get away with it.'

Against her will he had gotten her attention. She found herself listening to him and was disgusted by his logic and wanted to stop listening.

'Hey, but not me. I don't think like that. I know that foreigners have given us a lotta investment. My job, for one. I'm real grateful. I got so much to be thankful for.'

That last sentence in his American accent, mimicry from one of her own lessons, turned her stomach. She got up and went to the door of the compartment, but when she slid it open she could not move. A man in a gray uniform was standing inches away from her, the conductor.

'Chennai coming up, madam.'

'This man,' she said, gesturing at Amitabh, but without turning her head, 'this man is pestering me.'

'Passenger making nuisance, madam?'

'He is talking to me.'

The conductor spoke in Hindi – perhaps Hindi, how was she to know? – and his tone was familiar and almost friendly. Amitabh replied, as though bantering, exactly as he had described earlier, like a family member.

'Making unwelcome advances, madam?'

The conductor seemed unconvinced; it was like a conspiracy.

'No. But I wish he were sitting somewhere else.'

The conductor beckoned with his hand-puncher for Amitabh's ticket, which he examined.

'Passenger is holding valid ticket for this place, madam.'

'Never mind,' she said. She grabbed her bag and squeezed past him. She made her way to the end of the coach, where the vestibule door was open to the trackside.

The clicking of the tracks slowed, the wall of a culvert was visible, and soon the backs of houses, laundry hanging on poles protruding from windows, then there came the echoing of clattering wheels and a sudden muffled rumble as the train drew into the station.

She leaned out the door and hopped off before the train came to a stop, and so she stumbled slightly and almost fell, drawing the attention of the bystanders, mostly porters in red shirts and ragged turbans. She hurried down the platform, following the exit signs, to the front of the station, where she was set upon by frantic men.

'Taxi, madam!'

'Taxi, taxi!'

They fought each other, they struggled to be seen by her. They had hot frenzied eyes and red-stained teeth.

'I'm looking for the bus,' she said, pushing through them.

'Where going?'

'Hotel, hotel!' another man was chanting.

'Bus. Mahabalipuram.'

'Take taxi, madam. Special price.'

She kept walking through the mob, resolute, yet fearing that someone would touch her.

'Bus is not there,' a voice said into her ear, mocking her. 'Bus station is Mylapore side. I take you. Taxi just here.'

'Oh, God.'

She turned to escape this man and saw a crush of men in ragged shirts watching her and blocking the way. The heat here was heavy with humidity. Her clothes clung to her. Her face was already wet with perspiration. She wiped her face with her forearm and was bumped by the man saying, 'Taxi.'

'Fifty rupees, madam.'

'Forty,' she said.

'Okay, forty-five.'

A dollar. He hurried in a new direction, while she followed, the other men falling back. He led her into the glare of the sun, a parking lot, and not to a taxi but to an auto-rickshaw. It was too late for her to change her mind – she needed to get away from this station immediately.

She was glad for the breeze in her face, but the driver was talking incomprehensibly and sounding his buzzing horn; she was stifled by the fumes of the other vehicles, and jostled by the sudden braking. At last he bumped through a gateway where, among food sellers and people with suitcases, she saw rusted and brightly painted buses parked in bays, facing a low building.

'Bus to Mahabalipuram,' she said to a man sitting on a crate.

The man was eating peanuts out of a twist of newspaper. His mouth was full, his lips flecked. He pointed to a bus.

'Where buy ticket?'

He swallowed and chewed again and said, 'Ticket on bus.'

She walked quickly to the bus he had indicated and was relieved when she found a seat. Within minutes – anxious minutes for her – the bus filled with passengers carrying bags, some men with children in their arms, weary-looking women in saris, boys in baseball caps. Sooner than she expected, the bus shuddered and reversed out of its bay, and slowly turned, and swayed and banged through the gateway.

The bus was over-heated and made of loud metal, and when its sides flapped and clanked it seemed like a big old-fashioned oven with people cooking inside it, too many of them, pressed together, sputtering and dripping. Alice's discomfort verged on physical pain, but the sight of pedestrians out the window jostling on the sidewalk and the density of traffic made her glad she was inside this contraption rather than at risk in the street. All she had to do was relax and practice the yoga breathing she'd learned at the ashram, and before long – a couple of hours, a woman told her – she'd be at the temple by the sea, safe among elephants.

'You are going to . . . ?' the same woman asked, in the open-ended way of the Indian question.

'Mahabalipuram,' she said. 'Elephants.'

The woman smiled, and Alice was reassured. She was happier among women and here one was beside her, one in front, one squatting in the aisle; she felt their soft maternal bodies as protective. She closed her eyes, she inhaled deeply, she held her breath for a count of five, exhaled and breathed again. The bus stopped and started, toppling each time, the scrape of the brakes, the sucking of the doors opening and closing, smacking the rubber on the frame – all that was like breathing too, the labored breathing of a big overworked machine. More people got on, few got off: the bus was packed, it grew even hotter and now it was lumbering through a residential district, the dirty windows dazzled by the sun that shot from between the old buildings, honking every few seconds, and still Alice breathed and kept her eyes shut and was aware of the sun from the way it reddened her eyelids, and the warmth on her face gave her a sunbather's fixed smile.

When the bus began to roll on a straight road, the engine coughing, its tin plates flapping at its sides, somehow this unimpeded stretch induced her to open her eyes. She took another breath, looked up forward and saw Amitabh. He was holding a clear plastic bottle and swigging from it.

'Wadda?' he said.

Beyond the shock of seeing him, she was insulted and even felt violated by his accent. Now she hated hearing him speak English in that exaggerated American way. The very nuances she hated most were the ones she had taught him. In Bangalore she had learned that the most irritating traits of a person are the imitative ones, especially those you had yourself, when you looked at someone and saw a distorted image of yourself, the misery of teachers.

The bus was full. Amitabh, so top-heavy, gasping in his white wilted long-sleeved shirt, could hardly stand, and although he was speaking in his grating accent to her, his voice was mostly drowned out by the babble of the passengers, two screaming babies, the laboring of the bus's chugging engine, its oddly bronchial brakes, the banging of its loose metal doors and somewhere at the back the repeated clatter of a metal flap that made the bus sound like a tin box shaking down the road.

Most of the time Amitabh moved his mouth and smiled but Alice heard little except the din of the bus, and there was something smothering, deadening to her senses, in the smell of the sweating humans on board.

Now, outside the bus, every bit of the roadside looked safe to her – the shop fronts, the bungalows with their verandas, the rickshaws, the taxis, the fields of wheat. But if she got off at any of these shops – which were less and less frequent – he would get off too; and as long as she stayed on board, so would he.

Protected by the women around her, she drowsed and only woke – jerking upright, as though someone had slapped her – as the bus came to a halt, huffing, its abrupt silence as provocative as its noise had been. So soon? Her fears of arrival made her shrink in her seat.

'Are we there?' she asked the woman in the next seat.

The woman clawed at her long trailing braid and made no reply.

'Pit stop,' Amitabh said.

He was staring at her from between a crush of passengers, his fat face tightened in a smile, his tie rucked up and twisted against a child's damp head.

Because he was standing in the aisle he was among the first to get off. Alice waited until everyone else had left and then she did some yoga breathing and stepped out.

A crowd of people were pushing against each other at the counter of a roadside shop, reaching to be served, and some drifting away held bottles and plastic cups. Alice saw a hunkered-down woman breastfeeding a baby. She envied her concentration, her secure posture close to the ground, and had a great longing to change places with her. The woman had flung the shawl of her sari over her head so that it covered her and sheltered the baby, and she squatted in this silken tent of serenity unseen by anyone else.

She was afraid to look for Amitabh – she didn't want to see his face. But nearer the shop, against her will, she got a glimpse of the fat man holding two bottles of brown soda and she knew that one was for her.

He put them on the counter to rummage in his pocket for money. As soon as he turned aside and took his eyes off her, Alice went quickly to the far side of the bus, concealing herself from him.

A man leaning against the bus – this was the shady side – put his face up to hers, startling her. He had wild hair and a torn, fluttering, untucked shirt.

'Taxi?'

'Mahabalipuram,' she said. 'How much?'

His face went waxen in calculation, mute yet tremulous, his mouth pressed shut, the numbers vibrant on his tongue. Alice knew that look – an Indian guessing not at the value of something but at what a foreigner would pay.

'Three hundred rupees only,' he said.

'One hundred,' she said.

'Cost of petrol,' the man said, his voice becoming a whine as he bent over, assuming an insincere groveling posture to plead.

'Okay, let's go,' she said, and thought: I'm stupid, trying to escape and bargain at the same time. The man looked crushed. She said, 'Let's go,' and gestured, and he pointed to his parked car.

The man was wiggling the key and tramping on the accelerator as she got into the back seat. There was more room in front but she wanted some distance from this wild-haired driver. The car stank, the seats were torn, it was a jalopy; she prayed for it to start. After a gargling and clacking hesitation there was a powerful swelling of engine noise and the man pulled at the steering wheel with his skinny hands.

She did not dare to look back until they were on the road and traveling fast. Then she risked it and saw the shop, the parked bus, the gathering of passengers in a clearing of yellow dust by a shop. The road was empty and straight, lined by tufts of discolored grass.

'How far is it?' she asked.

'Far is it,' the man said.

'How many miles – kilometers?'

'Kilometers,' the man said.

He had numbers, he knew 'cost of petrol', but apart from that he had no English. He was simply barking back her own words.

'Mahabalipuram?' she asked.

'Mahabalipuram.'

But the speed made her hopeful, the clear road, the fact that she had slipped away from Amitabh. And she did not really need to know the distance. She had tried to speak to him mainly to assess his friendliness, sending out a signal, hoping it would resonate.

'You live here?' she asked, trying again.

He did not reply, he was shaking his head, pretending he had understood. She saw a small portrait of Sai Baba fixed to the dashboard, encircled by plastic flowers.

'Sai Baba,' she said. 'Me go darshan – Sai Baba – Bangalore.'

Even this broken English didn't work, and now she saw why. He was talking on a cellphone, holding it against his right ear, seeming to conceal it. He was mumbling in a language she took to be Tamil, rolling, bubbling words, like someone talking under a fizzing spigot in a narrow shower stall.

'Who are you talking to?'

He slipped the phone into his shirt pocket and said confidently, 'You talking to.'

He seemed dim but he was driving fast, with conviction. The car was not a taxi, just a rattletrap with ripped seats, but it was moving. The man's indifference to her, the way he was holding the wheel, caused Alice to consider her options, It would be foolish to continue on the road to Mahabalipuram. Amitabh would find her there. Give up the Penance of Arjuna, she thought; never mind the elephants, the animals, the grottoes, the temples, the carvings. Only one thing mattered.

'Stop,' she said. 'Stop! Do you understand?'

He kept driving. He seemed to be smiling in concentration.

'I want you to turn back.'

Nothing.

'Go Madras. I pay you. Three hundred. Please stop.'

Then he leaned and looked at Alice in the face – or was he looking behind her out the back window?

'Turn back now,' she said sharply, and thumped the broken seat.

The man did not react at once, but after a few moments, the time it took Alice to draw three long yoga breaths, he slowed down and veered to the side, struggling to control the car, his skinny arms fighting the shakes of the steering wheel, the tires bumping on the large loose stones on the shoulder of the main road.

He slowed some more, toppling thick tussocks of grass past a sign advertising a brand of toothpaste. Then he swung a hard left into a road that Alice saw only when he entered it. At last, she thought. The road was pinched by high grass on either side, a strip of grass in the middle, a country lane.

'Where are we going?'

He said something, gabbling, seeming to reprimand her: in this out of the way place he had taken charge. They all seemed to do it when she least expected it, not just Indian men, but Priyanka too. They would chatter and then all at once they would go dark; they'd turn, they'd become strangers, and she'd think, Who are you? and become angry and frightened. It had just happened again.

And then, ahead, she saw the big gray creature, like a piece of strange architecture, but moving, becoming a bizarre vehicle – the hindquarters of an elephant, filling the road. Amazing – she smiled and relaxed. It seemed a benign presence. The taxi driver slowed behind it and kept his distance. He could not pass it, did not even honk his horn, just drove at the slow speed of the elephant's deliberate plodding pace as he dropped his round feet on the road, big feet yet he picked his way forward with grace.

Alice was happy. She smiled at the great slow creature and sat back, watching the flicking of its tail, the brush, the wide dusty rump.

The elephant helped her see that the daylight was waning, the sky was bluey-green but the road was in darkness, the sun setting behind this tall grass.

The driver spoke a word, it sounded like 'bund', and he reacted, twisting in his seat, as though he heard something that was not audible to her. This had happened to her elsewhere in India, an Indian hearing something, saying, 'Listen,' making her feel deaf, because she heard nothing and only felt foreign.

She was still looking hard at the elephant when the driver stopped the car and switched off the engine.

'Where are we?' she said, and suddenly overcome by apprehension she got out of the car and slammed the door. She gave him the money she had been clutching. 'I don't trust you!'

The driver was not perturbed. He tucked the money in his shirt pocket with the phone. He was not even looking at her. He was looking past her, at the road they'd just traveled down. She saw the elephant had gone, and felt a pang, as though it had not walked away but had simply vanished, evaporated from her sight. She walked a little, heard a sound, and saw the car.

From his window the man spoke the word again, and she realized he was saying, 'Husband.'

He started the car, jerked it into the center of the road, and drove away in the direction the elephant had gone.

The other car was reversing but someone had gotten out of it, Amitabh, now advancing on her slowly, his white sleeves gleaming in the shadowy dusk, and seeming to fill the road, as the elephant had done.

'Hey, would I hurt you?' he said.

6

Now she had woken, and in the bad light of a dirty littered room in which she sat, wrapped in a gown, the mustached man was seated across the desk from her. He was holding a dark brittle-looking piece of paper, thick with smudged blue handwriting – like an ancient document from a vault. But she recognized it as a carbon copy of her statement, which she had dictated to the policeman earlier in the evening, after the nurse had examined her. She was cold, she was sad, she was someone else now.

'Just one or two questions,' the man said.

Alice sat feeling indistinct; part of her body was missing, she'd suffered an amputation – a portion of her mind, her torso where she'd been touched, the arm she'd used to defend herself. She was a shattered remnant of herself, the rest of her had been shivered away in the darkness, and she sensed those missing parts of herself as phantoms, numbed and useless, mere suggestions of physicality, as amputees spoke of a cut-off limb. She remembered his fingers and his face and she felt like wreckage.

Yet this man was smiling at her as though she was still whole.

'You say here that the alleged assailant is known to you?'

'He was in my class in Bangalore. A call-center English class.'

'And you know him by name?'

'He was my student.'

'He was traveling with you.'

'Following me,' Alice said. 'Stalking me.'

'When did you realize this happenstance?'

'As I said.' She yawned, she was weary, she had written it all. 'On the train from Bangalore.'

'Yet you persisted traveling in his company?'

Alice said, 'You said one or two questions.'

'We need to clear up these discrepancies.'

'What discrepancies? He stalked me. He chased me. He was on the bus. When I tried to get away he somehow got the phone number of the taxi I was in and he followed me.'

'You provided no details of the taxi.'

'He must have told the taxi driver to leave. I didn't see the license plate.'

'Yet you're sure you saw his taxi?'

'Of course. How else could he have gotten there?'

'You might have arrived together. It is rather a remote spot.'

'His taxi followed mine,' Alice said.

The man's obstinate finger was poking the paper. 'All taxis in this state are required to be in possession of a numbered disk, displayed on dashboard, also on rear of car. Can be on the wing. You have omitted this detail.'

'I was frightened. It was dark. I didn't see anything. I don't understand why you're asking me these questions.'

But she did understand. The man was insinuating that she was lying, that she had traveled with Amitabh and, this being India, she being foreign, was behaving in a way no Indian woman would dare to.

'My statement is the truth.'

'But there are certain significant omissions. Full and complete statement is required.'

'What omissions?'

He held the flimsy page trembling in his slender fingers. He said, 'Relationship to accused, first of all, is omitted. Traveling arrangement is omitted. What taxi or taxis? You say you were going to Mahabalipuram yet you were found in Chingleput district.'

The man looked up at her. He seemed too young to be so intrusive and so severe.

'An Indian woman would not travel alone with someone she distrusted. She would not travel alone, full stop.'

'Haven't you noticed,' Alice said, intending to be insulting, 'I'm not an Indian.'

The man adjusted his posture, shuffled papers on the desk, found one he wanted, studied it, tapped one line, and said, 'We have the results of your medical examination. It is noted that there is no sign of injury.'

'He raped me,' Alice said, choking slightly on the word, on the verge of tears.

'Yes, I see you assert that here,' the man said.

'He used his finger,' she said softly.

The man made a note and frowned. He said blandly, 'Unless and until that is proven this is an open case.'

'When are you going to arrest him?'

'When we have some inkling of his whereabouts we will do so with dispatch.'

'"Inkling of his whereabouts"? What's the matter with you? I told you he has a return ticket to Bangalore,' she said, sitting forward, trying to shout. 'I've already written my statement and I've answered those questions.'

'We have incomplete knowledge,' the man said, stonewalling.

'I spoke to your people!'

The man said mildly, as though to a child, 'When was the first time you met this man?'

Alice did not want to answer, but the man was attentive, his eager patience unnerved her – and the truth would come out in any case. There was no point in withholding what in time would become well known.

'I met him on the train to Bangalore in March.'

'How did you meet him? Were you introduced?'

'He introduced himself.'

'Just like that. "Hello, how are you?"' The man had begun to write on a pad.

'He was in my compartment.'

'What class of travel?'

'Sleeping compartment.'

'First class AC?' he asked, still writing but faster than before, scribbling, and he had been asking questions distractedly, breathing hard, his head tilted toward the privacy curtain at the side of the room, as though he was listening not to Alice but to something else, or perhaps calculating, as they all seemed to do.

'So you have enjoyed the acquaintance of the named person for some three-over months?'

Alice decided to say nothing. Everything she said

seemed to incriminate her, as though she were guilty of allowing it all to happen.

But fury overcame her and she said, 'Look. I was traveling on my own. He followed me. He had somehow found out my plans. You people seem to have ways of getting all sorts of private information.'

The man cocked his head and then shoved at the desk and stood up.

Alice said, 'When do I get a chance to tell my side of the story?'

'Excuse me,' the man said, seeming to go meek. He crumpled the statement into his canvas briefcase and looked at once very stern and very frightened, as though emboldening himself – yet indifferent to Alice's watching him. He screwed up his face and squinted, like a stiffened animal in the dark.

'Listen to me!' she said, her voice breaking.

But he had become an utter stranger in just seconds. He turned his back on her and pushed the curtain aside and was gone – there was not even the sound of his footsteps, a noiseless departure, another vanishing. From being a big persuasive presence he had become small and finally left without a sound, swallowed up.

That was what was most foreign to her now, the way people came and went, as they did in dreams, Indian vanishings, of which the elephant blocking the road had been an example. If the elephant hadn't been there, she'd have gotten away. Always it seemed insulting and disorienting, with dream-like irrationality, people showing up when she least expected them; people dropping from view.

Alice felt cheated again. It was worse than an inter-ruption – it was first an intrusion and to make it worse, the man had turned his back on her and seemed to flee, another abandonment.

She slumped and put her head in her hands, heavy, bereft, sorrowing in the empty room. She had never felt farther from home, and the India she had known slipped away and became not just unfamiliar – ruins and shadows – but hostile.

When she heard a sound, the rings on the curtain rod scraping again, she lifted her head and was startled to see a woman, a nurse, the one she'd spoken to earlier, and behind this woman a man in a khaki uniform. They stood just outside the privacy curtain, holding it open, peering in, the man holding a briefcase.

'Are you all right?' the woman asked.

'No,' Alice said.

'The inspector wishes to speak with you.'

'It won't take long,' the man said.

Alice saw on the man's face a look of pain. He seemed awkward, even sheepish, unwilling even to step beyond the curtain.

'All you've got are questions,' Alice said. 'How about some answers?'

'I will be as quick as I can,' the man said. He entered the room and took a seat at the table, while the nurse stood to one side. He opened his briefcase and slipped out a pad and pen. He said, 'We have requested a fast-track hearing. It can be held in Bangalore, in the first instance, if you approve.' He clicked the pen and stuck out his elbow, as left-handers often did. 'How well did you know the accused?'

'I've just told you,' Alice said.

'I'm sorry, I don't follow.'

'I told your man.'

'What man do you mean?'

'The other policeman. The young one. That just left here.'

The inspector turned accusingly to the nurse and said something fierce – it might even have been English, it certainly was a reprimand, but it remained incoherent to Alice. Yet Alice could tell that something had gone wrong, that there was tension between the policeman and the nurse in which her own misfortune, her pain, did not figure.

'I don't get it,' Alice said.

'We have no other man. I am assigned to your case.'

'So who was I talking to just a little while ago?'

The policeman had been facing away from her all this time, looking at the serious face of the nurse. He was still looking at the nurse, and now she looked appalled.

He said, 'Let's pray it wasn't one of these journalists.'

The story appeared the next day on the front page of the *Hindustan Times*. The policeman who accompanied her to the station handed the paper to her, folded, but why would he give it to her if there was nothing in it? Alice saw the story and began to read it. When she came across '*I met him in March on the train in my compartment*' she averted her eyes and turned the paper over on the seat so that she would not have to look at the headline: 'Alleged American Rape Victim Knew Her Assailant'.

She sat in the *Ladies Only* coach with three other women and two children. One of the children was a boisterous boy, first tugging at his mother's sari and then climbing onto a seat and jumping noisily to the floor, clamoring for attention. Alice disliked the fat boy and disliked the woman for her placidity. They were big pale mothers indulging the spoiled child, taking no notice of the small girl, who sat wincing at the boy's disruption.

A few days ago, Alice would have struck up a conversation with the women; she had believed such women to be strong, holding India together. She now saw them as complacent and hypocritical, bullies and nags to everyone except their sons, allowing them to rule. *My mother calls me Bapu. It means Dad.*

These women had betrayed her. That selfish pushy boy would grow up to be a tormentor.

'Katapadi,' one woman said, seeing a station platform appear at the window.

Skinny sharp-voiced food-sellers hovered at the open windows, calling to the women, holding teapots and trays of nuts and cups of ice cream.

The fat boy wailed for an ice cream and got one. He had a devilish face and though he could not have been older than six or seven he seemed to Alice like a wolf child, with a shadow of hair on his cheeks, a low-growing hairline on his forehead and a slight mustache. His fingernails were painted pink – Alice could see that they were chipped. His legs were hairy too. He sat with a thump next to her and poked her with his elbow.

Alice felt violent towards him and wanted to poke him back, slap his hairy cheek. She said, 'You're dripping ice cream on my bag!'

She knew she'd made an ugly face and shouted for effect, to insult the mother. The boy scowled at her and lapped at his ice cream.

'Rupesh,' his mother said, calling him wearily.

He went to his mother, who nuzzled him and hugged him. The other women cooed, as though to soothe the boy.

The women were on the opposite seats in the six-seat compartment, occupying the three seats on one side, the children dawdling at their legs. And they stayed there, facing Alice in the corner seat on her side, two empty seats beside her. An invisible frontier ran down the compartment, not a racial barrier, Alice told herself, but a cultural divide.

Alice crouched, feeling wounded, hating the journey, sorrowing, feeling like an amputee. A cleaner entered the compartment with a whisk-broom and a sack for rubbish. The Indian women tossed in the ice-cream wrappers and used tissues and orange peels. Alice twisted the *Hindustan Times* and tucked it into the sack of garbage.

Later, Alice was grateful for the women ignoring her. She slept soundly for short periods and was only woken when at stations the train screeched and halted; then she dozed again, as the train continued into the afternoon.

She said nothing when the women and children pulled out bags and turned their backs on her and got off at a station where more boys were shouting. Aching with fatigue she found she could not wake up properly, so she locked the door by working the bolt and she pulled down the tin shutter and slept deeply for a period of time, an hour perhaps, and was jolted awake – alarmed, gasping – when the door slid open.

'Bangalore City,' a man said.

She went tentatively to the ashram, where she was welcomed in a subdued way, gently, almost obliquely, as though she was fragile and had been injured. Alice thought, It shows on my face, it shows in the way I walk, in my whispers.

All topics unrelated to the assault seemed frivolous, and only Priyanka and Prithi dared ask about her experience. They seemed excited by her story. While seeming to commiserate, they wanted details.

'I have to see Swami,' Alice said, as a way of deflecting their curiosity.

In the past he had rebuffed her, but now it seemed that he too knew what had happened to her. Perhaps everyone knew. The devotee at Swami's gate did not ask her name. He nodded, he made a *namaste* with his hands and said, 'You can pass.'

Touching Swami's feet, Alice knelt before him. He placed his fingers on her head-covering and murmured prayers. He was smiling when she sat back and clasped her hands.

'Something terrible happened to me,' she said.

Swami was still smiling, his head slightly inclined, one of his familiar expressions, as though to indicate that he knew something she didn't.

'My dear child. You have seen devotees walking on hot coals?'

She nodded. Early on, they'd arranged it. She had been invited. The fire-walkers had made an elaborate business of it, praying before they set forth on the glowing coals, chanting as they hurried across, giving thanks when they were done.

'Their hearts were not burned. Feet only.'

But it was some sort of trick. Fire-walking was a con. There was a scientific explanation for not scorching your foot soles, nothing to do with heat. Anyone who was sufficiently confident could do it without getting burned, and Swami was using this as a parallel for that fat bastard trapping her and dragging her into the field?

'Swami, I'm sorry, I don't see the point.'

'You must separate body from mind. Mind must meditate and find peace. Body must be occupied with work. That way you will overcome tribulation.'

'I was injured,' Alice said.

'Injury is in mind. Rid mind of injury. Prayer will do it. Work also.'

'Have you ever seen a big suffering elephant chained to a post? That's how I feel.'

'That is a good thought. But take it further. But what if elephant keeps very still?' He held his hand before her to represent the standing elephant. 'If elephant is still, elephant is free – not chained to post. Elephant is Lambodar.'

'Lambodar?' she asked.

'One with Protruding Belly – Ganesh.'

Swami twinkled at his own neat piece of wisdom, as though Alice had handed him a limp ribbon and he'd tied it into a bow. He was so pleased with himself he began praying over her, using his hands, murmuring sticky-sounding words.

'That is Ganesh mahamantra,' he said. 'It comes from Ganapati Upanishad. It is used for beginning anything new in your life. If hindrances are there, hindrances are removed, and you can be crowned with success.'

Alice bowed and thanked him, she touched the hem of his orange tunic, and still bowing she backed away.

Crap, she thought.

'Swami is the answer,' Priyanka said. 'Always, Swami sees to the heart of things.'

Alice agreed because she did not want to be cast out, but what Swami had said seemed like a libel on her only friend, the creature at the stable, who was not Ganesh at all, not a god, but *hathi*, just a nameless elephant trapped by a chain.

She visited the elephant. At a vegetable stall on the way she bought a bag of carrots. The elephant wrapped the tender end of its trunk around each carrot and fed itself, crunching them, working his lower jaw, extending his trunk for more.

The mahout allowed her to spray it with the hose and, cooled by the water, the elephant danced back and forth, tugging its chain. If elephant is still, elephant is free – not chained, Swami had said. But the truth was that such an elephant, big and restless, was never still. It was always conscious of the grip on its leg, the clank of the chain, so what Swami had said was meaningless. The elephant was only free without the shackle.

Alice stood, beholding the elephant's eye, which was like the eye of a separate being, the eye of someone inhabiting the elephant's body, someone like Alice herself. The words trailed in her head: I will never be the woman I was before – horrible, that fat man has changed me forever. She sorrowed for the innocent woman, trapped and frightened on that narrow Indian road.

'No, no,' the mahout cried out, rushing towards her, appealing to her, looking tormented and helpless, because for the first time since the awful thing had happened Alice had begun to cry.

7

She had not gone back to Electronics City, she had not even called them. She knew she'd be unwelcome. She was stained, scandalous, an embarrassment, the subject of an investigation. But what did 'fast-track' mean? There was no sign of a hearing, only more paperwork – visa questions, a reprimand and a warning because she'd put down that she was a teacher at InfoTech and she had no work permit. More official forms were sent, with detailed questions about places she'd visited, people she knew, Indian citizens she'd met, names, addresses, specific locations. 'Attach additional sheets if necessary.' She was under suspicion, she had come to India to be free, and now she was under scrutiny and hated it. Everyone knew, of course they did. Only the elephant and its mahout still smiled at her as before.

She wondered, *Should I leave?* but did nothing. The weather had grown hot, no rains yet, dust hanging in the air, particles of it on her lips. She languished in the soupy lukewarm air of the ashram, where time was so clouded it was measured in months.

Miss Ghosh's secretary called her on the ashram's emergency number, the only one she had, and passed on Miss Ghosh's complaint that intrusive strangers were trying to get in touch with Alice. People who claimed they wanted to help were wasting InfoTech's time. You couldn't be more despised in India than being told by someone's secretary you were a problem. Letters and printed email messages were forwarded in bundles to the ashram. Using a phone card and the phone across the road at the ramshackle shop, Alice responded to the offers of help.

'We must meet you face to face,' a woman said.

Alice agreed and regretted it as soon as they showed up, three of them, but one was the speaker, the others silent, supporting her on either side. Alice met them just inside the gate of the ashram, the public entrance near the shoe rack, where there were chairs.

The two silent women stood; the woman who spoke sat on a white molded plastic chair. Like the others she carried a basket. She had a mean face and sunken mask-like eyes, and even trying to talk in a kindly way she sounded like a scold, saying, 'You are new to India. We are taught to be kind to strangers. We need you to bear with us.'

People offering favors in India always were in need of greater favors. No charity ever, there was only salesmanship.

The woman said, 'The smallest misstep can destroy a whole future. An elephant sees a mouse and it rears up and kills its keeper and tramples passers-by.'

Alice said, 'What happened wasn't a misstep. It was the worst thing that has ever happened to me.'

'I am not thinking of your future. The boy will be ruined.'

'I'm ruined,' Alice said. She thought, Oh, God, don't cry again, and could not speak.

'You think that because you are young. Worse things

will happen to you. Death will visit you and your family. This episode will seem like nothing.'

'It was like death. What do you know?'

'You are strong and quite young. You can go on living your life. You can go home.'

'I'm staying. I'm fighting this.'

Her face crumpling, the woman began quietly to weep. The other women consoled her. The one on the right, nearest to Alice, said, 'This is auntie. His mother is sick. She has taken to her bed.'

'A young man is being destroyed,' the second woman said, while still the aunt wept.

Alice looked behind her nervously and seeing no one from the ashram watching she said, 'Don't you see? He tried to destroy me.'

'But he failed.'

Alice lowered her head and whispered harshly, 'He raped me.'

'You are able to walk away,' the woman on the right said. Now her stern tone was apparent. 'He will be disgraced.'

'I'm disgraced. You're women – why don't you see it?'

The aunt recovered and dabbed her eyes. 'We are begging you.'

Then Alice found herself weeping with the woman, unable to speak.

The next day a man visited. He was kindly, with a black mustache that hid his mouth. He twisted its ends as he spoke, giving the big thing tips like tails. He wore a shirt and tie and a pale silk suit and in that terrible heat did not look hot.

'I represent the family of the accused,' he said. He handed Alice his card. He looked absurd on the white plastic chair, but it was the only place in the grounds where Alice could meet someone without being overheard. It was bad enough being seen like this. No one dressed like this ever visited the ashram.

Alice glanced at the card, the man's long name, the word *Solicitors*. The man took some papers out of his briefcase.

'This is a release form. Your signature is required.'

'I don't get it.'

'It is the wisest course. This way, no one gets dragged through the mud.'

'I don't care. I want him on trial, facing the charges.'

'Miss. Listen to me. You will also be on trial. Everything will be known about you. A thorough investigation will be undertaken and all the facts of the case made public.'

Another wordy Indian trying to sell her his opinion. She said, 'So what?'

'In some instances, unpleasant facts.' He tugged and twisted his mustache tips.

'I'm not signing.'

With one hand twisting a mustache tip, and seeming confident, the man said, 'For example, in Bombay, it has been established that you entertained a young American chap in your hotel room.'

'That's a lie.'

'We are in receipt of the desk clerk's signature on a sworn affidavit.'

It had to be Stella, entertaining Zack, but Alice said nothing.

'We are well aware that you have limited funds at your disposal. The family is prepared to compensate you. This can be negotiated.'

Alice said, 'Please leave.'

'A young man's life is in your hands.'

She wanted to say, 'Fuck him,' but instead she said, 'Not in my hands, unfortunately. In the hands of the law. I demand justice.'

A trait she deplored in herself was lapsing into pomposity when trying to control her anger. But that was preferable to the obscenity which she was inclined to scream into the man's face.

'This charge is like death in India. I assure you the family will fight it passionately. You may regret that you pushed so hard for justice, young lady.'

'You're threatening me,' Alice said, rising from her chair, a shriek entering her voice. 'In this holy place!'

The man stood up then and, with a frown of regret, thanked her. He walked to the gate, where his car was waiting.

Priyanka found her, dried tears staining her face, and spoke to her as though to soothe her, yet Alice heard what she said as scolding.

More people visited, offering conciliation, mediation, money; also making solemn promises, pleading with her to drop the case. One of them, a man in a homespun cotton jacket and a Nehru cap, left an envelope behind, a plane ticket to Delhi inside it. There was no return address on the envelope, so she couldn't send it back. She tucked it into her journal. She had done no writing since the day of the incident. She did not have the words to describe what had happened to her.

After the first wave of people begging and pleading, after another visit from a lawyer – and this one also had a document he wanted her to sign – there ensued several more waves of visitors, each less friendly than the last. Apart from the lawyers, the imploring people had come in shuffling groups, women mostly, weepers and grovelers. The darker unpleasant ones came singly. They were younger and tougher. They claimed to know all about her.

'We've been in touch with your friends,' one man said.

Alice said nothing. Was he talking about Stella, or was he fishing?

'We've taken statements from them.'

This was just a young man in a blue shirt and brown slacks and sandals, with dangerous-looking hands.

'I think you're trying to frighten me.'

'If you're smart you will be frightened. Take my advice. Drop this and go home.'

Alice was thinking how well these people spoke English, with diabolical accuracy, always with a rejoinder; and all of them on Amitabh's side.

That man left glowering, because Alice had fallen silent. Another man came the next day, as though to wear her down. He was older, better dressed, a gold chain around his neck, a gold bracelet on his wrist, an expensive watch.

'You're way out of your depth. You're lucky nothing has happened to you so far. Some of these blighters want to make a move. I don't know how long I can keep them away.'

His manner was so persuasive it roused her. She said, 'What do you mean?'

'I mean, maybe prevent you from testifying at a trial. Maybe prevent you from going anywhere.'

This was a direct threat to her life. Yet, like the others, he left her abruptly and even handed over his business card.

Some days passed, days of peace, she had almost forgotten the earlier visits, and then two men came. They said they had a message. They looked fierce. This hot weather, the humidity, their sweating faces, made them look villainous.

'You should be afraid,' one of them said.

He was nudged aside by his friend, who said, 'I am going to put this very plainly. Amitabh is betrothed. A match has been found. It's a good arrangement. But if this trial goes forward he is ruined. The other family will withdraw – no marriage.'

'Your fault,' the first man said.

Alice said, 'You want me to drop the charges so that Amitabh can go ahead with his arranged marriage?'

'That's the idea.'

'Does this woman know he's a rapist?'

'The charge will never be proven, so why waste your time?'

'That poor woman,' Alice said. And without her being conscious of their leaving, the men simply disappeared.

Priyanka was waiting for her at the far side of the pavilion, near the statue of Saraswati balancing her sitar. She took Alice by her damp and anxious hands and holding them she said, 'We're concerned that you have so many visitors.'

'I can't help it. I don't invite them.'

Priyanka released Alice's hands and took a step back,

a self-conscious move, like a formal dance step, as though she'd rehearsed this.

'The committee has met and decided' – she tilted her head, another affectation – 'with regret, that you'll have to leave.'

'When?'

'Forthwith. Oh, we can suggest some other places where you'd be comfortable.'

Alice had begun to walk away. Without turning, she said, 'I don't want you to know where I'm going.'

Her rucksack that had been such an awkward burden months ago was now much smaller. She'd given away all her cold-weather clothes. She had her saris, some T-shirts, the shawls. Since the assault she had become obsessed with covering herself.

There was one place for her to go – in a sense, the only place, but logical: the last place.

8

From her tiny room above the stable she could hear the snorting of the elephant. And she saw the gateway leading to the lane where she had stood the previous day, her pack on her back, a plastic bag in her hand – carrots for the elephant. The elephant had seen her first, had trumpeted, then nodded and tugged at his leg chain. He rocked to and fro on his great cylindrical legs. Hearing him, the mahout had appeared, and smiled when he saw Alice, and approached her. He summed up her predicament in an instant. He didn't need language or explanation. He worked with animals. He did not need to be told when one was lost.

He gestured with his hand decisively, clawing the air, saying 'come' with it, using his head too to be emphatic.

Alice smiled to show him she understood, and when she shrugged, seeming helpless, the mahout became active, began talking in his own language, and called to an open window. A woman stuck her head out, probably his wife, and she listened to what the mahout was saying.

Wiping her hands on a blue towel, the woman swept out of the ground floor door, her legs working quickly but invisibly under her sari, and went straight to Alice. She did not offer a *namaste*. She took Alice in her arms, enfolded her, and Alice began to sob.

She also thought, Is it so obvious that I look pathetic? How friendless I must seem.

She valued her strength, she believed she was tougher – too tough, she often thought – and here she was weeping in the arms of a stranger.

That was what the assault had done to her – turned her into a wreck. People say, You'll be stronger for it, but I will never be strong again.

He has broken me, she thought. She had not dared to think it in the ashram, where they'd seen her as a tough American – tough enough to turn into the street. But here, among these kind people, in the presence of the nodding elephant, she could admit to being what she had become, a weakling, in tears.

The woman took her to a sink and put a piece of soap into her hand and urged her to wash her face. Then she sat Alice at a wobbly table and brought her a dish of rice, a bowl of dhal, some okra, some yogurt, a sweetish paste, a lump of glistening pickle.

'I hadn't realized how hungry I was,' Alice said.

The woman was smiling, as though at her daughter. She understood Alice's gratitude. She brought out a framed photograph, a young woman in a cap and gown, a graduation picture.

'Mysore,' the mahout said.

Their daughter, obviously, looking proud, holding a rolled-up degree. Working in Mysore, probably Alice's age. They could relate. Their own daughter's absence made them sympathetic.

The mahout stood at a little distance, bandy-legged, in torn trousers and sandals, a turban knotted on his head, watching Alice eat.

Afterwards, the woman brought a bowl of warm water for Alice to wash her hands, a small towel, a broken piece of soap.

All this ritual, shuffling and serving; and then snatching air with her hand the woman gestured for Alice to follow her. When Alice bent to pick up her rucksack the woman waved her away. The mahout called out the window, and a young girl hurried into the room and heaved the rucksack, and unsteadily mounted the stairs behind them.

Up the flight of stone stairs there was a small room overlooking the courtyard, where the elephant was chained. The bed was on a low frame, near the window a table and chair, a colored picture of a seated god – perhaps Shiva, with a cobra hovering over him. On the floor a pale pink rug, at the far wall a bookshelf: most of the books in English, biology books, organic chemistry, physics textbooks. Of course, the daughter's room, daughter's schoolbooks. She was studying – what? Medicine? Nursing? Dentistry?

The old couple had no language to explain any of this, but no explanation was necessary. They had between them summed up Alice's predicament and they knew when to leave her alone in the room. Alice showed them some money, a purse of rupees, but they made motions of refusal and they backed away.

So she lay for a while on the hard bed, the clean sheet, her head empty, feeling stunned. Time did not advance, it rotated, twisting around her, defying her to name the day or month, as though she was in suspension. She may have dozed, for when she next looked at the window night had fallen and the elephant stood still, his broad back and the dome of his head gleaming in the moonlight.

Alice went downstairs to thank the woman. She was offered another meal, some of which she ate; and then she went to bed again and slept until dawn, when she became conscious of the warm animal odors that were like freshly baked bread, the elephant under her window.

In the crowded, traffic-ridden city of frenzied millions, this courtyard and stable was hidden and peaceful, smelling sweetly of new straw and elephant dung.

I'm so lucky, Alice thought. In this enormous hostile city, where her life had been threatened, she had found rescuers – well, she'd seen the elephant first and after that the people. At breakfast, she gave the woman an envelope of rupees, about four hundred, not even ten dollars. The woman made a show of refusing it, a ritual of indignation; but Alice insisted she take it, and when she did she felt better, for now there was a kind of contract. She would have time to think. It was easier among strangers.

The days that followed were dream-like and wonderful. She spent the mornings spraying the elephant with the hose – directing the nozzle into his mouth, into the pink nose holes in his trunk, and watched him spray himself, blowing water onto his back. She fed him, using the hayfork to make a stack of fodder, and she marveled at him eating. He could eat all day, shifting his weight from foot to foot, occasionally kicking the chain.

I have found friends, Alice thought. Once again, she lost the sense of time passing, and she realized this was so because she was content. India was not the huge country and the crowded streets and the stinks and the racket; it was this stable yard, and this food, and these kind people, and this elephant.

She could tell that the mahout liked her from the way he cheerfully involved her in the work of caring for the elephant, finding ways to please her.

She said, 'You have no idea who I am, and yet you're being good to me. Bless you, bless you.'

The mahout laughed, hearing this stream of English.

One day she took an auto-rickshaw to the ashram. The gatekeeper looked apprehensive,

'Just visiting,' she said.

'Swami at Poorthaparthy,' the man said.

She asked to see Priyanka, whose face fell when she saw her.

'I'm just here for my mail,' Alice said.

'We're trying to get over the hoo-hah,' Priyanka said.

'By hoo-hah, do you mean the fact that I was assaulted and raped?'

'We are bitterly sorry,' Priyanka said.

'Never mind. You have more important things to deal with. But would you mind holding my mail for me?'

'Of course. Not to worry, Have you found lodgings?'

'I'll let you know,' Alice said.

That day there was no mail of any consequence, but a few days later there was a large buff-colored envelope from the court in Madras, with a stamp and many signatures, explaining formally that the date of the hearing had been deferred, 'pending further enquiries'. So much for fast-track.

Someone had sent her a prayer printed on one sheet of paper, another envelope included a religious card, the scary-faced goddess Kali, the size of a playing card. The lawyer who had visited sent a form to sign – the same form, a letter with her name typed at the bottom, stating that she wished to drop all charges. Even Amitabh wrote, suggesting that they meet to discuss 'this matter'. The nerve!

She began to hate picking up her mail. And what had become of Stella? She thought of her now – probably she had left India, perhaps she was traveling with Zack, or living with him. Stella was safe. I am safe, too, Alice told herself; safe but in suspense.

Sleeping in the small fragrant room, rising early, attending to the elephant, beginning to make notes in her journal – about the elephant, not herself – and eating with the mahout and his wife became her routine. These days her accumulated letters were left at the front desk of the ashram. With Swami in his other ashram, there were few devotees around. Priyanka and Prithi were nowhere to be seen. They were obviously miffed that she had not revealed to them anything of her whereabouts.

At night in the dark, she told herself that she had a mission: she could not leave India until her case was heard and Amitabh was punished.

As though she'd sensed Alice's disdain, Stella wrote to her, care of the ashram. She'd read the story, she said. Zack was in pre-production for his Bollywood film. They were living in Bombay. *Zack says that his father might be able to help.*

Alice wrote various replies in her head, all of them

on the theme of I-refuse-to-be-patronized. But she did not send anything; she did not want Stella to know she'd received the letter. She did not want anyone to know where she was. It was a great plus to her that the mahout and his wife had no idea who she was.

More weeks passed, more delays, more ambiguous legal letters. It was a pettifogging culture. Instead of justice there was combat and an elaborate confrontation that was a form of evasion. The ancient quality of India, its ruinous, skeletal look, was a skeletal look, the result of delay. You would die before any promise was kept, but denial was another way of doing business. The legal system was based on creating obstacles.

In this mood, Alice became indecisive herself and was saddened to think that she had surrendered to this Indian lack of urgency. So she was surprised one morning when she went to the storeroom for the hayfork and saw the mahout blocking her way. He would not allow her to go near the elephant. Shooing her away, he indicated a door in the corner of the stable yard which led to the street. She understood what he was saying – it was an escape route. Should she find herself cornered, she could slip out and avoid the elephant's wrath.

She saw why. The tearstain dripped from the lower part of his eye, brownish on the rough gray skin. And the eye itself looked troubled, the great animal agitated, yanking its chain.

'Musth?'

'Musth. Musth.' The mahout made a gesture of

343

helplessness. The frenzy had come at last, it had possessed the elephant.

From her room, unable to feed the elephant, she looked down at the restless creature trumpeting, snorting, twisting his head, flapping his ears. Alice put her chin on her hands, resting her arms on the windowsill, and saw how the poor thing was much like herself, hobbled, trapped by the chain. She watched for most of the day, and saw the mahout leave by the concealed door. He had no role to play with the elephant so restless – more than restless, the poor thing was suffering.

She remembered how, months before, she'd misunderstood the mahout and imagined the elephant as half-demented with frustrated desire, chained against venting it, lust and anger mingled in its big body and leaking out of its eye. She'd written it in her journal. Now she was not imagining it.

In her meditative posture, listening to the moaning of the elephant, Alice made a decision.

The phone card that she'd bought months before and used once was still valid. She went out the way the mahout had gone, into the lane and a street of shops. She found one with a pay phone and, reading from a business card, she dialed a number.

'This is Shan.'

'It's Alice.' She took a breath and told him exactly where she was and how to get there; where the gate was latched, that he must secure it as soon as he entered the stable yard; that she would meet him.

He was relieved – she heard it in his expression of thanks, but she shuddered in disgust and hung up. She could not bear to listen to his gratitude in his strangled American voice, that hideous accent.

She was squatting in the stable yard, behind the elephant's post, in the darkness there, where the animal odor brimmed and stung her eyes. She was so still the elephant was not aware of her presence. She listened hard – was that a car in the side lane? Yes, the latch was lifted on the gate. The elephant heard, and snorted and swayed. He began to roar. She was glad for that sound – it drowned every other noise.

She did not act until she saw by the light of the streetlamp in the lane the gate being shut, the brace slipped into the slots, the door secured.

The elephant was straining forward. Alice saw Amitabh, greenish in the bad light, much fatter now, trying to judge the limit of the elephant's reaching trunk, and he was skirting the animal, believing himself to be safe, when he saw Alice, and called out softly, 'Hey, you.'

Then she pulled the long pin from the ring on the post, releasing the chain, releasing the elephant, releasing herself. And just before she slipped through the small door to the lane, which led to the world, she lingered. She saw Amitabh tumbled to the cobbles of the stable yard under the pounding feet of the rampaging elephant, twisted in the posture of a helpless victim, bellowing in terror in his own voice.

It was day again, just after dawn, in the *Ladies Only* coach on the Mumbai Express. The noise of the clattering train made for a kind of drama, like a sound track to the image in the compartment window: her face, with the Indian landscape passing behind her pale features. The bang of the wheels on the rails, like rough music, filled her head with the insistent reassurance of the train speeding her to safety. She began to chant,

Jaya Jaya Jaya Hey Gajaanana
Gajaanana Hey Gajavadana . . .